RAYLAN

Elmore Leonard

**WINDSOR
PARAGON**

First published 2012
by Weidenfeld & Nicolson
This Large Print edition published 2012
by AudioGO Ltd
by arrangement with
The Orion Publishing Group Ltd

Hardcover   ISBN: 978 1 4713 0049 3
Softcover   ISBN: 978 1 4713 0050 9

British Library Cataloguing in Publication Data available

Printed and bound in Great Britain by
MPG Books Group Limited

For Graham and Tim

CHAPTER ONE

Raylan Givens was holding a federal warrant to serve on a man in the marijuana trade known as Angel Arenas, forty-seven, born in the U.S. but 100 percent of him Hispanic.

'I met him,' Raylan said, 'the time I was on court duty in Miami and he was up for selling khat. That Arab plant you chew on and get high.'

'Just medium high,' Rachel Brooks said, in the front seat of the SUV, Raylan driving, early morning sun showing behind them. 'Khat's just catchin on, grown in California, big in San Diego among real Africans.'

'You buy any, you want to know it was picked that morning,' Raylan said. 'It gives you a high for the day and that's it.'

'I have some friends,' Rachel said, 'like to chew it now and then. They never get silly, have fun with it. They just seem to mellow out.'

'Get dreamy,' Raylan said.

'What'd Angel go down for?'

'Thirty-six months out of forty and went back to selling weed. Violated his parole. He was supposed to have made a deal through that Rastafarian ran the Church?'

'Temple of the Cool and Beautiful J.C.,' Rachel said. 'Israel Fendi, with the dreads, Ethiopian by way of Jamaica. Was he in the deal?'

'Never went near it. But somebody put the stuff on Angel, some doper lookin for a plea deal. Swears Angel was taking delivery last night. I doubt we walk in and find Angel sittin on it.'

1

From the backseat they heard Tim Gutterson say, 'He's looking at two hundred and forty months this time.' Tim going through a file folder of Angel Arenas photos came to a mug shot.

'Look at that grin. Nothing about him armed and dangerous.'

'He never packs,' Raylan said, 'that I know of. Or has gun thugs hangin around.'

The SUV was traveling through a bottom section of East Kentucky, creeping along behind the state troopers' radio cars, following a lake that looked more like a river looping around on its way down past the Tennessee line. A few minutes shy of 6:00 A.M. they pulled up to the Cumberland Inn.

The state troopers, four of them, watched Raylan and his crew slip on Kevlar vests, which they wore underneath their U.S. marshal jackets, and watched them check their sidearms. Raylan told the officers he didn't expect Angel would resist, but you never knew for sure. He said, 'You hear gunfire come runnin, all right?'

One of the troopers said, 'You want, we'll bust in the door for you.'

'You're dyin to,' Raylan said. 'I thought I'd stop by the desk and get a key.'

The troopers got a kick out of this marshal, at one time a coal miner from Harlan County but sounded like a lawman, his attitude about his job. This morning they watched him enter a fugitive felon's motel room without drawing his gun.

There wasn't a sound but the hum of air-conditioning. Sunlight from the windows lay on the king-size bed, unmade but thrown together, the spread pulled up over bedding and pillows. Raylan turned to Rachel and nodded to the bed. Now he

2

stepped over to the bathroom door, not closed all the way, listened and then shoved it open.

Angel Arenas's head rested against the curved end of the bathtub, his hair floating in water that came past his chin, his eyes closed, his body stretched out naked in a tub filled close to the brim with bits of ice in water turning pink.

Raylan said, 'Angel . . .?' Got no response and kneeled at the tub to feel Angel's throat for a pulse. 'He's freezing to death but still breathing.'

Behind him he heard Rachel say, 'Raylan, the bed's full of blood. Like he was killin chickens in there.' And heard her say, 'Oh my God,' sucking in her breath as she saw Angel.

Raylan turned the knob to let the water run out, lowering it around Angel, his belly becoming an island in the tub of ice water, blood showing in two places on the island.

'He had something done to him,' Raylan said. 'He's got like staples closing up what look like wounds. Or was he operated on?'

'Somebody shot him,' Tim said.

'I don't think so,' Raylan said, staring at the two incisions stapled closed.

Rachel said, 'That's how they did my mother last year, at UK Medical. Made one entry below the ribs and the other under her belly button. I asked her why they did it there 'stead of around through her back.'

Tim said, 'You gonna tell us what the operation was?'

'They took out her kidneys,' Rachel said. 'Both of 'em, and she got an almost new pair the same day, from a child who'd drowned.'

They wrapped Angel in a blanket, carried him

3

into the bedroom and laid him on the spread, the man shuddering, trying to breathe. His eyes closed he said to Raylan staring at him, 'What happen to me?'

'You're here makin a deal?'

Angel hesitated. 'Two guys I know, growers. We have a drink—'

'And you end up in the tub,' Raylan said. 'How much you pay them?'

'Is none of your business.'

'They left the weed?'

'What you see,' Angel said.

'There isn't any here.'

Angel's eyes came open. 'I bought a hundred pounds, twenty-two thousand dollar. I saw it, I tried some.'

'You got taken,' Raylan said. 'They put you out and left with the swag and the weed.'

Now his eyes closed and he said, 'Man, I'm in pain,' his hands under the blanket feeling his stomach. 'What did they take out of me?'

*　　　*　　　*

Raylan felt his pulse again. 'He's hangin in, tough little whatever he is, Sorta Rican? I can see these growers rippin him off, but why'd they take his kidneys?'

'It's like that old story,' Tim said. 'Guy wakes up missin a kidney. Has no idea who took it. People bring it up from time to time, but nobody ever proved it happened.'

'It has now,' Raylan said.

'You can't live without kidneys,' Tim said.

'Be hard,' Raylan said. 'Less you get on dialysis

4

pretty quick. What I don't see, what these pot growers are doing yanking out people's kidneys. They aren't making it sellin weed? I've heard a whole cadaver, selling parts of it at a time? Will go for a hundred grand. But you make more you sell enough weed, and it isn't near as messy as dealin kidneys. What I'm wondering . . .' He paused, thinking about it.

Tim said, 'Yeah . . .?'

'Who did the surgery?'

*   *   *

About noon Art Mullen, marshal in charge of the Harlan field office, came by the motel to find Raylan still poking around the room.

Art said, 'You know what you're looking for?'

'Techs dusted the place,' Raylan said, 'picked up Angel's clothes, bloody dressings, surgical staples, an empty sack of Mail Pouch, but no kidneys. How's Angel doing?'

'They got him in intensive care, maintaining.'

'He's gonna make it?'

'I think what keeps him alive,' Art said, 'he's half out but mad as hell these weed dealers ripped him off. Took what he paid for the reefer—if you believe him—and left him to die.'

'Didn't mention,' Raylan said, 'they took his kidneys?'

'I kept makin the point,' Art said. ' "Tell me who these boys are, we'll get your kidneys back for you." He commenced to breathe hard and the nurse shooed me out. No, but his kidneys,' Art said, 'were taken out by someone knew what he was doing.'

Raylan said, 'They were taken out the front.'

'They're always taken out the front. Only this was the latest procedure. Smaller incision and they don't cut through any muscle.'

'I'd like to see Angel,' Raylan said, 'less you don't want me to. I've known him since that time he was brought up for sellin khat. When I was on court duty in Miami. Angel and I got along pretty good,' Raylan said. 'I think he believes I saved his life.'

'You probably did.'

'So he oughta be willing to talk to me.'

'He's at Cumberland Regional,' Art said. 'Maybe they'll let you see him, maybe not. Where're your partners?'

'There wasn't anything pressing—I told 'em go on back to Harlan.'

'They took the SUV—how're you gonna get around?'

'We have Angel's BMW,' Raylan said, 'don't we?'

*   *   *

Angel was lying on his back, his eyes closed. Raylan got of hospital breath and said in a whisper, 'Your old court buddy from Miami's here, Raylan Givens.' Angel's eyes came open. 'Was that time you went down for selling khat.'

Now it looked like Angel was trying to grin.

'Did you know,' Raylan said, 'I saved your life this morning? Another five minutes in that ice water you'd of froze to death. Thank the Lord I got there when I did.'

'For what, to arrest me?'

'You're alive, partner, that's the main thing. Maybe a little pale's all.'

6

Pale—he looked like he was dead.

'They hook my arm to a machine,' Angel said, 'takes the impurities from my blood and keeps me alive long as I can wait for a kidney. Or I have a relative like a brother wants to give me one.'

'You have a brother?'

'I have someone better.'

Smiling now. He was, and Raylan said, 'You know I won't tell where you're getting this kidney, you don't want me to.'

'Everybody in the hospital knows,' Angel said. 'They send me a fax. You believe it? The nurse comes in and reads it to me. Tanya, tha's her name. She's very fine, with skin you know will be soft you touch it. Tanya, man. I ask her she like to go to Lexington with me when I'm better. You know, I always like a nurse. You don't have to bullshit them too much.'

'The fax,' Raylan said. 'You get to buy your kidneys back for how much?'

'A hundred grand,' Angel said, 'tha's what they offer. You imagine the balls on these redneck guys? They bring a surgeon last night so they can take my fucking kidneys and rip me off twice, counting what they stole from me. They say if I only want one kidney is still a hundred grand.'

Raylan said, 'The hospital knows what's going on?'

'I tole you, everybody knows, the doctors, the nurses, Tanya. They send the fax, then one of them calls the hospital and makes the arrangement. Nobody saw who deliver them.'

'The hospital knows they're yours?'

'Why can't you get that in your head?'

'And they go along with it?'

7

'Or what, let me die? They not paying for the kidneys.'

'When do you have to come up with the money?'

'They say they give me a break, a week or so.'

'You know these boys—tell me who they are.'

'They kill me. No hurry, get around to it.'

'And take your kidneys back,' Raylan said. 'I don't believe I ever heard of this one. You know the hospital called the police.'

'The police already talk to me. I tole them I don't know these guys. Never saw them before.'

'Or know who's telling them what to do?' Raylan said.

Angel stared at Raylan. 'I don't follow you.'

'You think your guys came up with this new way to score? They can take whoever they want off the street,' Raylan said, 'while this doctor's scrubbin up for surgery. Why should they be picky, wait for a drug deal to go down?' Raylan paused. He said, 'You want, I'll help you out.'

'For what? You find product in that motel room? Man, I'm the victim of a crime and you want to fucking put me in jail?'

Finally they reached a point, Angel on a gurney on his way to the operating room, Raylan tagging along next to it saying, 'Give me a name. I swear on my star you won't have to pay for either one.'

He watched Angel shake his head saying, 'You don't know these people.'

'I will, you tell me who they are.'

'You have to go in the woods to find them.'

'Buddy, it's what I *do*.' They were coming to double doors swinging open. 'I call Lexington with the names and they e-mail me their sheets. I might even know these guys.'

8

'They grow reefer,' Angel said, 'from here to West Virginia.'

Right away Raylan said, 'They're Crowes, aren't they?'

CHAPTER TWO

South of Barbourville Raylan turned off the four-lane and cut east to follow blacktops and gravel roads without names or numbers through these worn-out mountains of Knox County, the tops of the grades scalped, strip-mined of coal to leave waste heaps, the creeks down in the hollows tainted with mine acid. Raylan followed Stinking Creek to the fork where Buckeye came in and there it was, up past the cemetery, Crowe's grocery store, the name displayed in a Coca-Cola sign over the door, CROWE's GROCERIES & FEED.

He let Angel's BMW roll past the screen door standing open and came to a stop. He'd had the car washed in Somerset and wore a dark suit and tie for this visit, wanting Mr. Crowe to make a judgment about him. In its piece about Stinking Creek, *Newsweek* called Pervis 'Speed' Crowe the top marijuana grower in East Kentucky. Crowe said in the magazine, 'Prove it. I run a store for these poor people come up from the hollers with their food stamps. When's anybody seen me cultivatin herb?'

There he was behind the counter by an old-style scale he used to weigh potatoes, cuts of fatback, the shelves behind him showing sacks of flour and cornmeal. Eggs ten cents apiece reduced to four bits the dozen.

All these stores looked the same to Raylan, the same people coming in to buy necessities, then taking forever to spend ninety-nine cents on an angel food cake, some candy and Kool-Aid for their kids waiting, not saying a word.

A young girl starting to bud sat on cow-feed sacks in her shorts drinking an RC Cola. Raylan had bought Beech-Nut scrap in stores like this when he was a kid, wanting to hurry up and get enough size to become a federal officer, the kind went after armed felons.

The girl on the cow-feed sacks kept looking up at Raylan like she was wondering about him, thinking hard of something to say, until she found a sweet voice to ask him, 'Sir, would you think I'm bold to inquire what you do as your job?'

Raylan smiled. 'Which one's the question, what I think or what I do?'

Pervis Crowe, called 'Speed' in the magazine, said, 'Loretta, don't you know Drug Enforcement, you see a man wearin a suit of clothes? They come around sniffin the air.'

'You got me wrong,' Raylan said, 'I'm marshals service. We go around smelling the flowers, till we get turned on to wanted felons. I understand, Mr. Crowe, you have a couple of boys work illegal trades.'

Pervis said, 'You hold warrants on 'em?'

'I did, they'd be gone,' Raylan said. 'You wouldn't see 'em for goin on two hundred and forty months.'

'Where you been?' Pervis said. 'I don't know a judge hands down more'n a few years.'

'Doesn't matter to me,' Raylan said. 'I wondered if you're related to the Florida Crowes.'

10

'From some distance. How they makin it?'

'Doin time or dead,' Raylan said. 'I sent one to Starke while I was workin down there. I did wonder, is that Dewey Crowe one of yours? Wears gator teeth and joined that Heil Hitler club? Told me he was from Belle Glade.'

'I mighta heard of the boy,' Pervis said, 'but he don't raise my interest none.'

'Wants you to know he's bad,' Raylan said, 'but doesn't have it down yet. I'd like to meet your boys.'

'They're a different stock,' Pervis said. 'Wear clean clothes every day and drive Chevrolets.'

'Pickups,' Raylan said, 'with a .30-.30 racked in the back window. Otherwise they drive Cadillacs. I wouldn't mind talking to 'em, though it's not my reason to stop by. I thought I'd buy a jar and take it down memory lane. I'm on my way to Evarts and on to Eastover, where I dug coal as a boy.'

'You managed to get out,' Pervis said, 'before bad habits set in.'

'I was lucky,' Raylan said. 'I didn't mind going to school, found I liked to read stories.'

'Else you'd be wanted for bustin into drugstores,' Pervis said. 'Clean out the painkillers and sell 'em to folks want to stay numb, not have to think.'

'You carry those people?'

'The ones grow reefer in their backyard I keep on the books. They sell a crop and pay their store debt with hunnert-dollar bills.'

'Can I ask why they call you Speed?'

He was stringy and stooped in his seventies, wore a hairpiece that wasn't bad, though Raylan could tell Pervis set it on his head every morning. Had a neat part that was in it forever. Pervis let his expression sag into deep lines. He had not smiled

11

since Raylan entered the store.

'I sold ninety-proof whiskey clear as spring water, not a speck of charcoal in her. I sold it from a Ford looked like it was stock I used as my store. Never stopped runnin these hills and acquired "Speed" as my handle. You understand this was fifty years ago. I raced quarter-mile dirt and worked up to try NASCAR. Came up against Junior Johnson and saw my future get put on the trailer.'

'You sell groceries now,' Raylan said, 'and your boys run your other business.'

Pervis said, 'Finally gettin to it, aren't we?'

'I'm not Drug Enforcement,' Raylan said. 'Long as they got nothin on you I don't either. But I'm told you got fields of marijuana, a good thousand acres, from here to West Virginia.'

'What's good about it?' Pervis said. 'You plant a third for the law, a third for the thieves and what's left you sell to dealers, the ones makin the profit. I'm confidin this to you so we don't waste time lyin to each other. I didn't know your daddy, but I'll swear by your granddaddy. Six years I came over to Harlan and sold all the liquor he cooked and we did betten'n fair.'

Raylan said, 'I'm told he was a preacher.'

'Cooked all week and preached Sunday,' Pervis said. 'Boy, you don't know your own people.'

'I knew your boy Coover back in my school days till he quit to roam the earth, do whatever he wanted. And Richard . . .?'

'Been goin by Dickie since he was a tad.'

'What I have is a situation here,' Raylan said. 'I'm told your boys took payment for weed they never delivered.'

'You with Better Business,' Pervis said, 'check

on customer complaints? I might've heard about this. The DEA fella comes down here in his dress shoes and pays for product before he's given any. Anxious, in a hurry to get her done. Like cuttin a fart he believes is gas and messes hisself. I'm to take your word my tads cheated this man?'

Raylan said with a straight face, 'I know you love your tads. Now and then you notice them growin up to what they are today. But you heard it wrong. It wasn't a federal agent makin the deal, it was a wanted felon. I went to that motel room with an arrest warrant on me.'

Raylan gave Pervis time to step in and say something, but he didn't.

'I found Angel Arenas in the room,' Raylan said, 'without his kidneys.'

Raylan waited again, Pervis staring at him.

'Bare-naked in an ice bath.'

Pervis said, 'This boy's missin his kidneys?'

'They offered 'em back later on, while he's in the hospital, for a hundred thousand.'

Raylan waited again before saying, 'But he won't have to pay for 'em.'

Pervis didn't ask why, didn't say a word.

Raylan told him, 'We're on the case now, the marshals. Gonna stop this new business startin up.'

'You're tellin me to my face,' Pervis said, 'my boys cut this man open and took his kidneys?'

'I think they had somebody along knew how. Whoever he is,' Raylan said, 'I'm gonna find him.'

This time Pervis brought a pack of Camels from his shirt pocket, got one lighted and blew a stream of smoke like he was cooling himself off. He said, 'Well, I know it wasn't my boys. Who was it told you?'

'The man waitin to get his kidneys back,' Raylan said. 'He name my boys?'

'After a while he did.'

'He lied,' Pervis said, 'account of the broke deal. My boys farm reefer, they don't cut into a man's body for his parts. Even if they knew how.'

'They shoot a buck,' Raylan said, 'they know how to dress him out.'

He was on the edge with this old man, one time bootlegger, dirt-track driver, the man pinching his cigarette between his fingers staring at Raylan. Raylan said to him, 'Mr. Crowe, I respect how you feel, but I'm gonna have a talk with your boys, in your presence if you want. Have 'em come by the next day or so, or I'll hunt 'em down.'

'I always felt,' Pervis said, 'we're a good twenty years behind the times livin here, what we get by on. But it's how I like it. Now you tell me we're catchin up, gettin into this new business, sellin parts of the human body.'

'You brought yourself up-to-date,' Raylan said, 'wholesaling marijuana. Drug Enforcement thinks of your boys as hightech rednecks drivin around in Cadillacs, talkin to each other on cell phones.'

'You ever get to accuse my boys face-to-face,' Pervis said, bringing out a jar of moonshine from under the counter, a peach floating in the clear whiskey, 'this'll help ease your pain.'

*   *   *

Pervis put on his gray hat with the snap brim he'd been wearing the better part of his life, and went up the log steps two hundred feet to his home: a two-story white frame house he'd have repainted as

14

it showed wear. He went in the bathroom and took a leak, shook the dew off his lily and started going again, goddamn it.

Rita was on the couch in the sitting room watching *Days of Our Lives*. He got close enough to see she was asleep in her maid's uniform, her bare legs coming out of the skirt that covered her hips and stopped there.

Rita was a black girl, black as ebony, man oh man, the Queen of Africa Pervis found waiting in line for work. He said to her, 'You're on the dodge, aren' 'cha? You know how to pick this stuff? Don't matter. You cook?'

Rita said, 'What you have in mind?'

She was his maid and cooked all right, mostly Mex. Pervis paid her a hundred dollars a day every day at supper. A time came, he said, 'How much you have in the suitcase? The one in your closet?' He thought about it and said, 'Jesus Christ, you must have a hunnert thousand easy.'

'A hundred and five,' Rita said. 'But it ain't in the suitcase.'

'You leavin me?'

'I got to get into something, put the whole thing into weed you let me have cheap cause we in each other's hearts. Least once a week you feel stirrings in your dick, who is it says time to go beddy-bye?'

Pervis said, 'You want to sell weed?' Like he couldn't believe his ears. 'That's all? You want to be set up? Tell me what you want.'

Feeling better now, relieved. He'd help her out if she'd stay here in the house. They'd talk about it. Right now he had to see Bob Valdez. Sat down by the phone and dialed Bob's number. He waited a few rings, hung up, waited a minute and dialed the

15

number again.

This time he heard, 'Bob Valdez, at your service.'

'Bob,' Pervis said, 'you keep your cell on you. Have I told you that before? I believe I have.' He didn't give Bob a chance to say a word, told him, 'Stay put, I'm comin out to see you,' and hung up the phone.

Bob Valdez, the name he was going by at this time, was loaned to Pervis by the Mexican Mafia—what they called themselves—to act as security, watch over the patches and see they got their cut. Pervis would put up with it for the time being. This Bob Valdez had been a gun thug for mine owners during strikes. He had his own patch and drove a four-door Mercedes, a black one. He also had a tricked-out ATV, that little all-terrain number that climbed up the sides of mountains. Bob was a born American, but preferred acting Mexican in his ways. Today Pervis would tell Bob about this marshal bothering him.

*   *   *

They had breakfast in Harlan at the Huddle House, Art noticing the way Raylan broke up a strip of bacon in his grits, a pat of butter melting in it, and added salt, Art asking Raylan if he'd tried the jar Pervis gave him.

'It was good. The peach didn't mess it up any. I had a couple of pulls and gave it to an old coot on the street. It brought tears to his eyes.'

Art said, 'You know marijuana's now the biggest cash crop in the state?'

'Makes you proud,' Raylan said. 'We right on California's tail, and I guess Maui Wowee's.

16

It shows we're resourceful. Seventy thousand coal miners out of work, a bunch of 'em become planters. Last night on TV this news reader with the hair said marijuana was getting out of hand. He said you come across any patches, be sure to report it to the police. You believe it? The only people get worked up over reefer are ones never tried it.'

Art said, 'You haven't seen Pervis's boys.'

'Not yet.'

'You know he's called them by now,' Art said. 'You can kiss your BMW good-bye, they'll know it. DEA has a *Merc*edes they might let you have.'

Raylan liked the way this breakfast was going.

He said, 'The one I want is the doctor, and the only way I have of getting to him is through the Crowes, to tell me about him. Was the doctor working for a cut, so to speak? Or'd they grab one off the street. The doctor at the hospital said he was a pro. Used the latest method of extracting kidneys, the right spots in the belly, but didn't close up after. That was left to whoever used the staples. One of the Crowes? I want to ask 'em about it in a public place, so I don't get shot or beat up.'

Art said, 'Or we get the state cops to lean on 'em till they give up the doctor.'

'I don't know,' Raylan said, 'I'm starting to think it might be the doctor running the show. Calls the Crowes when he needs heavy lifting done.'

*　　　*　　　*

Pervis drove out to the camp in his Ford V8, a blower sticking out of the hood, and watched Bob Valdez approach from the barn. It was home to field hands who'd come to plant and return in ninety days to prune and trim Pervis's marijuana, the crops in this part of Knox County.

The day Pervis hired him he said, 'Bob, you keep what you make off your patch. You catch anybody growing weed on their own without my say, snap a varmint trap to their foot and fire 'em.'

Bob Valdez cocked a willow root straw close on his eyes in the afternoon sun. He wore a .44 revolver holstered on his hip and liked to stand around the yard with his thumbs hooked in his gun belt and make remarks to girls in the crew. He liked that hot-lookin black girl, Pervis's housemaid, and would stop by there when he knew Pervis was at his store. Rita would tell him, 'Mister ain't here.' Told him every time he pulled up in his ATV making a racket. A few days ago she said, 'Bob, you want to fuck me, huh? Mister finds out you come by, he can have your ass deported.'

'Hell you talkin about?' Bob said. 'I'm as American as Daniel Boone, born here in Kaintuck.'

'You gonna die here he finds out you messing with his maid.'

'You kiddin me?' Bob said. 'Mister's not once ever tried yellin at me. He knows better.'

'He never raises his voice to anybody,' Rita said, 'cause he don't have to.'

*   *   *

This time Pervis came by to tell Bob, 'I want you to do something for me.'

'I'm your man,' Bob said.

'A U.S. marshal come to see me name of Raylan Givens. You know which one I mean?'

'I'm pretty sure. Yeah, he was pointed out, wears

18

a good-lookin hat.'

'I want you to keep him away from my boys.'

Bob said, 'Oh?' He said, 'Is this guy a pervert?'
Bob tryin hard to look serious. He said, 'You want
me to become like a babysitter for Coover and
Dickie?'

Pervis stared at him.

Pervis said, 'In this part of the United States of
America, I got enormous pull. Way more'n your
Taco Mafia. I got judges doin favors for me and
state troopers among my best friends. I call 'em
down on you, you're in jail inside an hour. Bob, you
get smart with me again, that's how we'll play it.'

Bob said, 'Hey, come on,' managing a grin. 'I was
jus kid-din around with you.'

Pervis said, 'Keep this marshal away from my
boys or I'll hire somebody knows how.'

He got in his blown Ford V8 and blew away.

CHAPTER THREE

Coming out of the Huddle House Art said, 'Medical
schools use ten thousand cadavers a year. All over
the world there's a need for body parts.'

'Then why'd these guys,' Raylan said, 'only take
Angel's kidneys? Turn around and sell 'em back to
him the same day. Maybe this is a new way to work
it. They don't have to store the body and wait for
buyers.'

'That takes a lot of planning, pickin out the
victims,' Art said. 'I don't see these jitterbugs have
the patience. Angel's ready to make a deal, he'll
come up with the money. You come along and tell

19

him he doesn't have to.'

'What else am I gonna promise him? But what do these dumbbells know about the business of selling kidneys?'

'It's in the news,' Art said. 'The guy in New Jersey sold off parts from a thousand cadavers.'

Raylan said, 'I don't see the Crowes reading the paper less they're in it.'

'A hundred pounds of marijuana,' Art said, 'should gross you three hundred thousand—once you grow and cultivate it and get it to market. A human body with all its parts sold separate, the kidneys, the heart, other organs, the liver, the eyes . . . bone, tendons, the skin sold by the square inch, can get you up to a quarter million.'

Raylan said, 'The guy in New Jersey with the crematorium.'

'The funeral director,' Art said. 'He finishes the service and calls in his cutters. An hour later they've harvested all the guy's parts worth taking and shoved what's left in the incinerator.'

'That's different'n what we're lookin at,' Raylan said. 'Ours sounds more like a mom-and-pop operation. But, man, they can make the dough.'

'Say a doctor loses his license and is sellin dope scrips out the back door,' Art said. 'He's known the Crowes since whoopin cough and the measles.'

'Treated 'em for a dose or two once they reached puberty,' Raylan said. 'The boys live in different hollers and trade girls back and forth. DEA says once girls go up there they run home screamin.'

'This doctor drugs Angel,' Art said, 'but needs somebody to put him in the tub.'

'And before you know it,' Raylan said, 'the Crowes are in the body business. That make sense?'

'Does to me,' Art said. 'I meant to tell you, I brought Rachel back to watch over you.'

* * *

Raylan was driving an Audi Quattro, loaned to him off the DEA lot in Harlan. He said to Rachel Brooks next to him, 'I had this car one time before. I liked it, except the hood rattled at one-forty.'

'On these roads?' Rachel doubtful.

'Zero to sixty in five seconds,' Raylan said, 'we ever let her out.'

'Where we goin?'

'Up here to a cemetery, has a view of Pervis's store. He won't set up a meeting with his boys, we have to wait till they come visit their old dad.'

They turned off the Stinking Creek road where it forked at Buckeye and drove up a low rise to the cemetery, a field of gravestones marked MILLS and MESSER.

'A few have been here more'n a hundred and fifty years,' Raylan said. 'That one right there, John Mills, "Gone to the Mansions of Rest." What would you like on your stone?'

'I don't know,' Rachel said. 'Can I have a few years to think about it?'

'Gobel Messer's says "Meet Me in Heaven." Confident by the time he passed over.' Raylan put the car in gear and crept through the cemetery to the far side. He said, 'Now look straight ahead. That's Pervis's store over there through the trees. I make it sixty yards.'

Rachel got out her binoculars, raised them and said, 'I'm inside the store, nobody shopping this morning. Now a man's in the doorway lighting a cigarette.'

'A Camel,' Raylan said. 'That's Pervis. His boys should be along. Have to give their old dad his cut.'

'Of what?'

'The money they took off Angel.'

'How do we know that?' Rachel still watching the store.

'DEA says Pervis runs the show, he's Big Daddy. The boys hang out, get stoned and chase girls, till the dad tells 'em what he wants done. He's got Mexicans run the business in the field. Does it all from that dinky store. He's the marijuana king of East Kentucky, but DEA can't put it on him and make it stick.'

Rachel said, 'The Crowes' daddy's in the body parts business now?'

'No, and won't believe his boys are,' Raylan said. 'Wouldn't accept what I told him about the kidneys. Kept shaking his head. His boys would never cut into a human body, or stand to watch anybody doing it.'

'You believe him?' Rachel said.

'Yeah, cause he can't imagine himself doing it. I said, "They know how to dress a buck, don't they? Clean him out?" Pervis had a gun he'd of shot me. It was a dumb thing to say.'

Rachel was looking off.

'Finally here come somebody. Looks like a brother drivin the Cadillac. Only one in the car.'

She handed Raylan the glasses.

He raised them saying, 'DEA has this guy with the boys only a couple weeks. Drives Coover and Dickie around. His name's Cuba something. It's in my notes with a mug shot.'

She opened Raylan's folder and said, 'Cuba

22

Franks, forty-five-year-old African American . . . Come on, the man's in his sixties. Look at the lines, the old scars on his face. Five arrests, two convictions. Slim body, has that offhand strut.' She was watching Cuba get out and walk to the car's trunk.

'Check his hair,' Raylan said, handing Rachel the glasses. 'You ever see hair that straight on a brother?'

'Not around here,' Rachel said.

'He's got a bunch of white genes but not enough to pass.'

'Or maybe he did but didn't care for the life,' Rachel said.

'Lost his sense of rhythm,' Raylan said, 'but he's still cool.'

'Knows he is,' Rachel said, 'the do-rag matching the shirt. You notice the crease in the pants? Has to be careful putting 'em on, he don't cut himself.'

Raylan said, 'What you suppose he's doing for the boys?'

'You mean besides drivin 'em around?'

'Cuba comes along, the next thing, the boys are stealin kidneys.'

Rachel took her time. 'You want to know who's working for who.'

'I don't want to miss anything,' Raylan said.

He took the glasses again and watched this guy with the strange name lift a case of Budweiser out of the trunk and hold it in the fingers of one hand to hang down against his leg as he closed the trunk lid. Going toward the store he had the case in both hands again, kicked the bottom of the screen door for Pervis to come open it for him.

Raylan lowered the glasses.

'What's in the beer case?'

'I doubt any Bud,' Rachel said, 'the way he was holdin it.'

'I think it's the old dad's cut,' Raylan said. 'We'll get out of here and let Cuba run into us down the road.'

*   *   *

It's what they did, drove to where the buckeye fork came out and waited in the narrow strip of road.

Rachel said, 'The Crowes've been drivin their own cars since they're twelve years old. Like to drive fast.'

'Yes, they do,' Raylan said.

'Then why they sitting in the backseat now, telling their chauffeur where to go?'

'Or is he telling them things,' Raylan said, 'they never heard of before?'

'About body parts?' Rachel said. 'That what you mean?'

'He's coming,' Raylan said, watching dust rising into the trees, watching the Cadillac coming straight at them until it braked and rolled to a stop about thirty feet from the Audi's front end.

'Wants us to walk up there,' Raylan said. 'Look us over.'

'I've done it,' Rachel said and raised the binoculars. 'Now he's got his cell out making a call.'

'Who you think he's talking to?'

'The brothers,' Rachel said. 'I don't mean the *brothers,* I mean Coover and Dickie.'

They sat in the car waiting. Finally Cuba got out of the Cadillac and came toward them, taking his time.

'Got the stroll down,' Rachel said.

'Can feel he's a dude,' Raylan said.

'I might go for some of that,' Rachel said, 'he didn't boost cars.'

'Turn your little recorder on,' Raylan said. 'Gonna come up on your side.'

Cuba did, giving Rachel a nice smile as he leaned in, his hands on the windowsill.

'How you doin? Have some car trouble?'

Rachel said, 'Mr. Franks, we'd like to ask you a few questions and see your driver's license.' She held up her star hanging from her neck on a chain.

Cuba saw the badge as he straightened and looked at the sky before coming back to the window.

'What'd I do? You people been all over me since I got my job.'

'We're marshals service,' Rachel said. 'DEA's the one botherin you.'

'I still haven't done nothin. I'm workin as a chauffeur.'

Raylan leaned against the steering wheel to look at Cuba. 'You got your chauffeur's license?'

'I'm getting it out,' Cuba said.

'Driving the marijuana boys around?'

'I don't hear their business,' Cuba said. 'I find out they into reefer, I'm gone.'

He handed his license to Rachel.

She looked at it and said, 'How you work here and live in Memphis?'

'It's my home. I get time off, I go see my mama.'

'I'd go to Memphis,' Raylan said, 'for the ribs.'

'Now you talkin,' Cuba said. 'Best bar-b-que in the world's at the Germantown rib joint.'

'The Germantown Commissary,' Raylan said.

'Corky's is good.'

'I love Corky's,' Rachel said. 'They serve that pulled pork shoulder. Best anyplace.'

Raylan said to her, 'You're from Memphis?'

'Tupelo, Mississippi,' Rachel said. 'Lived across the tracks from Elvis's house.'

Raylan grinned. 'You'd see him?'

'He was gone by the time I was born. I got to cleanin houses and this white lady said I needed to go to college and paid my way, four years at Ole Miss.'

'I believe Ole Miss,' Raylan said, 'has the best-looking girls of any college in the country. Even Vanderbilt. Ole Miss, the girl's an eight-plus, she doesn't have to pass her SATs.'

'Excuse me,' Cuba said. 'Y'all have things to discuss, I may as well be goin.'

Raylan said, 'Cuba, why don't you get in the car so we can talk.'

'It's *Cooba,* how you say my name. But I haven't done nothin, I'm clean, done my time.'

Raylan said, 'Cooba? Open the door and get in the car.'

He did, and Raylan adjusted his mirror.

'What're you doing with the Crowes?'

'I drive 'em around. I was in the racing business, same as their daddy. Quarter-mile dirt, slide through the turns, man. The Crowes thought they could drive—have a pickup with juice? I scared 'em to death showin what real drivin's like. Throw it in reverse, hit the gas, pull the hand brake, and spin around.'

'Hey, Cooba?' Raylan said. 'Every boy in Harlan County knows how to do a reverse-one-eighty. Taught by their grampas. So why'd the Crowes hire you?'

'I 'magine so they can sit back, take it easy.'

Raylan said, looking at the mirror, 'The boys hired you or you hired them? Couple of dumbbells, do the lifting for you.'

'Yeah, I'm the boss,' Cuba said. 'I wait in the car someplace they havin a good time, I'm listenin to Loretta Lynn.'

'They call you "boy"?'

'They do, I'm gone.'

'It's a good cover,' Raylan said, 'working as their chauffeur. They don't get arrested you don't either. I bet you let the Crowes think they're partners in the deal. But you still tell 'em what to do.'

Cuba in the mirror stared, didn't say a word.

'How much of a cut they get for helping with Angel? Puttin him in the ice water? Once the doctor removed his kidneys.'

Now he was frowning.

'Like you don't know what I'm talkin about,' Raylan said. 'You wouldn't have to've been there. Less you brought the doctor to the motel. That how it worked? I'm thinkin the doctor must've hired you. Caught you stealin his car and signed you up. You look around for some dumb white boys and hire the Crowes?'

'You telling me,' Cuba said, 'I got somethin goin with takin people's kidneys and then sellin 'em?'

'I see you as the middleman,' Raylan said, 'between the doctor and the Crowes.'

'You want to talk to Coover and Dickie? Ask 'em about stealin kidneys?' Cuba said. 'I be anxious to see that.'

27

CHAPTER FOUR

Coover and Dickie Crowe were still boys in their forties. When they weren't driving around looking for poon, they hung out at Dickie's house the other side of the mountain watching porn. Coover's house was a mess and smelled. Dickie's was busy inside with his Elvis Presley memorabilia:

Fifty-seven photographs of Elvis in the front room, posters in the hall and kitchen. There were Elvis bobble heads; a bong looking like Elvis; a jar of dirt from the garden at Graceland; a photo of a cloud formation that looked like Elvis that Dickie paid a hundred dollars for; and a pair of towels Elvis used to wipe his face while performing, now doilies on the backrests of Dickie's La-Z-Boys.

Coover said, 'I thought you was getting rid of all this Elvis shit, tired of lookin at it.'

'When I get around to it,' Dickie said.

'Give it to the nigger, he can sell it.'

'I *said,* when I get around to it.'

Dickie had dismal hair he combed back and teased into a wave he sprayed to hold rigid. He wore starched white shirts with Hollywood collars that touched his earlobes, bought a dozen in Las Vegas for a bill apiece.

Coover had hair growing wild he never combed. Girls told him, Jesus, it didn't hurt to take a bath once in a while, clean his house, least use some soap powder on that pile of dishes. They told him he was gonna have rats nesting in his kitchen. Coover said, 'They's already some moved in.' He wore Ed Hardy T-shirts or the 'Death and Glory' track jacket that had a skull and dagger on it.

*   *   *

You'd never tell they were brothers. Dickie was picky and liked to scowl, his bony face sticking out of his Hollywood collars. Coover, stoned most days, did whatever he felt like. Dickie would say, 'I'm telling you for the last time, clean yourself up, or I'll shoot you in the ass while you're sleepin.' Coover'd say, 'Where you gettin the balls to do it?' They spoke like that to each other all the time.

Dickie said, 'You talk to Pap?'

'He started on me about kidneys,' Coover said. 'I'm like, "What're you sayin I done? You gone crazy?"'

'I give him a hurt look,' Dickie said. 'Ask him, "You believe me and Coove'd do somethin like that?"'

'I ast was he drinkin again.'

'He don't want to hear we cut into a body,' Dickie said, 'but he don't see nothin wrong with sellin the kidneys. He said, "You realize they's hundreds of people need kidneys?" And did I know they'd pay to get 'em? Pap said thousands of dollars. You know what he's tellin us, don't you?'

'Sayin he don't mind us bein in the kidney business,' Coover said, 'long as he gets his money.'

Dickie still had a grin on his face.

'You can't help but love old Pap, can you?'

*   *   *

Coover had let Cuba Franks take his car to deliver ten grand to Pervis, their old man's cut of what

29

they'd scored off Angel. It meant Dickie had to drive over to Coover's this morning, sit in the smelly house and talk about what they were into now, like this kidney business. Dickie wasn't sure he liked it.

Coover came in the front room from the kitchen to tell him, 'God damn rats are lickin the dirty dishes again.' He pulled out the top drawer of an old chiffarobe.

'What're you lookin for?'

'My Smith, goddamn it.'

'I been wantin to ask you,' Dickie said, 'did it bother you any puttin Angel in the bathtub?'

'Did it *bother* me?'

'All the blood.'

'It wasn't ourn, was it?' Coover brought a chromed Smith & Wesson .44 out of the top drawer. He said, 'I had to close him up and I did. I don't want to hear no more about it.'

'We didn't do one thing fast enough,' Dickie said. 'Even strippin him.'

'What'd I say? "You want him nekked, whyn't you bring shears?" But you know what I'm thinkin,' Coover said. 'We watch a few more times, shit, we'll know how to snip out a kidney. Me and you'll split the hunnert thou.'

'What if the guy dies on us?' Dickie said.

'The first time, yeah, we might cut somethin we shouldn't of, but we still got the kidneys. Keep the fucker alive and sell him back his own set, that's the ticket.'

'I'd just as soon,' Dickie said, 'not be in so big a goddamn hurry.'

'Look at it like learnin a trade,' Coover said, spinning the cylinder of his revolver to check the loads.

30

Dickie stepped to the door and opened it to let some air come in the house. He looked out and said, 'Cuba's back,' watching the Cadillac turn into the yard trailing dust. 'Hey, and another car's comin behind.'

Coover was going in the kitchen with his Smith, not looking around.

*   *   *

They were out of the trees now, driving into the yard, Raylan creeping behind the Cadillac, and the sound of gunfire—two shots fired, that flat, hard sound, and two more—got Raylan to swerve around the Cadillac, Rachel calling out, 'Where is he?' Raylan braking, rolling up to the porch.

'He wasn't shooting at us,' Raylan said.

Cuba Franks brought the Cadillac alongside and got out saying the same thing. 'Coover's cleanin his house is all, with his six-gun.'

Raylan was on the porch now, Rachel out of the car watching his back. She saw Cuba Franks step up on the porch with his cool stride but anxious now, she could tell. Her eyes were on Raylan and saw Dickie come out on the porch in his Hollywood shirt, Dickie looking like his pictures. She heard him say to Raylan:

'I'd swear you were drivin a Beamer.'

Rachel saw the way his long fingers lay against his thighs, then moved into the slit pockets of his Levi's.

Now Coover was coming out, bright-metal revolver in one hand, at his leg, a dead rat in the other, Coover holding it up by the tail.

'All the shootin,' Dickie said, 'that's what you

31

got?'

Coover's gaze went to Raylan, giving the marshal his mean look. He said, 'Another one of the fuckers is still in the kitchen. You like to try for it?'

'I shot rats when I was a kid,' Raylan said. 'Chase 'em out of the shithouses.' He said to Coover, 'All you have to do is go out'n the kitchen, huh?'

Coover squinted at him. 'Where I know you?'

'They're marshals,' Dickie said, 'him and the Negress.'

Coover looked toward Cuba. 'Set up those lawn chairs—they someplace—we can sit down and talk.' He said to Raylan, 'You can ask am I growin reefer and I'll tell you no. But first I ask you any God damn thing I want. How's that sound?'

'I only have one question,' Raylan said. 'How'd you and your brother get in the kidney business?'

*   *   *

Rachel stood by the Audi watching Raylan, Raylan the show.

Watched him facing Coover holding the bright-metal piece at his leg. Watched Coover swing the rat by the tail and let it go and saw it coming at her to land on the hood of the Audi. Rachel didn't move. Raylan didn't either, didn't glance around.

But said, 'Coover, you throw a dead rat at my car. What're you trying to tell me?'

Rachel unsnapped the holster riding on her hip.

Coover said, 'Take it any way you want, long as you know I'm serious.'

'You're telling me you're a mean son of a bitch,' Raylan said to his face. 'You know how many wanted felons have given me that look? I say a thousand I know I'm low. Some turn ugly as I snap on the cuffs; they're too late. Some others, I swear, even try to draw down on me. All I'm asking, how'd you come to take Angel's kidneys?'

Dickie looked at Cuba and Raylan said, 'I asked him the same thing. He told me talk to you.'

Cuba said, 'You see what the man's doin? I told him I have nothin to do with kidneys 'cept eat 'em.'

Coover was squinting at him now. 'I want to know what you told him.'

'Listen to you,' Cuba said. 'You ask me that? Get it in your stone head, I have nothin to say to this man.'

Raylan hearing a new Cuba Franks, one he hadn't met.

He said, 'Cuba, I got you on tape telling me talk to the Crowes.'

'*You* the one say you want to talk to 'em. I told you go ahead, I'm not stoppin you.'

'I know you were at the motel,' Raylan said, 'but you didn't show yourself to Angel, like these mutts. All I want is the doctor's name. Coover can get back to shooting rats, you can do what you want, till tomorrow.'

'You come in a man's home,' Dickie said, 'don't even have a warrant and talk like that?'

'I'm making it easy,' Raylan said. 'You want, I'll put you before a grand jury. Give us the doctor or do time.'

Dickie said, 'Coove, you hear him? He's threatenin us.'

'He's got a piece under his coat,' Coover said.

Dickie said, 'You got one in your *hand,* for Christ sake.'

33

Raylan turned enough to look at Rachel.

'You hear these bozos?'

'I sure do.'

'Coover raises his piece, shoot him.'

'If you'll move a step either way,' Rachel said.

He did, saying, 'I'll tend to Dickie.'

'Hey, come on,' Dickie said, raising his hands. 'I ain't even packin.'

'Here's my offer,' Raylan said. 'Give me the doctor or I'm back tomorrow with the warrants you want. You and your brother, once the court sees how dumb you are, might draw only forty months. Cuba's done time but still up to no good. He's looking at two hundred months on top the forty.'

Cuba said, 'You want to tell me what I done?'

Raylan said, 'It'll be on the warrant,' and looked at Coover. 'What's the rat killer want to do? I bet the weed's telling you things, huh? If you can believe weed.' Raylan turned to look at Dickie again. 'So we'll see y'all tomorrow?'

Rachel had her Glock in both hands, covering the scene.

Raylan, coming out to the Audi, kept his eyes on her. She let him get in and start the car before she opened the door.

'You tried to give him the idea,' Rachel said, 'short of kickin him in the crotch.'

'He wasn't up to it,' Raylan said. 'Stoned, what he'll tell his brother.'

'But what if he raised his piece?'

'You'd of shot him,' Raylan said.

*   *   *

They drove out of the yard Raylan saying, 'They're

34

gonna run and hide.' He paused. 'Or get in touch with the doctor. The Crowes, Coover's a chronic stoner. Dickie—'

'He don't want to get his hands dirty,' Rachel said.

'Dickie's the one to watch,' Raylan said, 'he's a sneak. Cuba . . . he's makin up his mind right now if he wants to be seen with these boneheads.'

Rachel said, 'Art's gonna want to know what we're up to.'

'We'll tell him we're in pursuit. We'll call again if we need help.'

'We not gonna try for warrants?'

'I never gave it a thought. We'll get state troopers on 'em instead. Find out where they go.'

Rachel said, 'Raylan . . . You expect they gonna take us to the doctor?'

'You don't think so?'

'I have serious doubts.'

'They don't come through,' Raylan said, 'I'll ask St. Christopher to find him for us.'

CHAPTER FIVE

The Crowes were still on the porch, Cuba inside making a phone call, Dickie telling his brother, 'All you had to do—Coover, goddamn it, I'm talkin to you. All you had to do was bend your arm, that's all, pull the trigger and shoot him through the heart. Same with the Negress. Get Cuba to dig a hole, nobody ever sees 'em again.'

Coover looked up at his brother and said, 'What . . .?'

'You're smokin Daddy's Own, aren't you?' Dickie said. 'Like smokin rocket fuel. Stick to Bitty's, Pap named for Mama when she took sick. Member how he'd call her his Little Bitty? He was good to Mama, wasn't he?'

''Cept he'd come home from drinkin with lovin on his mind and Mama'd throw kerosene at him, set him afire.' Coover grinning. 'Old Pap had to quit drinkin fore he stopped beatin her up. Hasn't had any since, I know of.'

*   *   *

Coming out on the porch Cuba said, 'Man, that kitchen's a rat café, find all they can eat. You hear 'em, don't you?'

'They mostly quiet as mice,' Coover said, and told Cuba, 'I'll give you a hunnert dollars you cook one and eat it.'

'How we did 'em in the ghet-to,' Cuba said to the fool, 'was well done, burn off all that hair on his ass. I never cared for rat. You eat a sick one you go to bed with a touch of the bubonic plague.'

'They're hardly any meat on him,' Coover said. 'You can chew his tiny bones. Hell, you can chew him up you take the skin off, it's the unhealthy part.'

'Get it crispy,' Cuba said, thinking: These hill folk gonna fuck up on the job. He said to the Crowes, 'I talk to Miss just now.'

Coover said, 'I keep forgettin her name. Lila?'

'Leela,' Dickie said. 'Like the song.'

Both fools getting the name wrong. Cuba didn't correct them. He said, 'She wants this next one straight, no reefer business, no people we know

36

givin us the kidneys.' Cuba said, 'Listen to me now.'
Meaning it. 'These next gigs gonna be different. We
leave the man in the tub and call a hospital. But see
then, we sell the kidneys to a body parts broker and
he goes with the best offer he gets, sellin to people
in the hospital. The sick person can't come up with
the money the parts broker wants, he crosses the
name off.'

Dickie said, 'Leela must be sellin to the broker
cheapen'n she could make sellin to the sick person.'

Like he just thought of it. Cuba said to Dickhead,
'You use the broker so you don't expose yourself
sellin to the market. See, but you can do one a
night, you want.'

Coover said, 'She ever talk about doin a woman?
Get her in the tub nekked. One with big ninnies.'

'You see 'em floatin in the ice water,' Dickie
said, 'the nips stickin straight up.'

Cuba said, 'I told her about the marshals
stopping by. Comin back tomorrow with warrants.'

Dickie said, 'We go and hide?'

'She say lay low for a while.'

'*Lay low*—' Dickie said. 'Her name's not Leela,
it's Laylo, ain't it? Same as the song.'

Cuba went out to the hardpack yard and phoned
her on his cell, looking up at trees, clouds hanging
over the ridgeline.

'How you doin? You close to the next job?'

Her voice said, 'I don't want to use those guys
again, they're more baggage than porters.'

'You want to cut 'em loose?'

'They know who I am.'

'They still don't have your name right.'

'Why don't you find a way to dismiss them,' Layla
said. 'All right?'

CHAPTER SIX

Months ago, before hooking up with the Crowes, Cuba first set eyes on Layla the Dragon Lady.

It was in the Blue Grass Room at Keeneland, the thoroughbred racetrack on the outskirts of Lexington; his boss Mr. Harry Burgoyne telling him, 'Go on wait at the bar till I motion you to come out on the floor.'

Meaning they'd be doing one of their Boss and Dumb African routines. Cuba watched Mr. Harry walk out to address tables of horse lovers applauding his winning the three-hundred-thousand-dollar Maker's Mark Mile not an hour ago.

The girl next to Cuba at the bar, Weezie, her dad one of the trainers, finished sucking up her Collins and said, 'Doesn't it piss you off the horse is called Black Boy?'

'They had to call it Black Boy,' Cuba said. 'What else you gonna call this stud's got all the fillies flippin their tails at him.'

The girl went off grinning to tell what he said and Cuba was looking at Layla the Dragon Lady, facing him in her dark glasses and shiny black raincoat a few feet away.

'Excuse me,' Cuba said, 'but can you tell me what is the time?' Giving the words that clipped African sound he got from cabdrivers in Atlanta.

He watched her slip off her sunglasses this overcast afternoon in April to show her brown eyes holding on him like bullets. She smiled and her eyes turned soft.

'That was funny, what you said to Weezie.'

Cuba checking her nice nose and mouth, that kind of lower lip on a woman he liked to bite.

'But,' she said, 'you forgot your African accent.'

He did, talkin about that fuckin stud Black Boy and trying to sound cool. He could ask how she recognized the accent, but didn't. Cuba took a moment and said, 'East or West Africa?'

Giving it back to this woman wanted to play with him.

She said, 'West, Nigeria. I spent an entire year in Lagos with a transplant team. Came back to my home base, UK Medical.'

Cuba said, 'I drove Mr. Burgoyne there one time, his kidneys actin up.'

'His kidneys are still working,' Layla said. 'It's his liver needs a rest.'

'Man likes his booze. Has a few he turns into a human being,' Cuba said. 'So you're a nurse, huh?'

She said, 'Why not an MD?'

'You wouldn't be playin with me,' Cuba said.

She told him she was a transplant nurse and Cuba said, 'You like foolin with people's organs?'

'When I can fool with them,' Layla said. 'It depends on who's doing the surgery. I've been assisting as long as some of the older guys've been switching organs, going on eleven years. I've seen enough kidney transplants I can make the switch myself and close up. One of the young guys, all he wants me to do is slap instruments in his hands and go to bed with him.'

She waited.

Cuba said, 'You go for the older guys, huh?'

'You're missing the point. The young guy comes out of the OR thinking he's God, he's just saved a

39

patient's life and expects me to reward him.'

'Yeah . . . ?'

'I tell him I'm worn out. I've worked twelve hours, pre-and post-op besides surgery, I'm beat. He can't believe I'm turning him down. We've had coffee a few times, he's told me to call him Howie if I want. He goes, "Come on, I've got an empty room lined up. We can make it a quickie or do the other."'

'You meet his desires?'

'Listen, will you? I can do the same surgery as Dr. Blow Job, who makes close to a million a year while I'm paid eighty-seven five. Does that mean I should go down on him?'

Cuba had to pay attention, quit thinking about biting her lip. She sounded pissed off, so he didn't think she gave the doctor with the hard-on what he wanted. Now she switched to Cuba, asking him what he did in his previous life, before he became Mr. Harry's boy. He told her he drove, raced dirt track, ran moonshine, dealt some reefer.

She said, 'How much prison time have you done?'

He saw it coming and told her, 'It took some years from me.' He said, 'You want my sheet? I'll see I can get you one. Cars, what I did time for, expensive ones.' Pretty sure he was telling this Dragon Lady what she wanted to hear.

It was that chick in the funnies she reminded him of, the Dragon Lady, used to be in *Terry and the Pirates*. Terry the ofay kid with the hair never got mussed. If he wasn't fucking the Dragon Lady Cuba believed he must go the other way.

Layla seemed calm now, staring at him with those brown bullets she could turn soft as he looked on.

Layla said, 'Cuba?'

'Yeah . . .?'

'I'm tired of hospitals. Tell me what you're tired of.'

Cuba saw Mr. Harry waving at him and said, 'You gonna see it in a minute.'

*　　　*　　　*

Time for the routine: Mr. Harry waving Cuba out to the tables of horse lovers, Mr. Harry holding a drink now. Good, ready to show his friends his idea of a regular guy. He watched Cuba coming around to the front of the room and Mr. Harry began to frown. This was part of the act, seeing Cuba in his black suit and black shirt, a bright lavender necktie popping out of the dark look.

Mr. Harry: 'Who said you could wear my colors with your chauffeur's uniform?'

Cuba telling himself to sound Ah-frican. A real African ever showed up at one of these he was fucked.

Cuba: 'Was your missus, Boss.' He waited a couple of beats before saying, 'It is your missus dresses me.'

This got a burst of laughs from the horse lovers.

Mr. Harry: '*Mrs.* Harry told you to wear my racing colors?'

Cuba: 'Because when we out, you always have me racing to get you to a men's room, so I wear your colors.'

Mr. Harry: 'When did I tell you to do that?'

Cuba: 'You never have, Boss, but I believe is what you thinking.'

41

Mr. Harry, to the room: 'I explained to Cuba that calling my winner today Black Boy was never meant as a racial slur.'

Cuba: 'Yes, sir.'

Mr. Harry: 'Tell my friends what you think of the name Black Boy.'

Cuba: 'I'm proud the horse was name for me since it wins all its fuckin races.'

Bursts of laughter.

Mr. Harry: 'Cuba, we don't use African words here in polite society.'

More laughter, but not as much.

*   *   *

Layla watched from the bar. She had told Cuba she was tired of hospitals; now he was showing her what he was tired of: playing the grateful darky, grinning with this asshole's arm around his neck, Cuba reciting his lines on cue.

Mr. Harry was telling the Blue Grass Room it was unfortunate Old Tom got sick and passed away on him. Old Tom, bless his heart, had become fearful of traffic, always drove with his foot on the brake. 'You weren't patient,' Mr. Harry said, 'it could make you irritable.' Mr. Harry paused for the Blue Grass crowd to laugh kindly at him. 'But now Cuba,' Mr. Harry said, 'he'd put his foot on the gas and leave it there. I asked him one time, "Cuba, you never stole cars by any chance, have you?" What'd you tell me?'

Cuba saying, 'I believe I tole you no, Boss, that is one thing the devil never made me do.'

Mr. Harry slapped Cuba's shoulder, told him, 'Get outta here,' the horse lovers laughing, and Mr.

Harry joined a front table making room for him.

*   *   *

Cuba walked back to the bar raising his hand to people applauding, Cuba nodding, grinning until he reached the bar and Layla set her drink in front of him. Cuba picked it up and finished the vodka without looking around. He said, 'You know how many times I been the grateful nigga?'

'Everyone believed you,' Layla said.

'What he said about Old Tom was bullshit. He hired me and fired the old man, why he took sick and died.'

'Watching your skit,' Layla said, 'I couldn't help thinking, one day you're gonna turn around, take Harry by the throat and strangle him in front of his friends. They'll think it's part of the act.'

Cuba said, 'Drivin him in the Rolls, I've thought of aimin the car to send it off a curve, top of the grade. I bail out and watch the man lose his ass. Car hits and blows up, like in the movies. Real life you don't get that much explosion. I'm drivin Mr. Harry . . . the man already has to take a leak. I see in my brights a stretch of road comin up, the side droppin away steep . . . I say to him, "Mr. Harry, get out your dick, we almost there."'

Layla's eyes on him turned warm. She said, 'I think I'm falling in love with you.'

'Try me out,' Cuba said, 'it won't hurt none.'

He watched her take a pack of cigarettes and a lighter from the pocket of her raincoat—expensive-looking, a shiny black one—waited till she was smoking it before he said, 'You know it ain't allowed in here.'

'If they catch you,' Layla said.

'You like to cause a scene?'

'They say anything I take one more drag,' Layla said, 'and put it out.' She moved closer. 'Something I've wanted to tell you about Harry's kidneys—'

'The time I brought him in?'

'He comes in once or twice a year.'

'The man takes a leak every twenty, thirty minutes. Set your watch by it.'

'That's his prostate. His kidneys aren't too bad. He has a pinched nerve in his lower back.'

'His sacroiliac fuckin with him,' Cuba said. 'I had that. Kept me in bed till a chiropractor fixed me up.'

'Harry tells us to get donors with his blood type ready.'

'You need a kidney,' Cuba said, 'I thought you had to wait in line.'

'Harry gives a million a year to the hospital fund. The donor gets a hundred grand the moment he shows up.'

'He wants a kidney so bad,' Cuba said, 'give him one.'

'Or take the old one out,' Layla said, 'and put it back in?'

Cuba grinned. 'Come out the hospital a new man.'

He saw Mr. Harry getting up from the table as Layla said, 'That's kind of what I'm thinking.'

Cuba heard her but kept watching his boss shaking hands with people at the table. He said to Layla, 'I expect to see you pretty soon now we lovers.'

She said, 'How about tonight?'

Didn't hesitate.

'Could be late, I get done haulin his ass around.'

'Come anytime. I'm in bed I'll leave a light on.'

'Tell me where I'm going.'

She laid her hand on a cocktail napkin, folded, and brought it along the bar to Cuba. 'It's all here,' Layla said, 'with a key to let you in.'

Cuba liked how her eyes turned soft looking at him. This was a cool woman with evil ways. The best kind. He said, 'Why don't you lift the kidneys offa Dr. Blow Job?' He said, 'No, he's too close. I think so's Mr. Harry.'

'I have an idea how we'd do Harry.'

'You're exposin your intentions,' Cuba said, 'to a lover?'

'As soon as I heard you're Ah-frican,' Layla said, 'I knew you were my guy.'

CHAPTER SEVEN

'You run out of gas,' Art Mullen said. 'You're on your way to Lexington and you run out of gas. This is after you stirred up the state cops, got 'em looking for the Crowes.'

They were in the Harlan marshal's office, Art standing over Raylan sitting down, trapped in his seat.

'What told you they were taking off for Lexington?' Raylan's boss said.

'It had to be where the doctor was.'

'How you know that?'

'It's where they do transplants.'

'But why do they take off to see the doctor?'

'He runs the show, he'll tell 'em what to do.'

45

'You thought about all that,' Art said, 'and decided not to get warrants. But you didn't look to see if you needed gas.'

'I thought I had at least one more gallon.'

'You know Rachel was against going to Lexington?'

'I don't recall her telling me why.'

'Because you're relying on St. Christopher to find the doctor for you, and there isn't or ever was a St. Christopher. Somebody made him up.'

Raylan said, 'Did you know that?'

'I think so,' Art said. 'But I've never asked him to find anybody for me. You're saying St. Christopher told you to go to Lexington?'

'I worked it out,' Raylan said, 'before I heard anything definite. You know there's a world-famous organ transplant hospital there? UK Medical. They transplant kidneys all day long, seventy miles away from where Angel's were taken.'

'That's what you're goin on?'

'I had a hunch. You have 'em, don't you?'

'How many hunches,' Art said, 'ever come to pass?'

'All right, we know the Crowes are involved. We pick 'em up, talk to 'em, give 'em a deal on their sentence for the doctor.'

Art said, 'If he's a resident at the hospital, he'll be there when we decide to look him up. We got something else coming up, a public meeting in Harlan County about a new mountaintop removal permit.'

Raylan said, 'Like settin the top aside to get at the coal. And all the coal dust settles on the people below. I was a laid-off miner I'd ask the coal company, "You don't have enough money? You

46

got to blow up our mountains?" '

'You want,' Art said, 'you can ask them yourself. They're coming in a week or so, when Ms. Carol Conlan gets back from the Bahamas.'

'You're kiddin, a woman?'

'She's the voice of MT Mining. Main office in Lexington.'

Raylan said, 'She ready for Harlan?'

Art said, 'Anything this lady wants, you pinch the brim of your cowboy hat and say, "Yes, ma'am."'

'While I'm waitin around, you mind if I scare up the Crowes?'

'If you can bring 'em in. You shoot 'em, you'll never find the doctor, will you?'

*   *   *

They were in Layla's motel room in Corbin, Layla packed, ready to return to UK Medical after two weeks off; Cuba here because he wanted to talk to her face-to-face.

'You tell me, dismiss the Crowe brothers,' Cuba said. 'You mean take 'em out.'

They sat at the table in the motel room sipping brandy with the coffee Cuba got from the lobby.

'The way to ask it,' Cuba said, 'did I ever shoot a dude look like he meant to take somethin belong to me, like my car or my life? See, that's different than askin me to go shoot somebody. Know what I'm sayin? You join a young boys gang, they tell you go on out and gun this dude from some other gang. Prove you got the *cojones*. There boys groove on it till they get taken out theirselves. I never was in a gang. I avoid any bloodshed isn't necessary to my state of being. The only time I used a gun—

47

this nine-mil Sig I have—two dudes try to jack the Mercedes I just got done jackin. Big crackhead young niggas come with baseball bats, tell me they gonna bang on the car less I get out. I shoulda sat there. It come to me later, they ain't gonna jack a car the windows broke out. But at the same time I thought I better defend myself. I pulled the Sig and shot both the motherfuckers they standin there waving the bats. Left 'em lyin in the street.'

'I can see it,' Layla said in her easy way. 'You left them for dead?'

'I never heard they made it or passed.'

She reached across the table to lay her hand on his.

'But if you don't do the Crowes they'll tell on us.' She said, 'Starting a new practice things always happen you didn't plan on.' She said, 'Once the Crowes are caught they'll give us up. You know that.'

'I suppose,' Cuba said. 'Only I never walked up to a man I've done business with and shot him. Or got into any kind of gig I ain't positive it's gonna pay off.'

'It's like learning a new procedure,' Layla said. 'Once you have it down . . . Our first week we scored both times, no surprises, four kidneys at ten each. I'm glad I found a good body broker. We can deal with some at the hospital, but you have to get the right ones when you're freelancing. If we do just one a week for a year, extract both kidneys, you know what we make? A million bucks. While Dr. Blow Job's working his ass off five days a week.'

'Your idea of usin masks,' Cuba said, 'made it a scene. The guy in the motel room opens the door, tired, just come off the road. Sees these faces

48

lookin at him—'

'They had to be the right ones,' Layla said.

'Man can't believe what's goin on. Starts to grin as I'm shakin his hand. You jab the needle in the man and I catch him as he goes down.'

'We started laughing,' Layla said, 'I think with relief. Remember?'

'It was *funny*,' Cuba said. 'We laughin in our rubber masks cause it was funny. I always felt, you don't have a good time doin crime, you may as well find a job.'

Layla grinning at him till she said, 'If I had any idea Angel knew the brothers—'

'I *told* you he did. You thinkin we sell 'em back the same day for a hundred grand, your mind busy. Hmmmm, maybe this is how we do Mr. Harry. The man still botherin your mind.'

'You're right,' Layla said, 'I was looking ahead. We know Harry can pay whatever we ask. Like a half mil for the pair?'

'Sounds about right,' Cuba said.

'But how do we collect,' Layla said, 'without exposing ourselves?'

'I was thinking,' Cuba said, 'we could take the Crowe brothers' kidneys.'

He waited.

'That's not a bad idea,' Layla said. 'The boys have to be good for *some*thing.'

'Take out the kidneys,' Cuba said, 'and forget about callin a hospital.'

'You're off the hook,' Layla said. 'Letting a person die isn't the same as killing him. Or is it?'

'A course not,' Cuba said, 'they two different things.'

'It's okay with me,' Layla said, 'either way.'

Raylan had to wait while Art was on the phone talking—Raylan believed—to Lexington, Art showing respect to whoever it was. 'Yes, sir, we're on that one. I was just now discussin the situation with Raylan . . . Raylan Givens . . . No sir, he's doin his job. Okay, I'll tell him.' Art hung up the phone and looked at Raylan across the desk.

'What're you doing?'

'Lookin for Crowes. What'd they want to know?'

'If you'd shot anybody this week.' Art picked up a photo from his desk, a color print, and handed it across to Raylan.

'We have a detainer on Bob Valdez, works security for Pervis Crowe. Though Bob actually works for the Mexican Mafia.'

'What they call themselves. I heard Pervis calls 'em the Taco Mafia,' Raylan said. 'Tell me why we let 'em grow weed here in the U.S.'

'I don't know,' Art said. 'Cause they're good at it?'

He watched Raylan study the color shot of a man named McCready, a laid-off miner.

'He was growing a patch of weed out back of the house. Bob Valdez shot McCready through the leg—you see him pressing the towel to his thigh— and the other guy snapped a varmint trap to his bare foot. Ed took it off, but you can see where it cut him.'

'Who shot the pictures?'

'His little girl Loretta, fourteen. She's been keeping house and going to school since her mama passed, Loretta ten at that time.' He handed Raylan

50

a few more photos. 'That's Ed while they're waitin for the doctor. See his foot? The doctor never made it, got tied up deliverin a baby. Loretta doesn't have a license but can drive. So she took her dad to town.'

'I met Loretta,' Raylan said, 'at Pervis's, she's havin an RC Cola. She asked if I thought she was bold she inquired what I did for a living. She's gonna have a hard time with boys, finding one good enough for her.'

'Anyway,' Art said, 'get the cops to ask Bob about his shootin McCready and bring him in to make his statement.'

'If Loretta said he shot her dad and has pictures of it . . . Why don't we arrest him? Get Loretta's statement, not Bob's. That girl comes right at you.'

'Handle it,' Art said. 'Meanwhile, two young men, both salesmen, woke up in hospitals without their kidneys. One in Lexington, the other Richmond, two days apart and the week before Angel lost his.'

'I remember seein it on the news,' Raylan said, 'but didn't relate it to anything we're doing—yeah, until we found Angel in the tub. I didn't know right away he'd lost his kidneys. You're the one tole me. No, it was Rachel, her mom had transplants. Then I wondered if the Crowes were in on the first ones, the salesmen. Their incisions were closed by a doctor. Angel's, somebody made a mess with the staples. Right away I think of the Crowes, Coover. Why didn't the doctor close Angel? He could've got tired of putting up with the brothers and walked out.'

Art said, 'Where you getting that?'

'It's what I would've done,' Raylan said, 'knowin

51

those dumbbells. A doctor working under pressure in a motel room, he's had enough of the brothers, leaves them to close up. But why'd he hire them to begin with?'

'To heft bodies,' Art said.

'Cuba Frank's there.'

'One thing we know for sure,' Art said, 'it wasn't the Crowes wearing the rubber masks. Both fellas said a man and a woman.'

'The president and Mrs. Obama out havin fun,' Raylan said. 'Making about twenty grand every time they put on their masks.' He said, 'Imagine you open the door and there the Obamas calling on you? They come in the motel room talking.' He said to Art, 'Who's playing Michelle?'

Art said, 'I guess the doctor brought . . . a nurse?'

'Who did . . . ? Cuba Franks?'

It stopped Art. Now he was shaking his head.

'What's wrong with me—Michelle Obama's the doctor.'

'It can't be anybody else, can it?' Raylan said. 'Don't we have tapes of their statements? What the two guys remember?'

'If you want to believe it,' Art said.

'It sounded good to me,' Raylan said. 'Michelle walks up and kisses the guy on the mouth.'

'They both said pretty much the same thing. How she approached, got real close—'

'She lifts her mask from under her chin,' Raylan said, 'to free her mouth and presses it into his. The last thing he remembers is getting turned on. As they come apart she hits him with the needle. He dreams of the First Lady tonguing him while she's taking out his kidneys.'

Art said, 'I wonder if she's black.'

Raylan shook his head. 'They both said she was white.'

*   *   *

Art said a couple times he wondered if she might be a doctor. Raylan said he did too, but couldn't see a woman stealing kidneys in a motel room. Even one pissed off at having her license pulled. 'I'm dyin to meet her.'

'Check on Bob Valdez first,' Art said, 'it having been handed down from above. Then I want the Crowes brought in while I'm getting the warrants.'

'If you get the right judge.'

'I have ways,' Art said. '"Your Honor, I just hope a law enforcement officer isn't gunned down in the line of duty by some weedhead while waitin for warrants."'

'And you get fined for being a smart-ass.'

Art said, 'You can't locate the Crowes, go see Pervis. This evening, no customers botherin him. You want,' Art said, 'threaten to burn his fields he don't give up his boys.'

Raylan was picking at a callous in the palm of his gun hand listening to Art. Raylan stopped picking. He raised his head to look at his boss with an expression of wonder.

'That's where they are, at Pervis's.'

'You threaten 'em,' Art said, 'they run home to their daddy.'

'I don't know why I didn't think of that,' Raylan said.

'You had,' Art said, 'you wouldn't of run out of gas.'

53

CHAPTER EIGHT

COAL KEEPS THE LIGHTS ON.

Raylan read the signs, the coal company rubbing it in. You want coal to heat your house? You have to accept surface mining and the mess it makes; the film of coal dust on your car sitting in the yard. Raylan followed the signs on barns and billboards, finally turning at one reminding him that JESUS SAVES and a mile later came to Ed McCready's property.

*   *   *

McCready lay in bed, his head propped up on a pillow so he could see Raylan, his gunshot wound cleansed and cauterized. He yanked aside the flannel cover to show Raylan his thigh bandaged all the way around. 'Went in my leg,' Ed said, 'turned south and went through the floor of the porch.'

'You're positive,' Raylan said, 'it was Bob Valdez.'

'No, it was some greaser,' Loretta said, 'drove up in his little scooter and shot my dad. Course it was Bob, who else?'

'I remember you at the store,' Raylan said, 'havin an RC Cola.'

Loretta said, 'I remember you too, don't worry. Bob walks up and shoots my dad with a .44 has a six-inch barrel. Soon as I find the bullet under the porch and give you the trap they put him on . . .' She said, 'Daddy, show Raylan your foot.'

'He can see it, it's right there.'

Swollen and bruised, ugly-looking.

'He shot my dad,' Loretta said, 'cause we had a patch growin among the tomatoes. Bob said, "You try and grow any more"'—Loretta putting on his accent—' "I deep you in a barrel of hot tar and set you afire." Threatenin to kill my dad.'

Raylan turned to Ed. 'He set the trap on your foot before or after he shot you?'

'After. I'm layin there bleedin,' Ed said. 'The other greaser pulls off my slipper. I'm sittin on the porch in my house slippers.'

'Before they showed,' Loretta said, 'Bob phoned and said to tell my dad, "Valdez is coming." You ever hear of anything like that?'

'I might've,' Raylan said. 'You sure took some award-winning pictures.'

'With my phone,' Loretta said, and pulled it out of her jeans to show Raylan. 'I got some other pictures of Bob, he comes by on his scooter. He'd pull out the neck of my T-shirt and look inside. I won't tell you what he said.'

'Has he ever, you know,' Raylan said, 'touched any of your like private parts?'

'The greaser shot my dad,' Loretta said, 'and you want to know if he felt me up?'

Raylan said, 'Lemme give you some advice, okay?'

'Don't call 'em greasers?'

'I mean, once you get serious about boys.'

'You kiddin? I already am.'

'All I hope you do,' Raylan said, 'is try to be patient with them.'

*   *   *

55

He watched the camp from high ground, a view through the trees that showed a slice of the hardpack yard and the barn where the Mexican pickers slept in hammocks. Some of them were at the two picnic tables now outside the barn having their noon dinner, Bob Valdez at the end of the table away from the stove. Raylan watched Bob through his glasses: his straw on his eyes, his hand on the rump of a girl serving his beans and rice. Raylan raised the glasses to outbuildings painted white, dressed-up cowsheds off in the pasture.

Inside, the plywood walls painted a flat white, Pervis had his hydroponic gardens, tended with care to maintain air temperature, ventilation, the feeding of nutrients to the water, and a 400-watt lighting system on twenty-four hours a day during germination, and reduced to twelve hours on and twelve off during the growing period. Once harvested, each of Pervis's hundred or so plants would yield an ounce of top-grade marijuana. It gave Pervis a cash crop every three to four months that grossed about fifty thousand dollars.

Raylan wondered if smoking it made you laugh at dumb things you'd think were funny.

Bob might have molested Loretta or he might not have. But he did shoot McCready in his bedroom slippers in front of his daughter, who took pictures with her cell phone Raylan could show Bob, if he needed to. Not down there with the help having their dinner, but off by those cowsheds. He was told Pervis put up signs that said AUTHORIZED BY STATE LAW. KEEP OUT. The way Pervis got around being robbed or arrested. VIOLATORS WILL BE PROSECUTED OR SHOT.

He'd drive down to the yard in the Audi . . . But

56

did he want to confront Bob at the table? Give him a chance to show off, all the help watching him? Raylan could hear Bob: 'Wha you talking about? I shot some old man was scaring me?' Bob playing to the crowd.

What Raylan did, he drove down to the yard following switchbacks until he came out in the open, angled toward the barn and the picnic tables—all the pickers watching him—raised his hand to Bob Valdez and kept going, drove around the barn and out to the pasture, the clean white cowsheds standing in the sun.

*   *   *

They came out for him in a pickup, Bob driving, and pulled up near the Audi.

Raylan stood a distance from the car, the pasture behind him, about sixty feet from the two getting out of the pickup, approaching now, Bob Valdez with his .44 slung low; the other one, another Mexican in a straw hat, carrying a twelve-gauge under his arm like he was out here to shoot birds, relaxed, a step behind Bob. He looked tired. Or he was stoned.

Forty or so feet now Bob stopped and grinned at Raylan.

'I didn't do it. Whatever it is you thinking.'

Raylan said, 'I got snapshots of you shootin Ed McCready.' Raylan's stare went to the other one. 'I got you snappin the coon trap on Ed's foot, Loretta takin the pictures with her phone. You ever hear of that? I got enough to put you in handcuffs and take you in.'

Bob said, 'Yes . . . ? Tell me what you saying.'

'I'm busy. I got something else I have to do.'

'Oh,' Bob said, 'more important than me, uh?'

'All I want to tell you,' Raylan said, 'replant Ed's patch, give him five hundred for the gunshot to his leg, his injured foot, so he won't have to sell Loretta to white slavers. I'm telling you to keep your hands off her. You do all that, we're square. You don't, I'll bust you for shootin him.'

'You kidding me?' Bob said. He sounded a little surprised. 'They two of us here. You got a gun on you somewhere?'

'Look,' Raylan said, 'I take it out I'll shoot you through the heart before you clear your weapon. Your partner, I'll wait for him to wake up. What'd you bring him for?' He saw Bob glance at the other guy. 'He's stoned,' Raylan said. 'Tell me you'll pay Ed so I can get back to work. I'm after a woman steals kidneys and sells 'em.'

Bob said, 'Yeah? I heard of that, selling parts of the body. What's a kidney bring?'

'About ten grand,' Raylan said, 'the going rate.'

'I couldn' do it,' Bob said, shaking his head and setting his straw again. 'Man, cutting in to some guy's body.'

'I couldn't either,' Raylan said. 'What kind of person would it take?'

He watched Bob shrug, maybe thinking he *could* do it.

Raylan said, 'You can't shoot a man, Bob, and tear up his patch. The man has to make a living.'

CHAPTER NINE

Cuba was trying to think of a way to get rid of the Crowe brothers without getting their daddy on him. The only trouble, they were staying with him now, moved into his house, Cuba believed, confident their daddy would protect them, keep them from going to prison. If they weren't his blood Pervis would have fired them years ago. Once Cuba did the two fuckups, the old man ought to thank him for taking a load off his mind. Except Pervis would have to narrow his eyes and swear he'd get the one did it. Cuba thought he might offer the old man consolation after, tell him, 'Least they won't go to prison and get cornholed every day by Negroes.'

Wait.

Or shoot the daddy first? Not have to worry about him?

*   *   *

Climbing the log steps to Pervis's house Cuba had to stop three times to rest his thighs. He had tried the store hoping Pervis was still there and found the place shut for the day. Cuba had made up his mind to do all three Crowes in whatever order they came along. He hoped Pervis would be first. After the old man it didn't matter.

Rita, the old man's housekeeper? Cuba had never seen her but heard she was hot-looking. Do her too? He reached the house and could smell weed as soon as he stepped on the porch.

Dickie and Coover sat next to each other on the

couch. It looked strange, the other chairs in the sitting room empty. Now he saw they were sharing a party bong, passing it back and forth: add weed, put a finger over the hole and take a hit. Coover looked up, saw Cuba at the screen door and waved at him to come in.

Both Crowes stoned, grinning at Cuba like they were glad to see him, the air in the room sweet with reefer.

Cuba said, 'Man, you two are havin fun, huh? Where's daddy, he home or out someplace?'

'Upstairs taking a bath,' Dickie said, holding up the bong. 'Want a hit?'

'When I finish my business. Where's Rita, soapin up the old man?'

'I don't think it's their day,' Dickie said. 'Rita's in the kitchen fixin us a treat.'

'Somethin for your sweet tooth?'

'Strawberry shortcake,' Dickie said.

'How's Rita, she sweet?'

'Coover tried to jump her one time—'

'Years ago,' Coover said.

'Daddy caught him and whipped Coove with a stick, a green one, like a whip.'

'Hurt like hell,' Coover said.

'Lettin you know she's daddy's girl,' Cuba said. 'Man, how long she been here?'

'About three years,' Dickie said in that weed voice, holding his breath.

'That long? Why's she stay?'

'The old man pays a lot,' Coover said, 'for his nookie.'

'Coove's been tryin to find her money,' Dickie said, 'but she's hid it good.'

'It's in the house somewhere? What's he pay

60

her?'

'Hunnert a day,' Dickie said.

'Jesus Christ,' Cuba said, 'and you can't find it?' He thought of sticking his head in the kitchen, have a look at this Rita, but said, 'How y'all like hidin out?'

'Nobody's lookin for us,' Dickie said.

'Your daddy's got friends,' Cuba said.

'Or that marshal can't get a warrant.'

'That's what I mean. It's good to have friends can do you favors.'

Cuba asked himself, You through being sociable?

He reached behind him, hands going under his limp cotton jacket to pull the 9 mm Sig Sauer from the small of his back, both the weedheads staring at it with dreamy eyes, Coover saying, 'What you got there, boy?'

Cuba put the Sig on the two from halfway across the room and shot both Crowes in the chest, Coover first, *bam,* exploding the bong he was holding, then Dickie, *bam,* as Dickie was screaming what sounded like 'No!' Cuba waited for the gunshots to fade and listened for sounds in the house. He approached the two sprawled on the sofa, then walked over to the front door, opened the screen and banged it closed. Now he turned his attention to the stairs, Cuba thinking the old man would be careful, look out a front window to see who left.

Un-uh, there he was creeping down the stairs naked, holding a big, must be a .44 revolver out in front of him. The man had a belly, the rest of him ribs and skinny white legs, his bald head shining, Cuba seeing Pervis for the first time without his toupee, said, 'Hey, old man,' got him looking this way and *bam,* shot him off the stairs, watched him drop the revolver grabbing for the handrail and fall nine steps to the floor. Cuba waited for the naked body to move, the man lying on his belly, staining the rag carpet with his blood, his right arm bent funny, looking broke. Cuba waited a few moments, turned to the hall that went to the kitchen and called out, 'Rita . . .?' Waited again and called, 'Where you at, girl?'

*   *   *

She came in from the kitchen drying her hands on a dish towel. Cuba watched her look at the brothers flopped on the couch; watched her stand over the old man, Cuba's gaze holding on her ass in the white slip she was wearing against her black skin. Had that saucy type of ass slim black chicks would arch their backs to show it to you. Cuba watched her stoop down to place the dishtowel over the old man's profile on the floor, and told himself to shoot her, get it done. But he said, wanting to say something, 'I believe he broke his arm.'

'Oh, is *that* all,' Rita said. 'I would have swore you shot Mister and the boys. One each—that's pretty good. I don't know why you shot the old man, less somebody paid you good money. You coulda done the boys you happen to be feelin out of sorts.' She said, 'Quit aimin that thing at me. Put it away. I don't know you and you don't know me, all right?'

Cuba said, 'I don't know you won't call the law,' and felt dumb saying it; he did. Like a straightman.

'I call and say I want to report some homicides?

The man wants to know who this is. I tell him I'm the one's been scoring dope out of your drugstores, with scripts a doctor writes for pussy.

'I tell the man go look at my picture you got on your wall.' She said, 'Honey, Mister was my savior, but he's dead and me and him are square.'

'You have to love him?'

'Only once a week, when he gets it up. Listen to him gruntin, like he's pushin his car stuck in the mud.'

'But worth it,' Cuba said. 'I understand the old man paid you a hunnert a day, pussy or no pussy. Three years, what's that come to?'

Rita said, 'You can slam a car door on my hand, I won't tell you where it's at. All you got left is to cap me. You still won't know. I don't have my money, I don't give a rat's ass what you do.'

Cuba said, 'Hey, we friends, we believe each other, what we say. I already got somethin goin with a fine woman. But I won't say you don't tempt me.'

'She's your girl?'

'We close.'

'She's white, huh? You one of those think you special get a white chick to fuck you?'

'Blow me,' Cuba said and they both started laughing.

'She's fine, she's cool—'

'Has money?'

'That's what we into, makin it.'

'Drugs?'

'People's kidneys,' Cuba said to shut her up.

But Rita said, 'Far-out,' serious, thoughtful. 'You take their kidneys and let 'em die?'

'We sell 'em back the next day.'

'Cool. For how much?'

Cuba said, 'Time for me to leave, get far away from here. You better too, you say they lookin for you.'

'I don't know,' Rita said. 'I'll think of something. Send me a postcard, tell me what you doin, all right?' She kissed him and it wasn't bad. She knew how.

Rita closed the door after him and locked it, hurried over to Mister, got her face down close to his and heard him breathe. She *knew* it. You don't kill this dog with one shot. Rita said to him, 'Honey, don't move. I'm on get you to the hospital.'

*   *   *

Knox County Hospital called the state police and they got on Pervis's case, called the marshals service to let Raylan know the two guys he had them looking for were homicide victims. Raylan visited the scene, saw Coover and Dickie dead on the couch and the bloodstained carpet where Pervis had been lying. The hospital said a black girl dropped off Pervis and must have left. They didn't know her name and Pervis refused to identify the girl or the one shot him.

He did tell Raylan, sitting at his bedside, 'He left me for dead. Shot me with a round that splintered a rib and messed me up inside.' Pervis raised the arm in a cast. 'I broke it fallin down the stairs.'

'While you're laid up,' Raylan said, 'why don't we see what I can do? It was Cuba Franks, wasn't it, the shooter? Through using your boys for his felonies? Shot you, you happen to be there. But was Rita brought you here, wasn't it? Why'd she take off?'

64

Pervis said, 'Why you grillin me when you think you know everything?'

Raylan said, 'Remember I told you they're taking kidneys from people while they're alive?'

Pervis kept his mouth shut.

'You're a hard-ass old man,' Raylan said, 'but I can respect how you feel. What I don't want is you goin to prison for taking out Cuba.'

Pervis said, 'It's time I did somethin for my boys.'

*　　　*　　　*

'He shot the brothers,' Raylan told Art Mullen—the two standing in Art's office—'while they're suckin on a bong. Coover's turn, he's popped and the glass shatters, got his shirt wet.'

'You noticed that,' Art said.

'His blood turned it pinkish. What's that remind you of?'

'Angel's bath,' Art said. 'Three kidney jobs in the last few weeks.'

'But only Angel's offered for sale. I told him, "Pray to St. Christopher you get 'em back" and he came through.'

Art said, 'What you're saying, St. Christopher got Dickie and Coover whacked so Angel wouldn't have to pay for his kidneys.'

'More or less.'

Art said, 'We're lookin for Cuba Franks, what he's been doing since his convictions. A year ago he chauffeured for a rich guy owns horses. Cuba Franks, says he's from Nigeria. Had the job for nine months and quit.'

'Wasn't making enough?'

'Got tired of putting on his African accent.

65

That's what Mrs. Burgoyne told us. Harry Burgoyne said, "That's what they do, they walk out on you. Only one African American I'd give high marks to and that's Old Tom. He died on me."'

'I know why Cuba quit,' Raylan said.

'Our office up there's still lookin for him. Nine months, he must know his way around.'

'Has friends there,' Raylan said. 'You don't suppose—'

Art said, 'Do I suppose he has a friend, a doctor at the transplant center, a woman?'

'Do you?' Raylan said.

*   *   *

Layla's voice said, 'Where are you?'

'I'm about to leave the hills for the four-lane,' Cuba said. 'The Crowe brothers left for heaven this afternoon, less they got rules against weedheads. I had to do the old man, since he was in the house.'

'You told me he has a cute maid.'

'Only what I heard. I was never up to the house before.'

'Was she cute?'

'She was too young for that old man.'

'She was cute, huh?'

'I let her go.'

Now silence on the phone.

Cuba said, 'She don't know me and I don't know her, how we left it.'

'You realize,' Layla said, 'if I'd been with you and we could've worked it? We'd have six more kidneys in one swoop. Eight,' Layla said, 'we throw in Rita. What do you think? Eighty grand.'

66

CHAPTER TEN

The Lexington office gave Raylan a partner whether he wanted one or not.

Bill Nichols, fifty-five, half his life a marshal; slim, about five-ten, hair cut short around a tan bald crown. He told Raylan:

'Fourteen I knew everything, shaved my head to become a hundred-and-thirty-pound white supremacist. Before I got any swastika tats, I got tired of getting beat up by these grown neo-Nazis dumber'n stones. I said fuck this and reversed my field, entered a seminary to become a brother, not a priest, a brother. Play softball, or walk around with my hands in the sleeves of the habit thinking of girls. I quit, went to UK, joined the marshals and married my wife, Julie, twenty-seven years now. We have three boys wanderin the earth, good guys, smart, three-point-fives or better. Max teaches English at a school in France. Alex designs book covers for Italian publishers and French, and Tim's writing his second novel in New York. The first one sold four thousand. I asked him what it's about, the one he's writing. He said the subtext is the exposure of artistic pretension. And my little girl, Kate, senior in high school, wants to be a marshal.'

'I'm gonna have to get busy,' Raylan said.

'How long you been married?'

'I'm divorced,' Raylan said. 'You ever look for the Nazi lovers beat you up?'

'Two of 'em are gone, overdosed. The third guy,' Nichols said, 'by the time I found him was a crackhead, his tats hard to read. I stood him against

67

a brick wall, put on leather gloves while I'm lookin him in the eye. I hit him one-two, both sides of his jaw. He went down and I stood lookin at him.'

Raylan said, 'He remember you?'

'I doubt it.'

'Something you had to do before you got too old,' Raylan said. 'It's a shame he wasn't a wanted felon.'

'So I could shoot him he resisted.'

'I meant you'd have a reason to hunt him down.'

Nichols said, 'You've shot and killed a man?'

'Yes, I have,' Raylan said.

'An armed fugitive?'

'More than one,' Raylan said.

'It doesn't matter how many, does it?'

'Not a bit,' Raylan said. 'Once or twice I might've been lucky.'

'You get to where you have to pull—'

'Knowing you better shoot to kill,' Raylan said.

Nichols gave Raylan a nod.

They knew each other.

*   *   *

They were in Nichols's Crown Vic leaving a two-story frame house on Chestnut—the address on one of Cuba's drivers licenses—that turned out to be a boardinghouse. Cuba Franks? Been more than a year anyone had seen him around.

The last address for him was out on Athens–Walnut Hill Road. Nichols knew it as Burgoyne Farms.

'Hasn't changed his address,' Nichols said, 'since he left. I have a brother, all he does is build fences for horse farms. Thirty-five thousand thoroughbreds born in the U.S. every year. Twenty make it to the Derby. One race you can't buy.'

Raylan said, 'You didn't talk to Burgoyne, did you?'

'Couple of young marshals did,' Nichols said. 'Mr. Burgoyne told them Cuba Franks walked out on him. He said, "It's what they do, get tired of workin and walk out." He means African Americans,' Nichols said. 'I'm finally getting use to saying it.'

'Burgoyne's wife,' Raylan said, 'thought Cuba got tired of putting on an African accent?'

Nichols said, 'She thought it was funny. You get the feeling she knew Cuba betten'n her old man did.'

'Cuba's our lead,' Raylan said. 'We get hold of him, he'll give up the woman doctor.'

They were moving east on New Circle, coming up on Richmond Road, where they'd turn south. Nichols glanced at Raylan.

'You saw the list of doctors? Thirteen workin on transplants?'

Raylan shook his head. 'I haven't seen it yet. There only thirteen?'

Nichols turned on to Richmond and looked at Raylan again.

'They're all guys. No women doctors doing transplants.'

Raylan did not want to give up the idea and said, 'You sure?'

'I have the list in my case,' Nichols said. 'All professors of surgery or associates.'

Raylan said, 'She's not an MD—'

'Least not at Chandler. It's part of UK Medical.'

'But she knows how to do it,' Raylan said.

'She knows how to take kidneys out,' Nichols said. 'She know how to put 'em in?'

Raylan had to think about it, looking at horse country cut with fences, thoroughbreds grazing, looking up to see their Crown Vic drive past, on Old Richmond now, on their way to Burgoyne Farms.

'She doesn't have to put 'em in,' Raylan said, 'does she?'

'That's right,' Nichols said, 'not if she's takin out kidneys to sell 'em. But I don't see an MD doin that.'

'I don't either,' Raylan said. 'But I'd like to find her working on transplants.'

Nichols said, 'She watches doctors exchange organs three times a week, about a hundred and fifty a year. She mops the doctor's brow under those lights and he likes her touch. They close up and he bangs her in the linen closet standing up.'

Raylan said, 'Yeah . . .?'

'Life in the OR,' Nichols said. 'He's playin doctor with his good-lookin nurse.'

'You're telling me,' Raylan said, 'that's the reason the good-lookin nurse is taking out kidneys in motel rooms?'

'I'm settin a scene,' Nichols said. 'Does getting banged in the closet have anything to do with her stealin kidneys? She knows how to take 'em out and finds out how to sell 'em. Money is what moves her. She sees how being Mrs. Obama once a week could make her rich. Still, I like the idea of human sexual feelings involved. Doing it standin up is all right with me.'

They were on Athens–Walnut Hill now, closing in on Burgoyne Farms. They'd called ahead and made arrangements to stop by for a visit that had to do with a former employee, if they didn't mind the intrusion?

Raylan said, 'You take Harry and I'll talk to Elizabeth. She gives her age as fifty-five, Harry's wife sixteen years, a second marriage for each.'

'You take Harry,' Nichols said, 'get him talking about African Americans and have some fun.'

'It's my case,' Raylan said, 'I'm going with Elizabeth.'

*   *   *

The maid took Raylan from the front door and down a hall saying Ms. Burgoyne would see him in the sun parlor. They came to a room as high-end formal as the rest of the house and Raylan said, 'Why's it called a sun parlor? It doesn't look like one.' He saw the maid in her yellow uniform look toward Elizabeth Burgoyne coming in from outside, her white cotton shirt hanging out of low-slung jeans.

'It's been the sun parlor for eighty-five years,' Elizabeth said coming in, the way it was done in the movies. 'Why call it somethin else?'

'It's all right with me,' Raylan said and told her who he was.

She said, 'You want to know about Cuba Franks. Why, what's he done?'

'We think he's stealing kidneys,' Raylan said. See what she'd do with that.

She said, 'Really?' Paused a moment and asked, 'What would you like, iced tea or a martini?'

'Whatever you're having,' Raylan said and watched her hold up two fingers to the maid in her

71

yellow maid's outfit. He'd bet ten dollars they were having martinis.

She said, 'I'd like your opinion about something, okay? All of my horse-country friends call me Beth. I think cause my mother does when she comes to visit. But my older friends—from a different life you might say—call me Liz. Which do you think I am, Beth or Liz?'

'You're testing my power of observation,' Raylan said.

'Come on, which am I?'

'Liz,' Raylan said.

'Why?'

'Because you had more fun with your old buddies than the horsey set.' Fifty-five—she looked no more than forty. A lot of dark hair she stood twisting around her fingers. 'You miss them,' Raylan said. 'I wouldn't mind hearing where you came from and how you met Harry—I bet it's a good story. But I need to learn about Cuba. I think you got to know him betten'n your husband did.'

'Harry,' Liz said, 'has no idea how to get next to people. His personality holds them off, his expression seems nailed on. Though he's not as stuffy when he's drinking, not nearly as boring. I think he'd love to be a stallion and get it on with the mares all day.'

'What do you do,' Raylan said, 'go to teas?'

She said, 'Yeah, I love tea,' and turned to the maid coming into the sun parlor with a pitcher of martinis and a bowl of anchovy olives.

*   *   *

They were both on the sofa now with the drinks, a

72

cushion between them, the pitcher on the cocktail table, Liz still talking about Harry.

'He'd have a few and he and Cuba would do their Boss and Darky show. Harry scolds him for what he's wearing, and Cuba says, "But, Boss, is your missus dresses me," and everyone in the Keeneland bar howls.'

'Why don't you get the horse people,' Raylan said, 'to call you Liz?'

She said, 'It wouldn't work. It would sound like Liz Taylor in *Tin Roof*. She had that Hollywood southern accent, like everybody's from Virginia.'

'You like acting a little nuts,' Raylan said. 'So does Cuba, the kind of action he gets into.'

'He was funny,' Liz said. 'We had all day to talk, if we wanted, Harry at the stables. We didn't meet to have sex, if that's what you're thinking.'

He was, but shook his head.

'Cuba was funny.'

'I believe it,' Raylan said.

'I'll be honest with you,' Liz said. 'It did happen now and then, but not on a regular basis. It would just, you know, happen, begin fooling around, you'd be crazy to stop.'

Raylan said, 'I've known that experience.'

'You understand,' Liz said, 'Cuba's a street guy, but very natural about it. I never had to ask what he was talking about. He told me what it was like in prison. He told me the difference between black chicks and white girls in bed'—Liz grinning till she said—'he told me about meeting someone, a girl.'

'A white girl,' Raylan said.

'He wouldn't say but I knew she was. He'd say, "What difference is it I see this person once in a while. I'm not gonna marry her." He always called her "this person." We'd meet and I'd have martinis or daiquiris, or pack the shaker with ice and pour in bourbon, sprinkle some sugar . . . And he walked out on me. I couldn't believe it.'

'I can't either,' Raylan said. 'This was about the time he left?'

'Disappeared.'

'I told you he's selling kidneys?'

'I don't believe that.'

'He sells them for ten thousand each.'

'Really?'

'He's done it three times, with help.'

'You mean the girl?'

'I think she's here at UK Medical.'

'A doctor?'

'A transplant nurse.'

Liz edged over the table to refill their glasses and drop in olives, saying, 'This is getting good. You're looking for the nurse, thinking he might've mentioned her to me, but he didn't.' Liz handed Raylan his drink and sat back with her own, nodding. 'I'll bet she's fat.' She sipped her drink and said, 'Why are so many women who work in hospitals overweight?'

'I've noticed,' Raylan said. 'Why are they?'

'He could have met her,' Liz said. 'Cuba drove Harry to Chandler at least twice to have his kidneys checked. They still work, despite all he drinks. He'd bitch, order the nurses around. One of them wouldn't give him his favorite dope and he tried to get her fired. I can't remember her name.'

Raylan said, 'I hope she's still there.'

'It was Layla. Like the Eric Clapton number.'

CHAPTER ELEVEN

Raylan came off the elevator and crossed the hall to a waiting area, vinyl furniture and magazines, Nichols in there reading *People*. He closed the magazine and picked up a file folder next to him on the couch.

'You have lunch?'

'Ham and lima beans,' Raylan said, settling into the couch.

'The days we're lookin at,' Nichols said, 'two of the nurses from this floor were away on leave, deaths in their family. Gladys, thirty-five years a transplant nurse, now a coordinator, came back and put her dad's death notice in the nurses' room. The other one's Layla.' Nichols brought a black-and-white head shot from the folder and handed it to Raylan.

'Thin face,' Raylan said, meaning she didn't appear to be fat.

'Five-six, a hundred and twenty pounds,' Nichols said. 'She's thirty-seven.'

'She's got great eyes,' Raylan said, 'they hold on to you. Who died in her family?'

'Nobody. Layla took a two-week leave to nurse her old mom back from death's door, coughing her lungs out, but didn't die, she's recovering, quit smoking.'

'Where's the mom live?'

'New Orleans.'

'You check it out?'

'Soon as I finish reading about Harrison and Calista gettin married after eight years keeping house. Then catch up on why Jake Pavelka says Vienna cheated on him, whoever they are.'

'Layla,' Raylan said, 'you notice her eyes. She makes you keep lookin at them.' Raylan squinted at the woman in the photo not quite smiling at him. He said, 'I'd like to know what she's thinking.'

Nichols turned his head to look at the photo. 'She's starin at the photographer thinking, You take one more I'm gonna get up and kick you in the nuts.'

'I don't see her impatient,' Raylan said.

'No, she's thinking it in a nice way.' Nichols looked at his watch. 'She ought to be out of surgery by now. She's helping Dr. Howard Goldman transplant a kidney. Like Layla doesn't know how.'

Raylan said, 'She's our girl, huh?'

'I don't see anyone else,' Nichols said.

They both got up from the couch: Raylan to stand in the opening to the hall, looking at the far end where they'd come out of surgery, Nichols to go check on Layla's mom.

*   *   *

Raylan watched them come out, both in white lab coats, Layla holding the door for Dr. Goldman, the young doctor doing most of the talking, Layla using her hands to gesture, shaking her head, talking her way out of what he wanted to do. Like get laid. Raylan had stopped him earlier in the day to ask about nurses. Stopped him and committed his name to memory. Howard Goldman, that was it. The doctor had no time for him, waved his hand in front of his face and kept going. Now, down the hall, he was opening his hands to Layla, the hands he had used to restore someone's life and it had given him a hard-on.

They were coming this way again.

Raylan walked up to Dr. Goldman—didn't look at Layla—and said, 'Excuse me, Doctor, but my sister's suppose to be here, seein about having a kidney transplant?'

Layla said, 'What's her name?'

'Raejeanne Givens,' Raylan said, his younger sister's name. 'I don't know why I don't see any family. I came straight from the airport.'

Layla said, 'Let's check on Raejeanne,' laying her hand on Raylan's arm and giving the doctor what Raylan saw as a kiss-off look with a shrug. Dr. Goldman walked past him without a word and on down the hall.

'I've been here an hour,' Raylan said, 'trying to get information. You just come out of surgery, huh?' He held out his hand. 'I'm Raylan Givens, deputy United States marshal. I'm sorry if I intruded on you and the doctor. I'm concerned about my sister.'

She said, 'Hi, I'm Layla. The doctor just finished a kidney transplant and you say Raejeanne needs one? That's funny, cause we don't have a Raejeanne scheduled for anything, not even an exam.' Layla raising her eyebrows with kind of a smile.

'It doesn't matter,' Raylan said. 'You didn't look happy talking to Howard. I thought I may as well step in, see if I could free you. You seemed to pick up on it.'

She said, 'You want to question me about something?'

'What I'm looking for,' Raylan said, 'is a doctor

takes out kidneys in motel rooms and sells them on the body-parts market.'

She was smiling now. 'You're crazy.'

'A doctor here can't have a gambling problem? Goes broke out at Keeneland and gets in debt to a shylock?'

'They bet playing golf,' Layla said.

'I understand,' Raylan said, 'to take out a kidney, you make your incision in the front.'

'How do you know that?'

'Talkin to guys. Two of 'em said it was a woman took their kidneys. I thought, Well, maybe the doctor had a woman's mask on. You put the donated ones in the front too?'

'You put them anywhere you want,' Layla said. 'What kind of mask was it?'

'Rubber, slips over your head. I think it was suppose to be Mrs. Obama.'

'Really.'

'Well, the other mask, I'm pretty sure, was the president.'

Layla said, 'The other mask . . . ?'

'The one Cuba Franks was wearing.'

Raylan let that hang to see if Layla could handle it.

She took a moment to shake her head and shrug in her white transplant nurse outfit. Layla said, 'I wish I could help you,' started to turn away and stopped. She said, 'Why can't the doctor be a woman?'

'I'm told all the MDs here are men.'

'She could be from another hospital.'

'You're right, except Cuba knows this place. He's been here once or twice with his boss. You know Cuba Franks?'

'I don't think so,' Layla said. 'I wish I could help you,' and started to walk away.

Raylan let her take a few steps before saying to her, 'Layla, you're not the one stealing kidneys, are you?'

He may as well get that said, thinking it would stop her and she'd turn around. Not Layla. She raised her hand over her head to give Raylan a lazy kind of wave, often seen in movies.

Again in the waiting room, with all its old magazines, he thought of what he'd say to her the next time. He wasn't sure until Nichols came in saying, 'She lied about nursing her mom back to health. The old lady's been in a home with Alzheimer's the past three years.'

*　　　*　　　*

Cuba was staying with Layla in her apartment on Virginia Avenue, the other side of South Limestone from the UK campus and hospitals; Cuba on the pull-out sofa, Layla with the bedroom to herself when they weren't using it. She liked to come home and have a drink while she took off her whites and sat down to watch the news in a T-shirt and panties. It would turn Cuba on and they'd go in the bedroom so Cuba could satisfy himself; her too most of the time. He knew when a chick was faking, always overdoing it. Layla never said a word and he'd wait for the gasp, the groan, like all the air was being sucked out of her. They'd watch TV then and have some more vodkas while he deep-fried supper.

This evening she came in talking about Raylan Givens and Cuba felt a tug in his gut and thought, Shit, though it didn't surprise him. The man kept on the job. He said to Layla, 'How'd he get on us?'

'You worked for the Burgoynes.'

'You layin it on *me*? They already lookin at dead Crowes.'

'You had to do it,' Layla said. 'But, you let the maid go, Rita.'

'I knew you'd bring her up.'

Layla stepped up to him in her nurse outfit, put her arms around his neck and kissed him on the mouth from tender to hard. Finally easing off she said, 'Don't worry about it. But I think we should hold up on doing Harry. The marshal would've talked to him. Probably asked his wife a few questions. You got it on with her, didn't you?'

'Not too much,' Cuba said. 'I been thinking, I go see Mr. Harry and apologize for leavin, this poor, uneducated Negro not knowin shit how to act. But that darky skit depressed me. I tell him I got a new gig we can try.'

'What is it?'

'I make up something—bring tears to his motherfuckin racist eyes laughing. I say I got a tape he can listen to. Bring him here and you pop him with the needle.'

'How does he pay us, say, two hundred and fifty thousand?'

'I'm workin on it.'

Layla said, 'We're not doing Harry just yet. I've been thinking, we could be gathering a few more organs. Gregg Allman just had a liver transplant, he can drink again—*yeaaah*! We'll extract kidneys, liver, lungs, pancreas. Hearts are too tricky. You have to keep it pumping.'

Cuba thinking, Like sellin used auto parts, a transmission, a manifold. She made it sound easy, reminding him that time, 'You don't do the Crowes they'll tell on us.' Her bein cool about it's what scared him. Like telling him to close the window so it don't rain in.

'This might blow your mind,' Layla said, 'but I'm thinking the one to do next is the marshal. We wouldn't even have to lure him. Raylan has more questions for me.'

Cuba's mind saw Dickie holding a gun while Raylan good as dared him to raise it. He said to Layla, 'Where you want to do it, here?'

'I was thinking right in the tub, instead of lugging him around, then add water. I don't see why we'd need ice.'

'How we get him out of here?'

'In the wee small hours of the morning,' Layla said, not quite singing it, 'we drop him out the window, put him in the car . . . Or we wait till he's coming to and walk him out to the car.'

'You haven't figured it out yet,' Cuba said.

'I'm thinking,' Layla said. 'We have until I decide to answer the phone.'

CHAPTER TWELVE

Raylan didn't want to be seen hanging around the fourth floor of Chandler, risk Layla spotting him and duck out. He stood outside, away from the entrance and watched nurses coming out till almost five. No sign of Layla. He went up to the transplant floor and found out she was off today. He called Nichols.

'You know it's Saturday?' Raylan said.

'It wasn't, I wouldn't be mowin the lawn.'

'Layla's off till Monday.'

'You call her home?'

'Her voice said leave a message and hung up.'

'You called last night you'd of had her in cuffs.'

'I wanted to give her time to get jumpy before I make my appearance.'

'I can stop mowin this minute,' Nichols said, 'you want me along.'

'I got to locate her first. I'll call her again or go over there, 156 Virginia Avenue, push her buzzer till she answers.'

'If she's home,' Nichols said. 'I'll call you tomorrow, see how you're doin. Come on over, we'll grill steaks, have a few beers.'

'I was gonna tell you,' Raylan said, 'I checked out of the Hilton, didn't work with my per diem. I took a cab to the office and got a Chevy assigned to me—it's okay—I'm not goin anywhere, but I'm now stayin at the Two Keys Tavern on South Limestone. I got an apartment upstairs, no charge.'

'You're kiddin me,' Nichols said.

'So UK students don't walk out skunked and get arrested or hit by a car. I spoke to management, I said if you have a spare room up there you can let me use while I'm in Lexington . . . I told him he'd have a U.S. marshal keeping the peace. The fella said he didn't want to shut the students down, especially on Crazy Night. I told him goin crazy's okay with me.'

Nichols said, 'You're a bouncer in a dive bar?'

'When I'm there. I don't think this'll take long.'

'You're youngen'n I am,' Nichols said. 'You might come out of there alive.'

'Martinis,' Raylan said, 'are only three bucks.'

*　　　*　　　*

Saturday evening he talked to the manager, a cautious but pleasant guy running a saloon on the edge of the University of Kentucky campus. Why wouldn't he be pleasant? He had droves of patrons, boys and girls coming in for rum or vodka in different flavors; for the three-dollar martinis; five dollars for a pitcher of beer, and for ten bucks you could drink all the beer you wanted. 'But just for yourself,' the manager told Raylan, 'or everybody in here'd get sloshed on the ten bucks.'

Raylan had on the suit and tie he'd worn to the transplant center yesterday. Hanging around in the Two Keys Tavern, there wasn't any doubt, this guy with the star on a chain was a lawman. He expected to get some remarks. They were all twenty-one going on thirty. A guy stared and Raylan would nod with his nice-guy look. He saw a lot of zip-neck sweaters over all kinds of shirts. He saw girls talking loud, girls making faces. They had a goldfish race in a plastic trough, hit the fish with water pistols to quit swimming in a circle and race, goddamnit. Not many beer drinkers seem to care about it. A celebrity deejay Raylan had never heard of came on and the crowd went crazy for about a minute.

He saw some good-looking girls here. One of them came up to him and said, 'My friends think you're a rent-a-cop and I bet them you're for real. Are you?'

Raylan opened his coat to show his star hanging on the silver chain. He said, 'I'm a United States marshal, miss. Tell me what your friends call you?'

A guy with some size standing there said,

'Anybody ever rip your badge off you, hangin there?'

'Not yet,' Raylan said. 'One tried but didn't make it. What do you do, play football? I'd take you to be an offensive lineman.'

This guy with shoulders on him said, 'I play defense.'

'What I meant,' Raylan said, 'I see you as a lineman becoming offensive to me. Twenty years ago I ever tried out for football here I'd be cut by the third day.' Raylan said, 'I'm gonna move the badge down to my belt, not get anymore remarks about it.' Raylan told him, 'In case you didn't know it, I'm one of the good guys. I've shot seven men in the line of duty, wanted fugitives, no women or students, and they all died.' Raylan smiled at the defensive lineman. 'You gonna have me telling marshal stories next.'

At 2:30 A.M. he put on his cowboy hat and went to visit Miss Layla.

*   *   *

Raylan used his burglar picks to open the front door without disturbing the manager. He went up the stairs to Layla's apartment and knocked on the door. He stood before the peephole in his hat—no way she wouldn't know him, and knocked again, giving the door three firm raps.

He waited.

She'd be looking at him by now, wondering how to play it.

'I'm not here to make an arrest,' Raylan said, his face close to the door. 'I want to talk to you about something.'

84

Finally he heard her voice.

'At three in the morning?'

'I been trying to get hold of you,' Raylan said. 'You told the hospital you took leave to nurse your mom back to health, but you never went near her. You know the time I mean?'

There was a silence.

Her voice said, 'I met my boyfriend. I actually *was* in New Orleans.'

'Let's get him to vouch for you,' Raylan said, 'and I'll quit worryin about it.'

'He's married,' Layla's voice said.

'I could have a word with him,' Raylan said. 'What's his name?'

'I don't want to get him in trouble.'

'I start arrestin people for committin adultery I'd never get home for supper and see my wife and kids. We have three boys and a girl.'

Layla's voice said, 'Wait till I put something on.'

Raylan imagined Layla standing on the other side of the door bare-naked and wanted to come back with a cool line, but couldn't think of anything that wasn't stupid and said, 'Okay,' and waited.

*   *   *

Cuba had pulled on his pants and was stripping the bedding from the sofa. He said, 'Raylan,' shaking his head. 'I could hear you lyin to each other.'

Layla had on a black kimono with touches of red here and there. She told Cuba to put on his shoes and wait in the bedroom. 'With your gun,' Layla said. 'We're ready, we'll do it here, right now. In the bathtub. Run water to wash out the blood. He comes in, we'll lie to each other some more. I'll

85

see how it goes, the kind of mood he's in. I'll have the needle ready.' She looked around the room. 'Maybe in the kitchen. I'll get him relaxed first.'

'When he ain't lookin,' Cuba said, 'you pop him with the needle?'

'And you take him out when we're finished,' Layla said. 'Get him to disappear.'

'Not hang him on a corner and call emergency?'

'He knows us,' Layla said. 'He gets on dialysis we're fucked.' She took time to look at Cuba and said, 'Am I right?' Cuba said,

'You always right, aren't you?'

*　　　*　　　*

She opened the door and said to Raylan, 'Follow me,' and took him through the living room to the kitchen, where two vodkas over ice waited on the counter. She watched him grin as she handed him one.

'To ease me down,' Raylan said. 'Tell you the truth, I came here with the same idea. Let you know I'm not gonna snitch on you, tell the hospital you didn't take off to see your old mom. She wouldn't of known you, you wore a sign with your name on it.'

'I told you, I met my boyfriend,' Layla said.

'His name Cuba Franks?'

Layla gave him a tired look, shaking her head. 'Whoever Cuba is, he's not my boyfriend.'

'He brought his boss to the hospital a couple times. Mr. Harry Burgoyne?'

'I still don't remember him,' Layla said.

'Cuba's easy to meet, for a fella's done hard time,' Raylan said. 'I thought he might straighten out his life, till he shot the Crowe brothers. Shot the dad too, but Pervis survived. Now the old man wants to do Cuba himself. Did you know that? For killing his worthless boys.'

Layla got out a cigarette and lighted it saying, 'Why don't you finish your drink and leave?'

'You haven't eased me down,' Raylan said, 'have you? The Crowe brothers did some work for Cuba one time. Lifted Angel Arenas on the bed to get his kidneys removed. I thought, Why didn't they do him in the tub, save messin up the bed? I guess they were still learning. The Crowes gave Angel a week to come up with a hundred grand—the second biggest mistake Cuba ever made, hookin up with the Crowes.'

Layla had to ask:

'What was his first mistake?'

'Getting involved with Miss Transplant,' Raylan said. 'Why he's hiding in the bedroom right now.'

She said, 'You can't just . . . search my apartment.'

'I've got cause,' Raylan said. 'Reason to believe a wanted felon's in there.'

'Why you've come after me all of a sudden,' Layla said, 'I'll never know.' She moved closer to Raylan leaning on the yellow-tile counter, his body against the fucking drawer she had to open to get the needle.

'Do you think I'd actually steal kidneys from the center?'

'You learned how watching for eleven years. Only you do your surgery in motel rooms.'

'I think you're crazy,' Layla said. 'You want to look in the bedroom? Go ahead.'

She threw her cigarette in the sink as he

straightened, leaving his glass on the counter, and watched him walk out of the kitchen in his cowboy hat. Layla opened the drawer and picked up the syringe.

Now the tricky part: walk up behind him and jab the needle into his arm before he saw her. She tested the needle, got a squirt and went after Raylan, almost to the bedroom, his left hand reaching for the doorknob, right hand slipping inside his suit-coat. Behind him now Layla said, 'Raylan . . .?' Saw him hesitate, start to turn his head and jabbed the needle hard through his coat and into his right arm. Saw his hand come out holding the Glock. Saw him look at her, his eyes turning dreamy, his knees giving up and he stumbled against the door, hat on, gun still in his hand, Raylan in his good-looking navy suit sliding to the floor.

'Cuba? You can come out now.'

Cuba opened the door to see Layla posing, holding Raylan's Glock and wearing his cowboy hat cocked on her head, a saucy angle. He looked down at Raylan, Layla saying, 'Let's get him in the tub.'

CHAPTER THIRTEEN

They dragged him to the bathroom and stripped off his clothes, everything, Layla using scissors to open the legs of his pants to pull them over his curl-toed cowboy boots, Cuba thinking they looked custom-made. Layla still had Raylan's hat cocked on her head, not knowing how to wear it. She took his legs, Cuba his upper body, straining to lift

Raylan over the side of the tub. Cuba thought he should be higher, so his chin wasn't on his chest; it didn't look right.

'We should move him up higher,' Cuba said.

She was looking at his privates, Cuba pretty sure she'd make a remark.

'Would you say he's hung or not?'

'A guy knows how to use what he has,' Cuba said, 'or he don't.' He looked at Raylan again. 'I want to ease him up so he's higher in the tub.'

Knowing she'd say something else.

'Why? What difference does it make?' She said, 'Do what you want, as long as he's on his back,' and left the bathroom with Raylan's clothes and his gun.

Cuba turned to watch her, in the bedroom now dropping Raylan's clothes on the bed. He watched her take off the hat and toss it by the clothes, *on the bed,* and almost yelled at her, *Get the hat off the bed, it's bad luck.*

He stopped to think, Like what?

They already had the worst kind of luck waiting for them, once they let a federal marshal die. It would be the same as a homicide, their intention being the same as killing him. She'd tell him okay, now dump his body somewhere while I clean up and get ready for bed. Only he wouldn't come back and get in with her. That would be the moment. That would be the time to keep going, 'Get out of town before it's too late'—Layla always singin that at him—'my dear,' and givin him the cool smile and all kind of lovin.

Or hang him on a corner and call the hospital.

He'd thought of that. Do it but don't tell her. Give the man a chance.

He looked at Raylan's head against the end

of the tub, chin stuck to his chest like he couldn't move it, and saw his face twitch, Raylan's face, like a fly was bothering him. Now his hand came up his bare chest to his mouth and Cuba turned to the bedroom. He saw Layla in there at the dresser laying out her things for the surgery, her scalpels, her swabs and alcohol, her staples she'd use to close him up. Cuba raised his voice to tell her, 'Girl, he's movin.'

He saw her look up at the dresser mirror.

'He's all right. I'll be there in a minute, maybe give him another shot.' She said, 'Get him comfortable and he'll nod off.'

Raylan heard her say, 'God damn it, I didn't bring gloves.'

Layla.

He heard her say, 'Not that it matters.'

*　　　*　　　*

He saw Cuba by the tub, his shape, his face coming down close and out of the smoke in Raylan's head.

Cuba said to him, 'Can you hear me?'

Raylan closed his eyes. He let his hand slip down his body to his groin and learned he was naked but could feel his toes in his boots. They kept slipping when he tried to push himself up, get a little higher. He heard Cuba:

'He's movin again,' his voice raised.

Layla said something about the fucking syringe; she couldn't find it. Now Cuba was saying, 'I could get behind you I'd pull you up, but they's no room. I'm on get in the tub and see can I push you up.' He said, 'Me and you got the kind of bodies the ladies die for. Our natures keeping us thin. None of

90

that runnin and weight liftin shit. You eat the right food you stay trim. I think the secret is only eat fried food, then work it off quick makin love to the bitches.'

Cuba, close to the tub, turned to the bedroom, Layla in there at the dresser. What was she doing? Cuba called to her, 'Girl, you puttin on makeup? Twice was enough—kissin the boys good-bye.'

Raylan opened his eyes to see Cuba turned from the tub, Cuba saying, 'You crazy, you know it? Dollin up while I prepare this man for his last thirty minutes on earth.'

Raylan heard her say, 'Do what you want,' Raylan staring at the Sig Sauer stuck in Cuba's waist, the grip showing, the barrel resting against Cuba's spine.

He turned to Raylan saying, 'I got to get in the tub to move you. All right? To *move* you. I ain't gonna cop your joint, I don't play that shit, so don't worry. You lyin there nothin you can do.'

*　　*　　*

Layla's voice came from the bedroom. 'Is he out?'

'He's all right, like shit-faced. I *know* can't stand up.'

'He might not've got the whole shot.'

Raylan heard her voice, her words, and could see Cuba with twenty-twenty vision he was so close. In the tub with him, bending over, trying to hug him and inch his dead weight up higher, Cuba straddling his legs. Maybe all they gained was an inch. He could hear, but it was like you were all the way taken down by shine. No, straight whiskey. With shine you felt you were quadriplegic and didn't dare

91

try to talk. Bourbon turned you alive.

Cuba said, 'I get a hold on you, you take hold of me and pull yourself up. You know what I'm sayin? Pull yourself up as I push.'

Raylan didn't know why he was doing this, wanting to move him higher in the tub. This time Raylan got his hands under Cuba's arms, trying to get a hold on Cuba's silk shirt and it tore down the middle. Cuba said it, 'You tore my good shirt.'

Raylan said, 'Fuck your shirt,' let his hands slide down Cuba's back to the Sig Sauer and slipped it out of his waist. Raylan and Cuba almost nose to nose in each other's eyes, Raylan wondering if Cuba felt him take it. He looked like he did. Raylan brought the Sig around to Cuba's belly and heard Layla say:

'What're you guys doing, getting it on?'

Raylan looked past Cuba's shoulder to see her standing in the doorway. She said, 'Cuba . . .?' She said, 'Cuba, his eyes are fucking open . . .' and she was gone—in the bedroom getting his gun, Raylan sure of it. Cuba staring in his face.

'She wants *me,*' Raylan said. 'Or maybe you, I don't know.'

He saw her in the doorway aiming his Glock at him, holding it in one hand and turning sideways to strike a shooter's pose and fired—he saw the gun jump—and fired again and fired again, and Cuba let out a gasp of air and slumped against Raylan, wedging the Sig between them.

He said to Cuba, 'You alive?' He didn't get an answer and said, 'Or dead.' He put his ear to Cuba's mouth, didn't hear a rattle of breath, but could smell it.

Layla said, 'Cuba . . .?'

'I imagine,' Raylan said, 'he's in Hell by now, the poor man. I'm placing you under arrest,' Raylan said, 'for taking his life. Lay down the weapon.' He couldn't say 'your weapon' since it was his. He hoped she'd drop it, the jolt setting off the semi-hair trigger and shoot herself. He felt sometimes he could talk to that gun he called Buddy, to himself. *Here we go, Buddy, stay loose.* He still had the Sig in his hand stuck between their bodies. But it was coming . . . and she was firing again, the Glock in both hands now. She fired four rounds at him ducked behind Cuba—Jesus, realizing he was using the man for cover. He pulled out the Sig and extended it past Cuba's shoulder and saw her right there framed in the doorway and put the Sig on her, and hesitated two, three beats and she was gone.

He lay there with Cuba on him thinking, You didn't shoot her. Why didn't you? She's standing right there.

*   *   *

Like that, she was in trouble.

She should have given him another shot before putting on her makeup. Cuba said the first two times were funny, kissing the Willie Lomans while they were still alive, not knowing shit what was happening. But lovin up a man drugged out of his head was creepy. Like kissing the dead.

It was in her mind to run, get out of here. Someone would have heard the shots and called the police.

Or, stay and make up a story.

Officer, I'm a transplant nurse at UK Medical.

93

We save lives, we don't shoot people.

Get rid of Cuba's clothes all over the place and the surgical kit.

Officer, I came home after putting in fourteen hours . . . stopped to have a bite to eat . . . I knew someone was in the apartment . . . and found these two shot to death. I did check their vital signs, not having any idea what they were doing here. I think the naked one's in law enforcement. He could have followed the other one, the African American, here. Tell them that. But why my apartment?

Don't think about it now. She had Raylan's Glock and had fired how many rounds, seven? If someone did hear the shots, one more wouldn't matter, would it?

Do it and get out. Think later.

*   *   *

It was work to free himself of Cuba, the man not helping any. Raylan lifted his body enough to push it aside and pull himself out of the tub. He checked the Sig, racked the slide to make sure it was loaded and stepped to the doorway.

Layla was on the other side of the bed with his Glock. She looked up and had the gun pointed at him in the same motion. Raylan didn't move, standing there naked in his cowboy boots holding the Sig at his leg.

She seemed at ease in her kimono asking him, 'How are you feeling?'

'Groggy,' Raylan said. 'Like I've had too many.'

She said, 'What's that, Cuba's gun? I hate to tell you, before you try to use it—'

'I checked,' Raylan said, 'it's loaded.' He said, 'I

don't want to shoot you. Okay?'

She said, 'I thought you wanted to arrest me,' sounding surprised.

'It's up to you,' Raylan said.

'Well, I don't see us shooting it out,' Layla said, raising both arms over her head, the kimono coming open enough to show her bare-naked under it.

She said, 'Would you like to pat me down?'

This was a first for Raylan: a girl with a gun in her hand exposing herself to him.

Get him horny and shoot him?

It's what she tried.

Swung the Glock down to aim eye-level at him and Raylan raised the Sig past his hip and shot her dead center, inches below the heart, the round punching her off her feet to go down grabbing at the bedspread. Raylan circled in his cowboy boots, picking up his suitcoat, put it on and took it off to stand in front of her naked. He stood looking down at her surprised expression, her eyes not yet losing focus, turning to glass. Layla said, 'I can't believe you shot me.'

Raylan said, 'I can't either.'

CHAPTER FOURTEEN

'You don't think of your manners and let the woman go first,' Art Mullen said, 'not when she's pointing a gun at you.'

They were having breakfast at A Touch of Country in downtown Cumberland. Raylan back from Lexington poking at his bowl of grits, burying

95

the pieces of bacon.

'You keep looking at it,' Art said, 'asking yourself were you too quick. The woman jabbed a hypo in you and took your gun. Finally you come to a showdown. She's aiming at you and you're still drugged out. You wonder if you might've been too quick on the trigger?'

'She was surprised I shot her,' Raylan said.

'Why? She thought you were a gentleman? Tell me what else you could've done.'

'I was surprised too,' Raylan said, 'I did it.'

''Cause you never shot a woman before?'

'I guess.'

'Why you think you had a choice?' Art said, trying to get Raylan settled in his mind about shooting the transplant nurse, Layla.

'She was standing by her things on the bed. I could see her okay but I was wobbly. She'd made up her face, put lipstick on, did her eyes . . . '

Art said, 'I don't see that makes any difference.'

'She's gonna take out my kidneys and—I don't know—wanted to look her best? I woke up naked, in the bathtub.'

'You crawled out,' Art said, prompting him.

'I had to move Cuba Franks off me. I still don't know why she shot Cuba.'

'She's trying to hit *you*,' Art said. 'Police have the rounds she fired from your piece.'

'See, but once we're in the bedroom, I don't remember if she shot at me.'

'You had Cuba's piece now, the Sig.'

'I did. I got him off me and went in the bedroom. I see her holding my Glock. She's in her kimono.'

'You remember that,' Art said.

'I may never forget it,' Raylan said, 'the kimono

hangin open.'

'You told the police she had your piece in both hands, holding it up above her head, and asked, you said, in a flirty way, "Would you like to pat me down?"'

'She did,' Raylan said, 'and I'm thinkin she's having fun with me.'

'Till she put the gun on you, your gun,' Art said, 'and you shot her right here'—Art touchin the center of his chest—'in the solar plexus.'

Raylan shook his head. 'I didn't think I was aimin.'

'You reacted,' Art said, 'like they taught you at Glynco. Shoot first, some dink's ready to put you down.'

'I'm still not sure what I think of Layla,' Raylan said, 'except I wouldn't call her a dink.'

Art said, 'She look like fun to you?'

'If I didn't already know her game. Yeah, I could have hung out with her.'

'You ever did,' Art said, 'I believe I told you, you'd be lying somewhere without your kidneys.'

'Even knowing who she was,' Raylan said, 'I came close to losing 'em. I go to arrest her and end up in a bathtub out cold. I was lucky to wake up, you know it?'

'But you aren't surprised,' Art said. 'You're the law, you expect what you say goes. You're like an old-time marshal, tells some guy he doesn't like to get out of Dodge by sundown.'

Raylan was grinning. 'You're talking about that mob guy, the Zip.'

'You think that situation was funny?'

'See, I was to tell him, get out of Miami Beach by sundown? It isn't like saying get out of Dodge.

I gave the Zip twenty-four hours,' Raylan said, 'to pack up and hit the road. The next day he's at the Cardozo havin crab cakes, only a few minutes left of his time, so I know he's armed. It's what the man does for a living, brought here from Sicily to shoot some guy and stayed. Bought himself a double-breasted pinstriped suit like Joe Columbo's . . . Did you know that?'

'He went for the gun,' Art said, 'you took it on yourself to shoot him, and got sent to your old Kentucky home most likely for life.'

'Yeah, but I went up two grades,' Raylan said, 'after being stuck for seven years. I think somebody upstairs liked me closin the Zip's file.'

CHAPTER FIFTEEN

Otis came out of his house and crossed the yard to where Boyd Crowder and some coal company man in a suit of clothes were looking at Otis's fishpond: the pond down to barely a foot of water, fish floating dead in a scum of coal dust.

'You know how many years,' Otis said, 'it took me to dig this pond, get it to look how I wanted? Stock it with channel cat, bluegill, some shiners? My grandkids used to come over and fish for the fun of it. Hook 'em and throw 'em back.'

Boyd said, 'I bet less anybody was hungry. Otis, me and Mr. Gracie here are with M T Mining? We go out to hear there any complaints. Folks in the hollers bitchin about debris coming down where we been stripping coal.'

Mr. Gracie said, still looking at the dead pond,

'All the rocks and soil once the coal's washed out, it's got to go somewheres.'

'You don't care it's full of acid,' Otis said. 'It kilt the stream fed my pond and now all my fish are belly up.'

He watched Mr. Gracie squat down at the edge of the pool, Mr. Gracie saying, 'Hey, I believe one of 'em's still alive. Look at the little fella flippin around in there wondering where the pond went.'

Otis stepped up behind him, planted his boot against the back of Mr. Gracie's suitcoat and pushed him to throw out his arms and go facedown in the scum-covered pond.

Otis said, 'Hard to breathe in there, huh?'

Boyd stopped grinning as Otis turned to him, Boyd saying, 'I don't think you shoulda done that.'

'Forty years in mines,' Otis said, 'the whole time yes-sirin these company pimps. Well, not no more.'

*　　　*　　　*

In the evening Otis put supper on to boil—potatoes, turnips with greens—but first he sat with Marion while she held her robe closed tight to her chest breathing through her mouth. He gave her a couple of her OxyContins and a jelly glass of clear whiskey she'd sip on for a while. She had black lung from breathing the air, not ever having gone down a mine shaft.

He heard a bulldozer start up, a big diesel, knowing the sounds of the equipment, the dozers and draglines. The wolfhound heard it and got up off the floor. They'd blow charges and push the debris over the side from the strip job up on Looney Ridge. But this sounded close. Who was working in the dead of night?

By the time Otis heard branches breaking, rocks flying through the trees—knowing it was too late to grab Marion and run—a boulder the size of his Ford pickup came down on his house like the end of the world and the frame house gave up furniture, the walls, no way to stop the hunk of mountain crushing the floor, blowing out the front wall taking the door and windows, slowed some plowing through the flower beds, on flat ground now, and rolled into Otis's pond to end its trip.

Marion, in her rocker holding her drink, coasting through clouds on oxy and shine, her back to the path of destruction, said to Otis, 'What in the world was that?'

Otis said, 'I'm gonna take you over to sister's while I go up and see the mine company, all right? I come back, we may as well stay the night there.'

Marion watched Otis put on his worn-out suit coat over bib overalls and stuff the pockets with shotgun shells. In this moment her mind sounding clear, she said, 'You finally had enough of mine companies, haven't you?'

*   *   *

The M-T mining office stood on a flat ridge shorn of trees and brush, carved away in the company's hunger for coal. Boyd had been hosing the pond stink out of his SUV while Mr. Gracie told him what he wanted done.

'Lemme get this straight,' Boyd had said. 'You want me to tip a boulder over the side and see if I can hit Otis's house with it?'

'You can't,' Mr. Gracie said, 'I'll get a man

100

knows how.'

'Cause Otis shoved you in the muck,' Boyd said, 'you want me to kill him?'

'I said bust up his house,' Mr. Gracie told him. 'You don't want to work Disagreements,' the most disagreeable man Boyd had ever known said, 'you can hit the road.'

'I'm kidding with you,' Boyd said. 'I don't mind hearin people complain. They know they never gonna get what they want. They vent their ire, so to speak, and feel like they took it to the edge.'

Mr. Gracie had Boyd spread newspaper on the seat of his car, got in with his smell of muck and took off home.

Boyd said, 'Pee-yew,' and went in the office trailer, a big double-wide all desks and drawing boards, no alcohol on the premises—half a pint of cheap vodka in a desk drawer, no naked girl on the calendar, nothing to make you want to work here.

This was before Otis came up the mountain.

*   *   *

First, headlights swept the trailer and a black stretch limo pulled up next to the office. Boyd watched a woman get out and he stepped to the door and opened it. He saw her talking to her driver, giving him a few words, and the limo took off. Now she turned to the trailer, in the light from the open door, and Boyd was looking at Carol Conlan, the one person everybody saw in the newspaper or on TV when the mine company had something to say. Jesus Christ, Carol Conlan coming in smiling at him, saying, 'You're Boyd, aren't you? The one dropped the rock on the guy's house.'

How'd she know that already? Boyd started to ask her, but Carol Conlan was talking on her cell now, telling somebody, 'I'm not going to hear that, Bob. Start over and give me a report I'm sure to love, okay?' She said, 'I have to go to the bathroom,' and set down her phone.

She said to Boyd, 'Where is it?' Boyd pointed and watched her go in and raise her skirt as she sat down, leaving the door open. Man, Carol Conlan.

She said, 'You did a job on that house.'

'Only took me the one boulder,' Boyd said. He picked up her cell from the desk and sniffed to see if it had her scent.

'I thought it was cool,' Carol said, 'flip the bucket and take out the entire house. What's the guy doing about it?'

'Otis? Nothin,' Boyd said, 'he's an old man.'

'That Mick fairy Gracie—you always call him mister?'

'It's what he told me,' Boyd said.

'He took it much too far,' Carol said, 'destroying the home when we have a public hearing coming up.'

Boyd heard the toilet flush and Carol came out straightening her skirt. She said, 'Now we're the bad guys. That pond sounded like it was nice before we fucked it up.' She said, 'I never liked Gracie much. I'll have your jobs switched around and make you the boss. We have anything to drink?'

'Half a pint of vodka and all kinds of water,' Boyd said and saw the good-looking company Disagreements woman make a face and pick up her phone.

'I'll call Brian, have him get a bottle of scotch. I hate vodka.'

*　　　*　　　*

Otis had shot an elk up near the summit of Big Black, the mountain covered in a forest of old pine and aspen: came on the stag so close they both jumped at the sight of each other. Otis put him down with one shot, bled him out and they had meat the whole winter. This time he followed switchbacks up the grade to what was left of Looney Ridge, the side of the mountain carved into contoured benches. They drilled holes in the rock above the veins, and blew charges to get the coal out. Otis's house—still a thousand feet down the mountain—would shake and pictures of his dad and Marion's kin would fall off the wall. He'd told her, 'By the war, they was a hundred and thirty thousand miners diggin coal in Kentucky. Now they's a few dozen up there scrapin it out with Cats. It ain't like coal mining no more.'

Marion asked him what it was like and Otis said, 'Livin on the goddamn moon.'

He saw the bulldozer standing at the edge of the fall line, he saw lights on inside the double-wide they used for their office, didn't care somebody was inside counting beans, Otis stepped out of his truck racking the twelve-gauge and began blowing out the trailer's glass. Paused and looked around at the earthmoving machines standing idle, shut down for the night. Good, he wouldn't have to shoot anybody come yellin at him.

Otis circled the double-wide blowing out windows, reloading twice on the way. He couldn't see was anybody inside till Boyd Crowder stuck his head out the door.

'Otis, you done?'

'I'm on come in there next,' Otis said, 'shoot up the office and put you out of business for an hour.'

'Otis,' Boyd said, 'I had the key to the dynamite locker I'd give it to you. I feel I owe you for the damage done your house, even though it was Mr. Gracie said to do it.'

'I don't *have* a house,' Otis said. 'It's gone.'

'All right,' Boyd said, keeping his tone down, 'but you got it totaled account of your fishpond.'

'What'd you tell Mr. Gracie,' Otis said, 'you gonna knock my house down soon as you get done kissin his ass? I remember you, Boyd, standin up like a man the time we struck Duke Power. But tell me what we got out of it.'

'Not much that time,' Boyd said.

'We got nothin. The whole country watchin, the company says they gonna play square with us. The country stops watchin. The company tells us it takes time to change ways of getting the coal out. They take twenty years thinking about it. It's how it is and always been. The company builds a slurry pool gonna hold all the mess they make washing coal. The wall busts and poisons dump in the stream feeds my pond. I work for those people or ones like 'em forty years underground. They kill my fish and don't think nothin of it.'

Close behind him Carol Conlan said, 'He's a threat.' Boyd turned his head to the side.

'He broke some windows.'

He felt the company lady pull out the waist of his Levi's and shove something hard against his spine. Boyd knew it was a gun, he'd packed guns stuck in there before. Now she was telling him, 'I know all about you, Mr. Crowder, how you become different people whenever you feel the need.'

'I follow my instincts,' Boyd said. 'Do the first thing comes to mind like my Higher Power is slippin me the word and I go with it. I've learned to think without arguing with myself.'

'Well, I've slipped you a Glock nine,' Carol said. 'A loose cannon's a high risk. He raises the shotgun, shoot him.'

'Otis? I told you, he broke some window's all.'

'I'm not going to court on this,' Carol said, 'while we're the bad guys, and I won't take risks with nothing at stake. We handle this right now. He raises his shotgun, shoot him.'

Otis, standing no more than twenty feet away, said to Boyd, 'Who you talkin to?'

'Tell him,' Carol said.

'I got a lady visitin,' Boyd said. 'One of the coal company high-ups come by to see how we're doin up here. I told her well, the mountain keeps gettin lower, don't it?'

Carol stepped into the doorway, gave Boyd a shove and he had to step outside. She said to Otis, 'I'm the one looks into whatever we disagree on.'

'You want,' Otis said, 'I'll disagree on what you done to my pond, my home. How do you like being disagreed with?'

Carol began with a pleasant tone saying, 'In a couple of days I'm coming back to put on a big open meeting and hear from both sides, friends of coal and complainers.' Carol changed her tone to a whine, pretending to rub her finger over a flat surface as she said, 'They's soot all over my organ I play at Sunday worship.' Herself again, Carol said,

105

'You know that old coal song? "We have to dig the coal from wherever mother nature puts it." That's what coal mining is all about.'

'It don't mention the mess,' Otis said, 'strip-minin makes of your home. You ever live in coal country you know that.'

'I was born and raised in Wise, West Virginia,' Carol said, 'till I went away to law school.'

'Was any soot on you,' Otis said, 'it's gone now. My wife's never been belowground, but she's dyin of black lung, sleepin next to me forty-seven years breathin my snores.'

'That's sweet,' Carol said, 'but I think you have revenge in your mean old heart, you say the company destroyed your home—'

'And his fish pond,' Boyd said.

'Blames the company,' Carol said, 'for his wife coming to the end of a miserable life.' She said to him, 'Otis, you're here to pay us back, aren't you? Looking at me thinking I'm the god-damn company. All you have to do is raise the shotgun.'

Otis stared at Carol, his face working into a frown. He said, 'The hell you doin to me?'

'I'll show you,' Carol said, put the phone to her face and said, 'Brian . . . where are you?' She said, 'Call the Harlan County sheriff. Tell him there's been a shooting up on Looney Ridge.' She turned to Otis. 'Some old man with a shotgun's gone crazy. That's it and hang up.'

'I ain't crazy,' Otis said, 'you are,' but didn't sound sure of himself, saying again, 'The hell you doin to me?'

She was close to Boyd as he finally reached behind him for the Glock, fitting his hand to the grip.

Carol said, 'What are you waiting for? Will you please shoot him?'

Boyd turned his head, raising his hands in kind of a helpless gesture, saying, 'I don't see the need, he can't hurt us none.'

Carol took a step and yanked the Glock out of Boyd's pants, shoved him out of the way, extending the Glock in one hand and shot Otis twice in the chest.

Boyd looked from the old man lying on the ground to Carol, now telling him in her calm voice to get Otis's shotgun and fire it from where he was standing. He heard her say, 'I'll tell the sheriff's guys Otis opened up and you stepped in front of me to save my life.'

Boyd said, 'I did?'

'You shot him, didn't you?' Carol said, handing Boyd the Glock.

'Wait now,' Boyd said, 'I don't have a license to pack this weapon.'

'It's registered to the company in my name,' Carol said, 'but what do I know about firearms? I was afraid of Otis and gave it to you while we were in the office.'

'I want to be clear about this,' Boyd said. 'You let me have the gun and I shot Otis when he opened up on us.'

'What's wrong with that?' Carol said. 'You're my hero.'

CHAPTER SIXTEEN

They were in Art's SUV driving out to the M-T Mining work site, 'Where Boyd Crowder shot and killed Otis Culpepper,' Art said. 'According to the police report maybe saving the life of this company woman by his action.'

'Or maybe shootin Otis,' Raylan said, 'cause he felt like it.'

They were coming into Lynch.

'At one time,' Raylan said, 'there ten thousand people living here. Population's down to eight hundred, not much deep mining now. Towns change as the style of mining changes. M-T's blasting away at the ridgeline, stripping the sides in layers down to what they dump over the side, the forest squattin below. I remember my buddies leaving high school, marrying a girl they knew all their life and going down in the mines. The boy can't wait to have this little girl in bed with him every night, a cutie till she loses her teeth. Wears herself out raising kids while he's out drinkin if he ain't down a mine. He gets a hunk of shale fall on him, he's laid up and can't work, so they fire him,' Raylan said. 'Remember Tennessee Ernie Ford diggin number nine coal, gettin older and deeper in debt?'

'Owed his soul to the company store,' Art said. 'That was the truth of coal mining. Get paid in scrip only good at their store.'

Raylan said, 'You saw those boys came in the restaurant?'

'Miners,' Art said.

'But you can't tell by lookin at 'em, can you? They might get dust on their coveralls sittin up on a dragline, but not a bit of coal dirt on them.'

Art said, 'Those boys were United Mine Workers at one time, like everybody else.'

'You're union, M-T won't hire you.'

'Leave 'em alone. They have to care for their families.'

They were approaching M-T Mining's Looney Ridge site. Art said, 'They dump the rocks and waste over the side and call it "holler fill."'

He slowed down to crawl past a company sign nailed to a tree. It said:

NO TRESPASSING
NO HUNTING
NO FISHING
NO FOUR-WHEELERS
NO SIGHTSEEING
NO NOTHING

Raylan said, '"Violators will be prosecuted," but nothing about investigating maybe a homicide, so we're okay.'

They were in the trees now heading up to the work site.

'Tomorrow's the meeting M-T's putting on in Cumberland,' Art said. 'Everybody welcome to air their beefs with the mine company.'

'No jobs,' Raylan said, 'and coal dust settling on everything you own.'

'They'll answer complaints,' Art said, 'and describe how they'll restore and dress up the bald ridges.'

'I hear,' Raylan said, 'they're puttin in a golf

course. All the laid-off miners can play a round of golf, since they're not doing nothin. The laid-offs and the working miners will yell at each other a while and that's the meeting.'

'You're bound to see some of that,' Art said, 'but this meeting—whether anybody knows it or not—is gonna be about Black Mountain. M-T's sneakin up on it.'

'They won't get it,' Raylan said.

'They haven't yet, but they're patient.'

'How high is it, four thousand and something?'

'Four thousand a hundred and forty-five feet above sea level.'

'How about top to bottom.'

'About twenty-five hundred.'

Raylan said, 'They won't stand for it being scalped down. It's full of nature, animals, deer, ATV trails . . . You know the tree huggers'll get up in arms.'

'You're talkin about people motivated by their emotions,' Art said. 'We'll see how they fare against a coal company lawyer.'

'This woman the company's sending?'

'Carol Conlan,' Art said.

'Five bucks she's a ballbuster.'

'Her dad was a West Virginia miner. I'm told she grew up in coal camps and went on to Columbia for her law degree.'

It didn't make sense to Raylan.

'Her dad's a miner, what's she doing workin for the company?'

'Ask her,' Art said. 'You're Ms. Conlan's security while she's here. You'll be in the limo with her, maybe driving. But you don't say a word less she speaks to you. Otherwise keep your coal-miner-

110

lovin mouth shut.'

'You're givin me this,' Raylan said, ''cause I went after the nurse on my own. Didn't have time to call for backup.'

Art was shaking his head.

'Carol Conlan asked for you by name, and got a judge to request the chief deputy to okay it, as a favor. This lady can have state troopers, any amount of protection she wants, and she chose you, Raylan. Tell me why she'd do that?'

'She's a vice president of a coal mine company, I guess she can have anything she wants.'

'But why you?'

'I don't know.'

They followed a sweep of road that climbed across the side of the slope to the top of Looney Ridge. Art pointed to a bulldozer.

'The one Boyd used to dump the rock on Otis. Boyd said it must've taken a bad hop and hit his house.'

'An act of God,' Raylan said.

'That's what Boyd called it. He did, an act of God, "Since man can never tell what the Lord has in mind for us." He said the company's agreed to pay the wife for her loss.'

'Her husband or the house?' Raylan said.

*   *   *

They came in view of the office trailer, none of the broken windows replaced.

Art said, 'Look who's coming out, with a broom.'

Boyd Crowder in a white shirt and maroon tie— the M-T colors on their signs—and wearing new chinos.

111

Raylan stepped out of the car.

'Boyd, what they got you doing, cleanin up?'

'I find myself,' Boyd said, 'when I least expect always in the winner's circle. I'm on Carol Conlan's staff, helping her out while she's gettin ready for the meeting.'

'That's why you're driving the limo?'

'I'm not above takin the wheel,' Boyd said, 'she's got some scudder in the backseat, cuttin him down without ever raisin her voice. Raylan, when you're always right, you don't have to talk loud.'

'You get along with her?'

'We discuss different aspects of life as they apply to surface mining . . . the kind of complaints the company gets. She wants to know about any new ones she hasn't heard.'

'Ask her,' Raylan said, 'why she told you to shoot Otis Culpepper.'

Boyd looked tired shaking his head. 'Man, you always get on me, don't you? The old man was firing his scattergun before I got off a round.'

Raylan was showing a faint grin.

'You saved Carol's life?'

'She says I did.'

'Where was she when Otis fired at her?'

'As I recall, by the trailer, havin come out the door.'

'He shoot up the trailer?'

Boyd said, 'Hey, come on. All I know is he didn't hit Ms. Conlan. All this on account of the old man's fishpond, the pond dead, Otis claims, from all that gob the mine poured into the streams. I said, "Otis, don't fish get old and die, like everybody else?" He wouldn't listen to me.'

'Carol here yet?'

'She's stayin at a home in Woodland Hills, one this fella has a piece of the company owns and lets her use. Casper Mott, you remember him?'

'Little guy,' Raylan said, 'living on top of a mountain.'

'M-T bought it off him. He held out, said he was puttin in a bridle path and rent out horses. M-T wanted his mountain so bad they gave him stock in the company. Casper turned from nature boy to coal company showboat and got rich. He likes Ms. Conlan, so he'll be at the get-together.'

Raylan said, 'You know when I go to work?'

'In the mornin,' Boyd said. 'I pick you up and then get Ms. Conlan. She wants to talk to you, make sure you're what she wants.'

Art stepped up while they were talking, Boyd giving him a nod, then saying to Raylan, 'Got your boss watchin out for you; good,' and looked at Art again. 'See he don't shoot Ms. Conlan, now he's got a feel for shootin women.'

'I recall,' Art said, 'he shot you one time. You're mouthin off at Raylan, your gun right there on the table.'

'Havin supper Ava fixed for me that time,' Boyd said.

'Yeah, Raylan shot me dead center, but the Lord made him miss my heart by a hair and I survived it.'

Art said, 'I bet the Lord's havin second thoughts.'

'Hey, come on,' Boyd said, 'me and Raylan are buddies now, both workin for the coal company.'

*　　　*　　　*

In the SUV again, circling down the bare mountain, Art said, 'I admire your control. He made that

113

remark about shootin the nurse, you didn't deck him.'

'I am practicing self-control,' Raylan said, 'for when I'm with Ms. Conlan. Boyd's right, I've shot a woman, but I've still never hit one with my hand.'

CHAPTER SEVENTEEN

She came out of the tall pillars across the front of the Colonial in Woodland Hills and walked up to Raylan and Boyd waiting by the limo. She didn't look at Boyd. She offered Raylan her hand saying, 'Carol Conlan.'

Raylan, his expression pleasant enough said, 'Ma'am,' touched the brim of his hat and gave her hand a squeeze. 'I'm Raylan Givens.'

'I know, I've been reading about you, the one who shot the nurse.'

Raylan waited.

'The write-up in the paper called you brave. Are you?'

'I try to be whatever's required.'

'Would you give your life to save mine?'

That took him to the heart of his job here. Raylan paused. 'It would depend on the situation.'

'What does that mean?'

He said, 'Carol . . . once I'm dead and gone to heaven, how do I know I've saved your life?' There. If she didn't care for him calling her Carol, fire him.

But she seemed to let it go. What she said was, 'Raylan,' in a mild voice, 'wouldn't heaven know if you saved my life or not?'

He had to smile saying, 'You got me.'

114

Carol said, 'Let's get in the car.'

*   *   *

Boyd, way up in front at the wheel of the stretch, couldn't believe it. The two buddy-buddy already. He watched them in the rearview mirror, next to each other on the backseat; Ms. Conlan, her legs crossed in expensive-looking tan slacks, a preppy black sport coat, sunglasses. Raylan sitting up straight but looked at ease, still wearing his cowboy hat, Ms. Conlan going easy on him, not scaring the shit out of him yet. Boyd looked at his controls now and turned the speaker on back there—to tell the driver what you wanted without raising your voice— and kept it low, both their voices coming to him, Ms. Conlan asking Raylan about the nurse who stole kidneys, saying she read about it in the paper.

*   *   *

'You know what I've wondered?' Carol said. 'If you ever got it on with Layla. She was attractive, wasn't she?'

'You're askin me,' Raylan said, 'since she's good-looking, did I try to get her in bed?'

Carol paused. 'Did you?'

'By the time we met I was on to her.'

She wouldn't let go of it. Now Carol said, 'But if you didn't know what she was up to . . .?'

'My boss asked me the same thing. He said if I hooked up with her, not knowing what she did, I'd be laying in an alley missing my kidneys.'

'So you set out to arrest Layla the transplant nurse and shot her instead.'

115

Raylan waited. It wasn't a question.

'What was it like,' Carol said, 'shooting a woman? Was it different?'

'I can't say you get use to shooting *any*body. As a rule, women aren't into crimes where they'd get shot by people in law enforcement. So we don't get that many opportunities to shoot women.'

Let her chew on that.

She didn't seem to mind it, saying, 'With Layla, did you hesitate?'

'I had, I'd be dead,' Raylan said.

She seemed done with shooting women and said, 'You've worked as a coal miner.'

He didn't answer and Carol said, 'Isn't that true?'

'My boss told me not to open my mouth unless you asked me a question. Yeah, I dug coal, when we weren't on strike.'

'Do you still think like a coal miner?'

'I don't have his problems, finding work, getting pushed around by the company.'

'Your attitude about the companies hasn't changed.'

'I think miners' complaints are all real. A miner's injured on the job, he keeps working or you fire him.'

Carol held up her hand to Raylan and said in a quiet voice, 'Boyd, where'd you put the Cokes?'

Raylan watched him look at the mirror.

'They're on the other side from you, by Raylan.'

Carol said, 'Turn off the speaker.'

'Oh, was it on?'

She said to Raylan, 'He lies, doesn't he?'

'It's his nature,' Raylan said. 'I'm looking at him for shootin Otis Culpepper.'

Carol said, 'You know I was there.'

'I understand you told the authorities you were by the trailer,' Raylan said, 'when Otis fired his shotgun at you.'

Carol nodded, brushing her blond hair away from her face. She said, 'I was coming out,' and started to smile. She knew what he was about to tell her but Raylan said it anyway.

'No buckshot hit the trailer where you were standing. There aren't any marks or dents in it.'

She said, 'Then he missed, didn't he?'

'From thirty feet, where Boyd drilled him.'

Carol said, 'Raylan,' and put her hand on his knee. 'Your job is to look out for me. You don't *investigate* a matter that would bring me in as a witness, I don't have time. Just watch my back, all right? I think this meeting could become physical.'

She was through talking about Otis, Carol looking out the window now.

'It's so green . . . the trees in the hills come so close. Like they want to envelop us.'

'Pretty soon,' Raylan said, 'you'll see the ridge going bald, but it still causes people living below to fuss. Now they have rocks and bare earth envelopin them.'

'Be nice,' Carol said.

*   *   *

Boyd didn't hear them once she caught him listening.

He'd look at the mirror and he'd see them talking most of the whole way to Cumberland on 119. He turned on the speaker—hell with her—saying, 'You like, I could direct your attention to

117

some points of interest.'

Carol's voice said, 'No, we wouldn't.'

He thought of what he'd recite had she let him. Lynch, we're not goin there, but you might be interested to know Lynch is where colored miners lived. Excuse me, Americans of the African persuasion. Benham now has a tourist attraction. Portal 31, where you can pay to ride down from the surface and see what a mine looks like cleaned up and tidy. There's a Johnny-on-the-Spot you never saw in a working mine, any the tourists have to take a leak. Finally they were coming to Cumberland, driving past nice-looking houses on the outskirts, Boyd telling them we have arrived. Approaching Cumberland High he pointed to the red and gold flag flying. He'd tell Ms. Conlan looking out the window, 'I don't know if our Indin brothers have complained about it yet, but look at that sign. Cumberland High School, Home of the Redskins.'

*   *   *

Cars and pickups were parked along the front of the school—early arrivals—more cars on the other side of the road. Boyd headed for the lot next to the school, not many cars in there yet, and passed an open space directly in front of the building. Saw a colored guy in a chauffeur suit standing in the space like he was guarding it.

Casper Mott's driver.

It *was*. It put Casper in the stretch parked in front of the space, by the walk that went up to the school. There were people with signs standing across the walk from one another. On one side, COAL KEEPS THE LIGHTS ON, and opposite them on the other side of the walk, was the same sign with words crossed out and one written in that said COAL KILLS.

Boyd saw the chauffeur in his rearview step out in the road and wave his arm for Boyd to come back, Boyd easing the brakes on and heard Ms. Conlan tell him to stop and he did. Told him to back up and Boyd said to Ms. Conlan, 'We never gonna fit in that dinky space.' All right, she'd get out here, and opened her door saying to Raylan, 'See you in school,' and walked back to the stretch, the chauffeur holding the door open now. Raylan watched her stand there talking, most likely to Casper, before she got in.

Boyd said, 'That colored fella drivin, I believe was a fighter one time, from Lynch.'

'Reggie Banks,' Raylan said. 'Promoters'd take him around to different coal camps. Pay a miner ten bucks to go two rounds. Reggie had style. Shuffle his feet like Muhammad Ali, fake you out of your jock and hit you with a right he called his stinger. Reggie'd get a hundred bucks to fight five guys in a row, two rounds each.'

Boyd said, 'You know him, huh?'

'I fought him back when we were diggin coal.'

'He take your head off?'

'He came close. But we got to know each other.'

They parked in the school lot and walked around to the front of the building, Raylan nodding to miners he knew.

One of them holding a GOT ELECTRICITY? THANK A MINER sign said, 'Raylan, I hear you're on the company's side this time.'

'Till tomorrow,' Raylan said.

Another coal lover in his sport shirt and

119

M-T company hat said to Raylan, 'I'll meet you out here after, you want. Teach you respect for the company.'

'You don't see me right away,' Raylan said, 'practice falling down till I get here.'

The two sides were yelling things at each other now and Boyd said, 'Come on,' and they walked toward Casper Mott's limo, Boyd saying, 'Aren't you suppose to be keepin the peace?'

'I'm in this, but don't have a say.'

Reggie Banks stood by the door waiting to open it, saw Raylan coming toward him and said, 'Man, you still pickin fights?'

They touched fists, Raylan saying, 'Reg, you still off the sauce?'

'Not in two years, nothin. Had me drivin fast till I went to AA and got calmed down.'

'What're they doing in the car?'

'Waitin till they ready. Or the company lady's given 'em their bonus, one.'

Raylan heard a tap on the window, from inside.

'Time to let 'em out,' Reggie said. 'Man's too wealthy to open the door hisself. Somebody told him he was a man of leisure, don't have to do nothing he don't want to. Dumb as mud he ain't schemin with his money. I wonder, does he put on being simple as a child.'

Reggie opened the door and little Casper Mott came out grinning at Raylan.

'Boy, hey, you lookin good. Ms. Conlan tells us you're her security.' He added, not moving his mouth, 'I'd stay as close to Carol as I could get, but not believe a word she tells you.' He reached up and gave Raylan a hug. 'Hey, I've got a guest with me's an old friend of yours.'

He turned to the car and the man came out ducking his head and Raylan was looking at his hairpiece shaped for life.

'Mr. Pervis Crowe,' Casper said.

There he was, wearing a suitcoat with wide lapels and a tie and his toupee. Now he was an old friend? Pervis took hold of Raylan's hand saying, 'They's matters we disagreed on, but I always saw you as a man. Even tellin about my boys stealin kidneys. You kept bein yourself, not puttin on how smart you are.'

Raylan said, 'I'm sorry about your boys.'

Pervis held up his hand. 'I let 'em become nitwits. They had plenty time to straighten out, so I'm not takin blame. I swear I couldn't stand to have 'em around.'

'I get Pervis here for the day,' Casper said. 'Tomorrow he has to be home—Rita's coming. She visits every two weeks—set your watch by it.'

Raylan glanced at Pervis listening, not seeming to mind.

'She puts on her maid's outfit,' Casper said, 'and her and Pervis play house all day.'

Raylan looked at Pervis. 'You mind him tellin your business?'

'He talks, he sounds like a woman. Everybody knows she lived with me for years. I set her up.' Pervis said, 'Rita's the smartest dealer in the state.'

'All I'm tryin to do,' Casper said to Raylan, 'is show my good buddy how to get rich.'

'I got enough,' Pervis said, 'without sellin any my properties.'

Carol was getting out of the car now.

Raylan watched her come out telling Casper, 'I'm not here to make Mr. Crowe an offer. I've told

121

you that. My job is to hear complaints and work out disagreements. Listen to what miners have against the company that's giving them jobs.'

Casper was grinning. 'Honey, we know each other, we been across the table. You're gonna set all your girlish devices on poor Mr. Crowe and get him to sell.'

'You mind my asking,' Raylan said, 'what you all are talking about?'

'Big Black Mountain,' Casper said, 'the highest peak in the state of Kentucky, and Pervis owns it.'

CHAPTER EIGHTEEN

Once they were inside the school, people in the hall turning to look at them, Raylan leaned close to her saying, 'I wondered what you were doing in the car. You changed your pants.'

Carol said, 'You're the only one noticed.'

'I know the difference between linen slacks and forty-nine-dollar Levi's.'

The folded pair she'd brought along; they fit her snug. Raylan kept this observation to himself, but then the Devil made him say, 'A tear across one of the knees is popular.'

'You can be annoying,' Carol said, 'but I'm not letting you go. I want you at the side of the stage where I can see you. I'm going to use you, Raylan, the most popular guy here with all your celebrity. I'm going to make a point that comes close to home.'

'I was a miner at one time,' Raylan said, 'and live to tell about it?'

'Wait for my questions,' Carol said.

*   *   *

In the gym, Carol got up from her chair next to Casper Mott's, gave his shoulder a pat and walked up to the mike, its stand in the middle of the movable stage at the far end of the Redskin gym. She looked out at three hundred folding chairs all occupied, signs sticking up in the crowd; unemployed miners in clean shirts and dirty baseball caps outnumbering the ones with jobs three to one, maybe more, their wives waiting to have a say.

She glanced to her right, where Winona sat at her stenotype machine. Carol had listened to Casper reading the names of court reporters. He came to Winona's, mentioning she was Raylan's ex, and Carol said get her for the meeting, whatever she wants. Casper asked should he bill M-T, and Carol said, 'I would.'

To Carol's left, Raylan stood where he'd mount the stage if he had to. While she was still seated Carol had watched him looking at Winona, trying to catch her eye. But she couldn't tell if he did without turning around.

Beyond Raylan, off to the side of the crowd, Boyd was talking a mile a minute to a girl Carol saw as a babe, in heels and a showy yellow dress, the neck cut just low enough. She had to be Ava, attractive but still a babe, the one who'd shot her husband while he was having supper. Boyd's brother. Ava was living with Boyd now—he'd mentioned it—as brother and sister. Carol asked him why.

Boyd said, 'We're seein can we trust each other

123

enough to fall in love and make it work.' Whatever that meant.

Carol didn't ask.

She took the mike from the stand now and said, 'Good afternoon. I'm Carol Conlan, a vice president of M -T Mining.'

She got a wave of boos, a few whistles she believed had nothing to do with her job, and questions fired at her:

'When's M -T gonna do right by us?'

'Lady, we miss a day sick we're laid off.'

Carol said, 'My dad mined coal in West Virginia. I grew up in coal camps, so I know what you all are talkin about,' her accent taking her closer to West Virginia as she spoke.

A voice in the crowd asked her: 'How'd you escape the life?'

'I got out on a scholarship to college, worked my tail off studying about industry, supply and demand and the coal business. I went on to get a law degree and was hired by the company that's given you fellas your jobs.'

A man's voice said, 'They's way less jobs workin mountaintop. What are all us miners sittin around the house suppose to do?'

Carol said, 'Times change, don't they? You're drivin a car now stead of a team of mules. The blacksmith used to shoe your mules, what's he doin? He's gone, workin at something else now. Most coal mines are still underground, but you know it's changing. There more and more surface operations workin today.'

From the crowd: 'You mean desecratin the mountains.'

Carol said, 'We restore the mountains, don't

124

we?'

The same voice: 'Wait a hunnert years for the trees to grow? I doubt we'll be around.'

She had something to say about future generations, but saved it. A man in the front row was standing now. He said: 'My name's Hazen Culpepper from over by Mayfield? I like to know why one of your gun thugs shot and killed my brother Otis for breakin a few windows.'

Carol softened her voice saying, 'Hazen, I can't tell you how sorry we are. But it wasn't a gun thug shot your brother. We don't hire gun thugs.' She said, 'Otis lost his home because of someone carelessly dumping debris from a work site. I don't blame Otis for gettin mad, but—and I hate to say this—your brother fired a shotgun at me. He was ready to fire again and one of our employees intervened.'

'You mean Boyd Crowder,' Hazen said, 'standin over there against the wall?' He said, 'Boyd, you tell her Otis missed?'

'Ms. Conlan was *there*,' Boyd said. 'She saw him.'

'Then you're both liars,' Hazen said. 'Otis don't miss with a twelve-gauge. You shot him when he wasn't lookin.'

Raylan watched Hazen walk over to Boyd and say something to him, a few words, on his way through the crowd, having hands put on him, patting his shoulder. Raylan caught a whiff of Carol's scent and turned his head to her standing next to him.

She said, 'You're not going to arrest him?'

Raylan said, 'Which one?'

Now a woman in the front row stood up and said to Carol, 'You don't live anywheres near a mine, do

125

you? You know what it does for people livin below? It covers everything you own in coal dirt. It's all over the house on every surface. Is that why they call it surface coal? It's in your bathtub, your well— you can't drink the water no more. Every mornin a coat of coal dirt coverin my car. I have to wash my car before I can go to work.'

'Wait now,' Carol said. 'You're surprised it gets things dirty? Ma'am, it's coal. You live in the heart of coal country. A boy comes home from playin, his mom says, "Junebug, your hands are black as coal. Wash 'em before grampa gets after you." This old man with fifty years of coal dust you're complainin about, embedded in his pores. Ma'am, coal powers more than half the electricity in the U.S. Do we quit minin coal cause it's dirty? My dad use to come home so filthy all you could see were his eyes. The coal industry mines forty million tons of coal a year. Half of it's taken from the surface.'

A woman's voice said, 'You people dig it all up, what's future generations gonna do?'

'What have future generations ever done for us?' Carol said. 'I'm kiddin. You know who said that? Groucho Marx. Listen, I don't think we should worry our heads about running out of coal. I know we've got enough in the ground for the next two hundred and fifty years.'

A man's voice piped up: 'We can have windmill power right now, like in Holland. Clean wind, no soot blowin on us.'

'If the wind lovers ever get it right,' Carol said. 'The trouble is, wind turbines can cause health problems, headaches and sleep disorders, kids having nightmares.'

Man's voice: 'All this strippin goin on, your

company gets rich while we're the poorest county in the state, most of us laid off.'

'It tells me,' Carol said, 'we got to do more strippin, get more work for you fellas.'

A miner's voice: 'We work for a time, the company digs while the price of coal is high. The price dips, the coal company files bankruptcy, forfeits its bond, and slips away in the night.'

'You know they're always risks,' Carol said. 'It costs a fortune to set up a mine operation. They don't find as much coal as expected, they have to try again someplace else. Mister, it's the price of coal on the market keeps us in business.'

'You clear out,' a voice said, 'without cleanin up the mess you always leave behind. A 'poundment breaks loose where you're holdin three hundred million gallons of slurry, fulla poison, toxic chemicals, and it pours down in the holler and contaminates the water. You know what your boss, the CEO of M-T Mining, called it?'

'An Act of God,' Carol said. 'I believe my boss, bless his heart, is sincere when he says that. He's a churchgoer, he believes the Lord moves in mysterious ways we don't always understand. Why couldn't it be an Act of God? The Lord tellin us, if you gonna build impoundments to catch slurry, then God damn it, try buildin one that holds.' Carol said, 'Sometimes we have to learn the hard way.'

She was getting sounds of approval, whistles, a woman saying, 'A-men' and Carol felt closer to the crowd.

She said, 'I know the pay's decent for surface-mine work. I believe it comes to eleven hundred and twenty dollars a week,' and said right away, 'Raylan Givens,' extending her hand in his direction, 'I bet most of you know him. A judge assigned Raylan as my personal bodyguard. I asked His Honor, "What do I need protection for? Aren't we all friends?"' That drew some noise. 'Raylan works for Uncle Sam, he's a federal marshal and has been decorated a number of times, I understand, for drawing down on outlaws.'

She let the miners hoot and whistle, then turned to Raylan saying, 'Marshal, may I ask if your salary as a law enforcement officer is in the neighborhood of eleven hundred a week?'

It surprised him and he hesitated, taking his boot from the first step to the stage. Raylan said, 'Base pay startin out? It's around there.'

'About the same as a surface miner's.'

'Well, there's overtime . . . '

'But you start out with a weekly salary not much different than if you were diggin coal. Isn't that right?'

'It's pretty close,' Raylan said. 'Except marshals are paid fifty-two weeks a year. I've put ten years in, that's five hundred weeks I've been paid without a miss. I take a day off—sometimes I have to—I come down with a ferocious hangover . . . '

Raylan paused, letting the miners come alive yelling remarks at him, 'Tell it like it is,' shouting, 'Day off's a day of pain!'

'I take a sick day,' Raylan said, 'I don't get fired.' He waited a beat and said, 'Even get paid for it.'

*   *   *

Carol saw it coming. Raylan finished and the gym erupted in applause, those piercing whistles, miners yelling his name—'You tell her, Raylan!'—and

Carol realized she'd blown it. She'd let Raylan in, let him go on when he said, 'Except'—and nailed it in a few words—'there's a big difference between my pay and a coal miner's working for a company that shuts down when they feel like it,' Raylan giving them something to cheer about, the crowd applauding and yelling remarks.

Carol announced to the crowd, most of them standing now, 'Let's take a break, all right? We have refreshments waiting in the front hall. Then we'll come back and have at it again, okay? Meanwhile I'll have a talk with Raylan, let him know he's supposed to protect me, not step on my lines.'

The hill folk probably wouldn't get it. They weren't listening anyway.

She saw Raylan talking to miners gathering around him and turned to Winona sitting by her steno machine. Carol walked across the stage toward her.

'Winona? Hi, I'm Carol. We're so pleased we could get you for this meeting.'

'I wasn't sure why you wanted me,' Winona said. 'Other than I was married to Raylan at one time and you're curious about him.'

'My,' Carol said, 'you speak right up, don't you?'

'I wondered why you wanted a court reporter for this. Because it's what I do and you can ask me about Raylan? Or because you like reading transcripts?'

Carol walked away, got her chair from the middle of the stage and dragged it over. She sat down saying, 'Which do you think?'

'You've heard all the complaints before. I think you'd like to know about Raylan. From a woman once married to him.'

Carol said, 'Did he fool around?'

'Not once in six years.'

'How can you be so sure?'

'He'd walk in the house and if he had, it would be on his face, but never was.'

'He left you, didn't he?'

'I left *him*. We're in bed he'd start talkin about offenders. I had different moves I'd have to put on him.'

'You're married to a real estate man now.'

'Sorta. I can't say the marriage was made in heaven. I thought I needed security.'

'It's obvious you don't,' Carol said. 'You want a job?'

'I'll never in my life go to work for a coal company,' Winona said. 'I'm surprised you did, your dad a miner.'

'He died,' Carol said. 'I was at Columbia and switched my major from English lit to mining management and joined the company.'

'And save your love for your dog?'

'I have a cat. That's what I call her, Cat. "Hey, Cat, whatcha doin, huh?" She never purrs.'

'I don't blame her.'

Carol said, 'What kind of moves worked best?'

'On Raylan? All of them. Being seductive wore me out.'

Carol said, 'You're after him again, aren't you?'

'I'll bet what you owe me,' Winona said, 'you don't get him in bed.'

Carol said, 'What about in the limo?'

*　　　*　　　*

Raylan got away from the miners grinning at him, telling him he ought to run for judge, and walked over to Boyd and Ava by the wall.

Boyd straightened. He said to Raylan, 'I believe with hope in my heart you're gonna arrest that Mayfield hick. You're standing there, you heard him threaten me. Tell me you are so I can go sit down.'

'He didn't threaten you,' Raylan said, 'he called you a liar.' He turned to Ava saying, 'Ms. Crowder,' with that hint of a grin he put on, 'you're a double-dip ice-cream cone in that yella dress.'

Ava said, 'Raylan, I'd let you have a lick, but I'm with Boyd. We're seein how it goes right now before our relationship becomes serious. If you know what I mean.'

'Well, you've had a taste of Crowders,' Raylan said. 'Married Bowman and had to shoot him. I'm not criticizing you. You believed he had it coming.'

Ava said, 'Thank you.'

Boyd said, 'Hey, leave us alone, all right?'

'I'll tell you,' Raylan said, 'I'm lookin at ways to bring you up for shootin Otis, Carol telling you to do it. Bring her into it, you might get your plea down to second degree. Only have to do twenty years.'

Ava took Boyd by the arm saying, 'I don't want to hear this.'

'He's lyin,' Boyd said, 'accusing me of a premeditated act, so he can get at you when I'm gone. Force himself on you.'

Ava seemed to hesitate, losing a step, dragging Boyd toward the door now. She turned her head past his shoulder to look back at Raylan.

CHAPTER NINETEEN

The morning of the day of the meeting, God told Pervis he ought to use Dewey Crowe as honey to attract the insects.

Pervis had sat almost bolt upright in bed. God's message was in his head, so he knew who the bugs were: Casper Mott and others who wanted his mountain, Big Black. He phoned Rita, Rita having everybody's number.

She said, 'It's tomorrow I'm coming, not today.'

'I know,' Pervis said, 'I want to make sure I'm home from Cumberland and hear you come in the door sayin, "I'm ho-ome." I get that tug in my groin. What I'd like you to do, locate Dewey Crowe and let me know where he's at.'

Rita said, 'What is it you need fucked up?'

See how smart she was?

Rita was back in a minute. 'He left word he's in Harlan. Will be at the Dairy Queen from noon on, takin orders.'

'Oh yeah, he's sellin whiskey.'

*   *   *

Noon on the dot Pervis called Dewey's cell. Dewey, no life in his voice, said, 'Yeah?'

Pervis said, 'That's how you answer a phone?'

There was a pause. Dewey came back on showing life.

'Is this Uncle Pervis I'm speakin to?'

'You recognize my voice.'

'Yes sir, and pleased to hear it.'

132

'You goin to Cumberland tomorrow for the meeting?'

'What meeting's that?'

Pervis said to the nitwit, 'The one at the high school. Am I gonna see you there?'

'Yes sir, I was thinkin of goin.'

'Boy, what're you doin in Harlan?'

'Sellin hooch I get in Cumberland and mark up.'

'You doin all right?'

'I clear least two bucks a fifth.'

The boy needed help, bad.

Pervis said, 'Since I lost my two sons, you're the only Crowe left to carry on what I consider my life's chore. You understand what that is?'

'Is that true? I'm your only kin?'

'I'm not leavin you my business,' Pervis said. 'I'm referrin to my property, Big Black Mountain.'

There was a silence.

'Sir, you telling me you own Big Black?'

Pervis believed everybody in East Kentucky knew it but this moron. Pervis said, 'I do, and when I'm gone the mountain'll be entrusted to you.'

'I'm gonna own it?'

Nervous excitement in his voice.

'Do anything I want with it?'

Already close to selling it off.

'You have to promise me,' Pervis said, 'you won't ever part with it. Casper Mott finds out you're gonna inherit my mountain, he'll have me run over by a coal truck and work on you to get it. I'm gonna let him know today there's no chance of his buyin it off me.'

Dewey said, 'Casper Mott, he's already rich as kings.'

'The day you sell Big Black you'd be richer. But

133

I'm countin on you to preserve the highest peak in Kentucky for the enjoyment of the people livin here. You have to promise me, Dewey . . . you listenin?'

'Yes sir?'

'You won't ever sell it. You'll pass the mountain on to your heirs'—if the moron ever had any—'with their promise they won't sell it either. You give me your word on it?'

'I get the mountain when you're gone?'

'It's how it works you inherit somethin.'

'But I can't make any money off it?'

'You want your mountain stripped of its majesty?'

You bet he did.

'I'll meet you tomorrow in Cumberland,' Pervis said, 'in front of the high school. I want to see you wearin a clean shirt, a suit if you have one and no gator teeth. Boy, you're heir to the richest mountain in the state of Kentucky. How's that make you feel?'

Dewey said, 'Well, yeah, Jesus.'

'You won't say a word about it this evening.'

'No sir.'

Like hell he wouldn't.

*　　　*　　　*

Noon there he was in a borrowed suit too big for him, no gator teeth showing, standing by the school doors checkin out girls' asses.

Pervis got out of Casper's limo and hung back, letting Casper go on ahead with Ms. Conlan and Raylan. He saw Raylan take her arm and she brushed his hand away. Casper had said before she

134

got in the limo what he'd like to do to her. Suck her toes, play around with each little piggy with his tongue . . . Pervis asked him did he ever lick his way up to think of havin sexual intercourse with Ms. Conlan. He said Oh sure, lots of times. Pervis believed Casper would try to set him up for Ms. Conlan, who'd make the pitch for his mountain. Pervis wouldn't mind hearin it even though he'd give the mountain to Rita when the time came and she'd hold on to it till she got tired of hearing offers pitched at her and finally pick the best one. She'd have dudes comin at her and she'd set one or two aside for fun, fun bein the girl's nature. He'd like to see what Raylan'd do if Rita ever came after him. There was Raylan stayin close to Ms. Conlan in the crowd, Casper tryin to keep up.

Pervis waited for Dewey to spot him and come pushing past people to get to his old uncle.

'You all dressed up,' Pervis said. 'You feelin good?'

Dewey said, 'Yes sir, I'm proud you're trustin me with the mountain.'

'I'm *en*trustin you with it,' Pervis said. 'That don't mean I trust you.' Let the nitwit chew on that. 'I have a heart condition,' Pervis said, 'can kill me any time it wants. I've seen my will lawyer and put you in for the mountain. But you're not gonna tell anybody about it, are you?'

Dewey said, 'No sir, I'll swear to it on a Bible.'

'Say this wop gangster has you. Gonna stick your hand in a fire less you tell him your secret.'

Dewey was shaking his head.

'No,' Pervis said, 'what the wop says, he's gonna cut your nuts off and feed 'em to the squirrels you don't tell him.'

135

It seemed to give Dewey pause, till he squared his narrow shoulders in the borrowed suit and said, 'Uncle, this here's nobody's business but mine.'

* * *

They sat in the crowd and listened to the first part of the meeting, Pervis with Dewey next to him, bored, squirming, Pervis directing his attention to Ms. Conlan softening her accent for the boobs sitting here listening. She gave Raylan the floor and he pulled the rug out from under her, Pervis thinking, Good for you, boy. But it wouldn't hurt Ms. Conlan none. The way she'd see it was coal miners looking for a hero. She wasn't solving disagreements, she was the coal company.

The first part ended and Dewey asked Pervis if he'd like a drink, he had some whiskey in his car.

Pervis said, 'We'll have one and then I'm goin home.'

'But you come in Casper's limo,' Dewey said, 'you don't have a car with you.'

'You're right,' Pervis said. 'I'll take yours and leave it at the Dairy Queen.'

* * *

Carol sat with Casper in his limo having a cigarette while the tree huggers, sworn enemies of mountaintop mining, presented their arguments to the crowd in the gym.

Casper said, 'How you gonna give the company side you don't hear what they're talking about.'

'They're saying shame on us for letting our mountains go bald,' Carol said. 'Our beautiful

136

countryside gone to hell. Twelve hundred miles of streams filled with debris. Waste dumped on their homes. I've heard it.'

'They gonna throw flooding at you,' Casper said. 'Cut down the forest they's nothin left to catch the rain, soak up the water. You know animals are coming down from those bare-ass mountaintops? Foxes, skunks, coyotes. Fella told me he has to put his garbage on the roof of his house, keep it out of reach of bears.'

Carol said, 'Really, there are bears?'

'Blasting causes damage to homes in the area, cracks the foundation—you have a house close to a mining operation—she can depreciate on you ninety percent. This home bein all the man's got.'

'Coal's his life,' Carol said, 'in his family for generations. I've already talked about more work. Give us the mountains and we'll give you jobs.'

'You don't have enough to offer. Man's out of work, falls behind in his payments, the bank takes his house. You gonna get health questions too,' Casper said. 'More kids gettin asthma, all the coal dust in the air.'

'But a lower incidence of black lung,' Carol said, 'mining from the top?'

'I suppose,' Casper said. He watched Carol light another cigarette off the one she was smoking. 'I know you want that parcel a thousand feet from Big Black's summit.'

'I don't see that coming up at the meeting.'

'Everybody knows you're sneaking up on the mountain, the jewel in the crown, known to be fulla coal. I bet it'll be a question thrown at you. Gonna talk to Pervis about it?'

'As long as I'm here.'

137

'Like it isn't your only reason.'

'I'll open his eyes to possibilities.'

'Open his fly,' Casper said, 'he might make you a deal.'

* * *

She had told Raylan to wait by the car, outside. He asked how close he should stay to it. She looked at him—maybe she couldn't think of anything good to say, so she didn't. Carol got in the limo. After a while Casper came out, said hi and went behind the limo to take a leak, hitting sheet metal, Raylan wondering if Carol was supposed to hear him. Casper said hi again and got back in the car.

This was when Dewey Crowe came out of the school lighting a cigarette.

CHAPTER TWENTY

Raylan walked up to him saying, 'Dewey, I saw you in there during the meeting, but couldn't make up my mind what side you're on.' He didn't appear to know what Raylan meant—for the mine company or against it—so Raylan said, 'I saw you hangin out with Pervis, the old man treating you kindly, putting his hand on your shoulder?'

'Pervis says I'm like his son,' Dewey said.

'Which one, Dickie or Coover?'

'Neither. He said I'm like a son he never had.'

'You seemed close, Pervis smiling, and he isn't known to smile much.'

'He's got a kin now,' Dewey said, 'to look out for

138

his property when he's gone.'

Raylan said, 'Who's the kin?'

'*Me,*' Dewey said. Got his voice normal again and said, 'I'm his heir when he passes. Me and some colored girl he uses for his wants but no kin to him. I'm his only relation he knows of.'

'Both of you Crowes,' Raylan said, but at some distance from each other. 'Where's old Pervis? I haven't seen him in a while.'

'He took my car and went home. Actually,' Dewey said, 'I offered it to him, Pervis wantin to get away from people botherin him about property I'm due to inherit.'

'You're telling me,' Raylan said, 'he's leaving you Big Black when he's gone?'

Dewey grinned. 'I didn't say it, you did.'

'I get it,' Raylan said. 'Pervis doesn't want you to tell anybody.'

'Not till he passes. I'm not to dare think of sellin it either.'

'Trusting you with his mountain.'

'*En*-trusting me.'

'Well, hell,' Raylan said, 'you need to get home, don't you? Ask Casper to give you a lift, or Ms. Conlan. They both have limos, plenty of room.'

'I don't know either one to speak to.'

'Tell 'em you're Pervis's kin,' Raylan said. 'That ought to get you a ride.'

He watched Dewey approach Casper's car and knock on the window. Raylan heard him say he was looking for a ride back to Harlan.

Heard him say he was Dewey Crowe.

Heard him say Pervis was his uncle.

'Pervis Crowe, same as mine. The one owns Black Mountain.'

It got the limo door to open, Casper stepping out with a gesture, please, for Dewey to join them.

*   *   *

They had him sit next to Carol in the dark, Casper taking a seat he flipped open to face them. Carol saying, 'Dewey, really, Pervis Crowe's your uncle?'

'He is,' Dewey said, 'and I'm the only kin he's got. I come out of Florida—he knows they's Crowes down there, see, but never heard from any of 'em. I come up here and introduce myself, I see the old man's eyes fill up as he takes me to his bosom and hugs me. He said, "You have come at a time in my life when I most need a kin."'

'Why is that?' Carol said.

'I took it to mean his end is near, his tired old heart telling him he's a goner fore too long. You know Pervis has this colored girl worked for him years? He'll leave her something, any trinkets he has from the time he was married.'

'But he's surprised,' Carol said, 'an honest-to-God kin has shown up? Why does he believe you?'

Dewey said, 'Why wouldn' he?' not liking her tone of voice. 'We both Crowes. He knows some of his people live in Florida. I come here wearin gator teeth, he knows I'm a Crowe from down there.'

'And proud of it,' Carol said. 'Let's say he believes you. If he's giving trinkets to his former cleaning woman, what's he giving you?'

'None of your business.'

She smelled good, but Dewey did not like her tone.

Carol said, 'Casper, how much have you made

140

selling your mountains?'

Casper said, 'How many million? You ought to know. M-T Minin checks pay all my bills. Bought me a house, this car.' Casper said, 'You ever hear of a limo can go a hundred and forty miles an hour? Get out on the highway, anywhere you go, it's a trip.'

'What engine you got in her?'

'I think they just did a job on the one's in it.'

'I got a '87 Hornet,' Dewey said. 'Leaks oil.'

Carol said, 'What's Pervis drive?'

'An old Ford with a blower.'

Carol said, 'Pervis is a sleeper.'

'He's got more money'n God and never shows it.'

Carol said, 'He told you he's leaving you his mountain?'

Dewey grinned. 'I didn't say it, you did.'

*   *   *

The next thing they were telling him to leave, Ms. Conlan asking would he excuse her? She had to get ready to go in there and talk, okay?

Casper jumping out and held the door open, Dewey feeling Casper's hand on his shoulder.

'Casper will give you a ride sometime in his souped-up limo.'

Casper shrugged.

'You get the mountain we'll give you a hot limo just like it,' Carol said. 'Bye.'

Casper hopped in and the door closed.

Dewey turned to see Raylan standing there watching.

'You hear her?'

'Some,' Raylan said. 'I think what she meant, she

141

isn't sure you're gonna ever own the mountain.'

'I never come out and told her I was.'

'She reads minds.'

'I didn't care for her tone a voice,' Dewey said, 'like I was the help. She offered me a ride home, I turned her down. It wasn't easy. I begun sniffin her perfume, I'd be sniffin her all the way to Harlan. But I prefer people that believe me I tell 'em somethin, they don't put on airs.'

'You told Carol you're gettin Black Mountain?'

'I never come out and told her. I let her figure it out once I said I'm Pervis's heir.' Dewey frowned then like he was in pain. 'I hope my Hornet don't quit on him, have the old man irritated at me the time he's got left on earth. I feel I got to take care of the old man, see he leaves with a smile on his face.'

Raylan said, 'You goin up to Stinkin Creek?'

'Pervis ain't been there since his boys were kilt. He took a property off Piney Run, mile or so north of Harlan. Pervis says he can't look at the bloodstain all over his rug, remindin him Dickie and Coover are gone.'

'I think he'll find peace,' Raylan said, 'never having to worry about them again.'

'Hey, they were harum-scarums, I *know* that. Still, it's hard to lose your boys,' Dewey said, 'you watch 'em grow up from tads. It can break your heart you let it. Pervis's got that colored girl comes to visit.' Dewey shrugged, shaking his head. 'It takes all kinds, don't it? They's always things about people hard to figure out.'

'You have to walk a mile or so in their moccasins,' Raylan said, 'before you understand where they're coming from.'

'You say so,' Dewey said.

Raylan watched him shrug and walk off in his Doc Martens.

* * *

Raylan walked up to the limo and knocked on the smoked window.

'You know there's a whole gym full of people waiting on you?'

The window rolled down.

'I'm waiting for them to get restless,' Carol said, 'so I can calm them down. Where did Dewey go?'

'Home, once he lines up a ride.'

'You know Pervis would never in sound mind give that idiot his mountain.'

'I don't think he would,' Raylan said, 'but I don't know it for a fact.'

'We'll see Pervis tomorrow,' Carol said. 'Get him to admit it.'

Raylan said, 'What do you care what I think?'

Carol said, 'I want you on my side for a change.'

The window already rolling up.

* * *

People standing around outside smoking would come over to Raylan, offer their hand and say he'd sure told her and ask where she was, hidin in the limo? Raylan would say Ms. Conlan's resting up, you people getting to her pretty good. Some would say they'd had enough company talk and were heading home. Raylan was surprised to see Hazen Culpepper walk up to him.

'I thought you'd left.'

143

'I may as well. I don't see you doin anything about Otis.'

'Like what? I could do anything I would.'

'Sit her down in one of those rooms you got and shine a light on her. Get her to talk.'

'The sheriff's people already have Ms. Conlan's statement,' Raylan said. 'Otis fired at her and Boyd shot him, saving her life.'

'You believe that?'

'I asked her myself. Otis fired a twelve-gauge at you from thirty feet and didn't even hit the trailer? Ms. Conlan said, "He missed, didn't he?" and will swear to it. That's where we are. I doubt her word, but there's nothin I can do about it.'

'Otis fires his scattergun,' Hazen said, 'he don't miss. I'll swear to that in court.'

'We ever get inside a courtroom you can say anything you want. But we aren't near to gettin there,' Raylan said. 'You try to settle this yourself, I'll have to come get you. Understand? I know how you feel. We can both stew over this without it doing either of us any good.'

'My brother killed,' Hazen said, 'ain't something I can put out of my mind.'

'I understand,' Raylan said. 'But getting Boyd's my job, not yours.'

'You ever forget it,' Hazen said, 'call me. I'll come remind you.'

Another time they'd be good friends. Raylan offered his hand to Hazen, already walking away.

Carol came out of the car, Casper following. She said to Raylan, 'That was Otis's brother, wasn't it? I thought he'd left. What's he looking for, revenge? Boyd gets the chair or what's his name will shoot him. Hazen?'

144

Casper said, 'Or shoot the two of you, you were both there.'

She gave him a look.

Casper said, 'The intended victims.'

'Why is everyone picking on me?' she said in a normal tone. 'We go inside, I'll do five minutes of warm-up, get some of the crowd on my side, and the bleeding hearts will take their shots. Why do I want to turn mountains into dunes? "Lifeless dunes," I was told one time. I've forgot their line. But what we do is lay waste to beauty, to grandeur, to God's idea of a pretty nice place . . . that's full of coal.'

Raylan listening, watched her light a cigarette.

Casper said, 'You then put a curious look on your face.'

'It isn't curious, it's a look of curiosity. Wait a minute. Wasn't it God put all that coal under the grandeur?'

'It stops them in their tracks,' Casper said.

'I say, "Heck, if God put it there . . . " Or I might say, "Hell, is God tryin to hide it on us?" I smile. "Playin a game on us?" I tell them, "But gettin it out gives you men jobs and heats your homes," and I go through all the coal rewards.'

She turned to Raylan.

'I'm warmed up. How are you doing? Wait. "Har you doin, big boy?" I start thinkin that way and it comes out of my background naturally.' She said to Raylan, 'You don't comment? My security, Marshal One-Liner?'

'I haven't thought of anything,' Raylan said, 'worth saying.'

'You just did it again. You make one-line declarations. You sort of mope around, so to speak, while your mind is flicking lines at you.'

Raylan said, 'Wait'll I tell Art.'

Carol said, 'See?' She said, 'When I finish my chore we'll go back to the house—where you picked me up and told me how smart you are, but it didn't work, did it?'

Raylan said, 'When I take you back to Woodland Hills, my time's up, isn't it?'

Carol said, 'I'll let you decide.'

CHAPTER TWENTY-ONE

She talked all the way back to Woodland Hills.

'The woman asks, "What's the matter, don't you like beauty?" Like I'm color-blind, void of any appreciation of nature. I was tempted to go with the usual, the more heavy-handed. "You'd rather look at the view than your husband having a job?" But I tried something else, agreeing with her. "Of course I'd rather have the view. I watch the work going on, your husbands operating those giant machines, and all I can wonder is, How long will it take us to restore that grandeur, home for all of our animal friends." I don't know why I said that, it just came out. So I added, "And some like skunks who aren't especially our friends."'

In the limo going back to Carol's place, Raylan said, 'You could hold your nose as you're saying it.'

'Isn't that obvious?'

'Get a laugh,' Raylan said, 'from the ones who don't know you're putting them on.'

Neither spoke again—Boyd watching then in the rearview—until they pulled up the drive to the

Colonial and Carol said to Raylan, 'I want you to come in with me.'

Boyd wasn't told anything. He sat there.

*   *   *

She took him into a paneled study with pictures of horses and furniture covered in Black Watch plaid, the room done, Raylan believed, by someone other than Casper. He said, 'Casper loans out his house to the company, doesn't worry about guests looting the place? Ones he doesn't even know?'

'You think I'm a looter?' Carol said.

She was at the tea table bar pouring, Raylan believed, cognac. He wasn't sure until she handed him a wineglass half full and he raised it to his face, Raylan thinking, Don't clink glasses with me.

She did and he clinked hers back.

She said, 'Snifters require care. These glasses are easier, quicker too, and I'm dying of thirst.'

It was dark in the house, lamps on, and almost dark outside.

Raylan told himself she was taking a moment with the sip of cognac to become a different Carol, someone he hadn't met before. He had watched her all day going from down-home to mine company executive with the facts. Now she looked up at him and said:

'Tomorrow Boyd and I are driving up to Piney Run to see Pervis. He's staying there while, as he puts it, he shakes off the deaths of his boys. I have to admire Pervis. He makes his bullshit sound nearly as authentic as mine. I do my West By-God Virginia accent and they believe me.'

'You want to know,' Raylan said, 'did Pervis will

Black Mountain to Dewey or not.'

'He wouldn't,' Carol said. 'I might make Pervis an offer, or, it might not be the right time.'

Raylan was thinking of Carol offering Otis Culpepper a settlement for his property. And Boyd shooting him.

She came close to Raylan, moving in on him, saying, 'You've seen me at work playing different roles. It's exhausting. Well, finally it's done and I get to be myself.'

Looking at him over her glass.

Raylan believed if he took her glass and set it on the bar with his, he could put his arms around her, give Carol a soulful kiss, and he'd get laid.

Man, she was right there waiting.

It turned out he didn't have to take their glasses and set them aside. She did, and turned to him, he believed, not having a lot of time; wanting him to get to it. He wondered if she'd be serious and do a lot of gasping or grin, having fun?

He wondered why she was so sure he'd want to jump her.

Picks some guy to be her security and says, 'Him.'

Because she read about him and Layla. Carol wondering what Layla saw in him.

He didn't care for what he was doing here.

Raylan said, 'Carol, I'm sorry but my time's up,' and offered his hand.

She said, 'You're turning me down?' Surprised but not showing it much. But then she said it, 'I'm surprised.'

Raylan said, 'You aren't the only one.' He gave Carol a kiss on the cheek and got out of there.

*　　　　*　　　　*

148

His cell buzzed.

Raylan in the front seat with Boyd. It was Winona. 'Am I interrupting something?'

'I'm on my way home,' Raylan said, 'the Mount-Aire Motel. I got a cabin almost off the property, but still hear these people from Ohio revving their ATVs.'

Winona said, 'She bet me she'd seduce you.'

Raylan said, 'I hope you bet a pile.'

'She make the moves on you?'

'She's standin in the room nekked, I told her I had a headache.'

'You dog—call me tomorrow,' Winona said. 'Okay?'

Boyd said, 'She took all her clothes off?'

Raylan's cell buzzed again.

It was Art. 'You at her house?'

'I'm in a car,' Raylan said, 'on the way to Harlan and still a virgin.'

'I'm proud of you,' Art said, 'staying pure. You through with Ms. Conlan come on back, I got something else for you.'

'I'm near done,' Raylan said, 'but want to check on Carol in the morning. I think she's gonna try to pull something. I'll call you later.' Raylan said, 'I'm sittin with Boyd Crowder listenin to every word I say,' and turned off Art before he could start yelling at him. He said to Boyd:

'What time you seeing Pervis tomorrow?'

Boyd said, 'Oh, that's where I'm goin? You know more about my future whereabouts'n I do.'

'What I keep thinking,' Raylan said, 'Carol must've offered that old man a settlement before you shot him.'

149

'Which one?' Boyd said, looking at Raylan. 'You mean Otis, you're beatin a dead horse.'

CHAPTER TWENTY-TWO

Pervis was sitting in his white socks, his drawers and an undershirt. 'A wife-beater,' Rita told him. 'I'm not your wife, so you can't ever get mad and hit me.'

'You're my precious girl,' Pervis said, 'I'm givin my business to, my fields, my leaves of grass, my mountain . . . and my store, everything.'

'What I always wanted,' Rita said, 'run a store and get paid in food stamps. You not puttin me on you say all I'm gettin?'

'You know my heart's pure,' Pervis said. 'You get the works, every last thing I own.'

'You be the first man ever gave me anything from his heart. Usually it's from lower down.' Rita came over in her pure white shirt hanging over her pure white panties and curled up on Pervis's lap saying, 'You don't think Dewey'll give me a hard time?'

'The poor soul's waitin for me to pass. The way I'm feelin, it may never happen.'

She kissed Pervis's bare skull and stuck her tongue in his ear. 'You want to wait a while for the main event?'

'I thought we'd smoke a little as I build up steam.'

She ran her hand over Pervis's bare skull.

'You gettin your head tan. That's what's different about you. You not wearin your rug no more,' running her tongue over his skull. 'You look

150

younger without that old thing, you know it? Got some sun on you for a change.' She got up and went in the kitchen still talking. 'I know we got salt pork. You want, I'll fry up a mess of eggs.'

'You bet,' Pervis said. 'I'm hungry enough to eat the ass out of a skunk.'

'Honey . . .?'

'Yeah . . .?'

'You know you got a coffeepot on the stove has a gun in it?'

'For varmints,' Pervis said.

'It's a .38.'

'For big varmints.'

*　　　*　　　*

What Raylan did the next morning, he watched the house where Carol was staying from a patch of trees in Woodland Hills, kept watch close to two hours before the limo arrived. He saw Boyd get out and ring the bell, Boyd waiting now. The door opened for a moment and closed and Boyd returned to the limo.

A half hour went by before Carol came out in her Levi's and heels and slipped into the front seat next to Boyd.

Raylan got in the Audi he'd been using and followed the limo through Harlan and out past Baxter.

About a mile up 413 Raylan saw the limo pull off the road and he braked to a crawl and saw Dewey—it *was*, in his suit too big for him—walking up the road, Raylan thinking the limo was waiting for him. But now a few seconds later a red pickup was coming up on Raylan with M-T MINING on the door as it passed, and pulled in behind the limo. Raylan turned into a service station long out of business. In his rearview there was Dewey running toward him.

Dewey in the passenger window now saying, 'Raylan, I wonder could you help me out. I loaned Pervis my Hornet to get home? Only it wasn't where he said he'd leave it, so I'm thinkin he took the car home . . . if he didn't run out of gas and left it somewheres.'

'Get in,' Raylan said. 'You know who's in the pickup?'

'Rifle mounted in the window,' Dewey said. 'You start yelling at him about his driving? Better think about it first. They're company people in the truck. Look—the guy gettin out—goin up to the limo, leans in . . .'

'Jumps back,' Raylan said. 'Five dollars Carol raised the window on him.'

'That one by the car's Billy the Kid.'

Raylan said, 'He's fifty years old he's a day.'

'He musta been Billy the Kid at one time and it stuck. I'm told he's known to have shot people.'

'That mean nobody's seen him do it?'

'The ones got shot did,' Dewey said. 'I know he's one of M-T's intimidators. Goin to talk to Pervis about his mountain. See if he'll listen to figures. He don't, he better have a good reason.'

Raylan said, 'You know why they're called intimidators?'

'Means they pack.'

'We called 'em gun thugs,' Raylan said.

He watched Billy get back in the pickup—another guy in there with him—and start up. Raylan got in line and followed the limo and the company truck all the way through Piney Run to Pervis Crowe's rented house.

*   *   *

Rita saw the limo from the kitchen window, she turned off the fire under the salt pork and went out to the sitting room, still holding the cooking fork.

'Honey, we got company.'

Pervis said, 'You gonna stick 'em with that?'

Rita said she'd get his pants and ran upstairs to the bedroom. She brought his Levi's he called his dungarees—Pervis at a front window now—and helped him put on a shirt.

'Who do we know comes to visit in a stretch?' Rita said, stepping into a pair of denim shorts.

'Must be the company woman, Ms. Conlan,' Pervis said, 'come to buy a mountain.'

'How much she gonna offer?'

'She starts, we'll say, "You kiddin?" We won't tell her you own the mountain,' Pervis said. 'See how high she wants to go.'

They watched a pickup now easing its way up the grade to stop behind the limo.

'Company woman,' Pervis said, 'bringin some company people.' He looked at Rita. 'You turn off the stove?'

She went out to the kitchen and Pervis watched two men step out of the truck. He recognized Billy the Kid as the skinny guy put on his hat, cocking it over one eye. The other one, standing there in kind of a lazy slump, Pervis believed went by the name of Wayne. He looked hungover.

'They's another car,' Pervis said, 'pullin in behind the company truck.'

153

Rita came from the kitchen smoothing her white shirttails over her shorts, saying, 'How many's that woman need?'

Pervis waited till he saw a sight for sore eyes step out of the Audi and said, 'It's Raylan, bless his heart.'

Rita said, 'Yeah . . .?' Watching Raylan with keen eyes and heard Pervis say:

'And Dewey. What in the world he bring Dewey for?'

* * *

Dewey hurried to catch up to Raylan while counting the people in the yard, Raylan turning to him.

'You gonna go up there and say anything?'

'Ask Pervis where my Hornet's at.'

'I mean about the mountain.'

'I told you last night she guessed I'm gonna own it, and I let her think it. She makes a deal with the old man before he passes? I get a stretch limousine goes one-fifty full out. I figure ought to sixty—that's a load to get off from standin still—but she'll do it'n less'n ten seconds.'

Raylan was looking at the two thugs waiting for him, Carol and Boyd closer to the porch where Pervis stood calm as could be, his girl Rita right there close by.

Dewey said, 'The company woman ever wants to offer a deal at a future date, I'll get some tips from Casper, smartest man I ever met.'

Raylan said, 'It's four to four I count you on my side.'

'Me and you,' Dewey said, 'Pervis and his colored girl?'

'That's our team,' Raylan said. 'You don't have to say nothing you don't feel like it, all right?'

'You come due to own a mountain,' Dewey said, 'they's all kind of people asking about it.'

He hung back now watching Raylan approach the two company thugs in the yard.

*   *   *

'Kid,' Raylan said to the middle-aged, guy, 'Tell me what you're doing here.'

'Mine company business,' Billy the Kid said. 'It sure ain't none of yours.'

Raylan said, 'You come armed?'

'One I'm licensed to pack. So's Wayne here.'

Carol called to Raylan, 'Leave them alone. They're my security people.'

Raylan said, 'You afraid of Pervis?'

She didn't bother to answer. Raylan watched her turn and walk toward the house, Boyd still facing Raylan until she stopped and looked back at him.

'You coming?'

The company thugs turned and followed Boyd.

Pervis stood on the porch waiting, Rita close by, hands on her hips, slim brown legs coming out of her shirttails.

Carol, turning to Pervis said, 'You going to invite me in?'

'What for?' Pervis said.

'Talk about mineral rights.'

'I'm not sellin none today.'

Billy the Kid was facing Raylan again. The Kid turned his head to say something to his partner and now Wayne, wearing dark sunglasses, was looking this way like he'd just now woke up. The Kid

155

seemed alert but anxious, loosening the hat on his head, an old businessman's Stetson, and setting the curled brim over his eye again.

Pervis said, 'You want to talk business—' and stopped, the company woman looking at Raylan. Pervis said, 'Miss, I'm talkin to you,' and waited for Carol to look up at him.

He said, 'You come to talk about buyin my mountain, tell me why you bring these thugs along?'

Carol said in her nice tone of voice, 'Mr. Crowe, I represent M-T Mining. I come to Harlan, I know full well I'm not gonna win any popularity contest.'

'You sure aren't,' Pervis said, 'puttin on that West Virginia voice. Case we forgot your dad mined.'

The Kid said, 'Grampa sees how it is. Talks hard to us, huh, in front of his nigger puss.'

Raylan saw Rita's hands ease down to her thighs.

He said, 'Pervis, why don't you and Rita step in the house while we finish up here.'

He said to Carol, 'Pervis is thinking how you did business with Otis Culpepper and what Otis got out of the deal.'

'They musta got Otis drunk,' Pervis said, 'and shot him he's got his eyes closed. That's what I think of this company girl's story.' He said to her, 'Honey, you want to talk bout a mountain I'm leavin to my kin? He swears he'll honor my wishes and never sell it.'

He looked out at Dewey standing across the yard, not close to anybody, and waved to him.

'Come on up here, boy. Show this girl we standin together on this.'

Raylan said, 'Go on up there,' getting Dewey out of the way. Watched him edge around the gun

156

thugs heading for the porch. Watched Dewey step up there as Pervis put his arm around his shoulders.

'Tell this little girl,' Pervis said, 'a time comes I ever pass, you ain't sellin. Remember what I said about my gravestone?'

Dewey standing small under Pervis's arm, people in the yard watching him, said, 'You want it up on top of Big Black.'

'Laid to rest in the trees,' Pervis said.

'Yes sir, you don't want no trees cut down.'

'You don't either,' Pervis said, 'or any coal taken out of your mountain.'

Raylan watched Dewey hesitate, a look of pain on his face. He said, 'No matter how much they offer me.'

'Mr. Crowe,' Carol said, 'if I thought for a moment Dewey was your heir, I wouldn't be here to make you an offer, would I?'

'Since I'm never gonna sell it,' Pervis said, 'I believe you're thinkin of puttin a gun to my head and have me sign a deed over to you. Then have the Kid shoot me and make up a story how it happened.'

Raylan saw the Kid adjust his hat again as if he was taking a bow, the Kid acting like he was in a movie.

They were getting to it now.

Raylan said to Boyd, 'You have a gun stuck in your pants? I like to know who's in this and who's watchin.'

It was the Kid, not Boyd said to Raylan, 'You got one way to find out,' sliding his hand down to his belt.

What Raylan did, he pulled his Glock, raised it and shot the hat off the Kid's head, saw him look stunned, dropping a chromed-up revolver in the dirt, his hand going to the top of his head, then looking at his palm to see if there was blood, Raylan doubting he saw no more than a speck, his hair parted clean. Wayne, at this time, was working to get a gun cleared of his coat, finally drawing another chromed-up piece as Rita stepped off the porch pulling the old man's .38 from under her shirttails and swiped the barrel across Wayne's skull. Wayne stumbled, dropped his piece and stood in the yard looking bewildered. What Rita did next was put the .38 on Carol saying to Raylan, 'You want, I can shoot her.'

'Hey, come on,' Carol said. 'I came here to talk business and Raylan pulls a gun.'

'On your two thugs,' Rita said. 'I could shoot you and put a gun in your cold hand.'

'We're done,' Raylan said, looking at Boyd again. He hadn't moved. 'You thinking about the time I shot you and you rose from the dead? It only happens once in your life.' He turned to Carol again and she said:

'Were you actually aiming at his hat?'

'I hit it, didn't I?'

Raylan looked at the two gun thugs, both sitting on the ground now, wobbly.

'You gonna take these two with you?'

'They're fired,' Carol said, and took a moment before saying, 'you know I grew up in coal camps—'

'You keep reminding us.'

'To make the point,' Carol said, 'I know hill people are a different breed, strange to outsiders. But you've been something of a new experience for me.'

'Anything happens to Pervis,' Raylan said, 'I'll

158

come lookin for you.'

Carol said, 'You promise?'

She walked off—not looking at Boyd—walked to the limo and got in and made a U-turn in the yard, skinned past the pickup and the Audi and got out of there.

Raylan turned to Boyd.

'I guess you're fired too.'

'You asked me a question,' Boyd said, 'what side I'm on. What did I say? Nothin. Was this scudder answered you, I didn't. You don't know what I was gonna say, do you?'

'Doesn't matter,' Raylan said. 'You pulled, I'd of shot you. I think you believed that, so you decided to watch.'

Boyd said, 'Raylan . . . I don't hold ill feelings against you, even for shootin me that time. I admit, it was in my mind to shoot you but only if I saw it comin to that.'

'Boyd, you told me that time it was your in*ten*tion,' Raylan said. 'I let you watch today, so now we're square, all right? You need a ride, put the Kid and the other one in their truck and take 'em home.'

Boyd said, 'Raylan . . .?'

'We're through talking for now,' Raylan said, walking up to the porch. He looked at Pervis. 'You ever see Carol again, call me, and I'll get marshals on her.'

'She don't worry me none,' Pervis said. 'I got Dewey here lookin out for me.'

'I'm devotin my life to it,' Dewey said.

Rita had come up by the porch. She said, 'I told Pervis he ought to be ashamed of himself, Dewey has to wait till you pass. What if the mountain, it

159

turns out, ain't worth diddly, the coal Dewey's been waitin for years already dug out?'

Pervis said, 'I always tried to be optimistic in life.'

Dewey looked from one to the other.

'But everybody says it's full of coal. Ain't it?'

'Everybody prayin for a job,' Rita said. 'Hoping for work.' She looked at Pervis. 'I don't think it's fair, leaving a dead mountain to your only kin.'

'Well,' Pervis said, 'I could give him a pound of my top-grade weed, should last him a while.'

Rita was nodding. 'Two pounds would be more generous of you. Two pounds of Daddy's Own. Dewey could smoke it or sell it, get happy either way.'

'What would be the street value of that,' Dewey said, 'I was to sell a pound of it?'

*   *   *

Raylan said to Art Mullen, 'Rita's telling Dewey, he wants to, he could mark it up to ten grand since it's Pervis's top-grade smoke. I thought it sounded high, but Dewey's eyes lit up and that was it.'

They were in Art Mullen's office in Harlan, the front of his desk stacked with papers and wanted dodgers. Art said, 'A girl twenty-three years old, a senior at Butler University, was arrested in a raid on a poker game.'

Raylan started to grin. 'The cops bust in the dorm and find 'em playin for matchsticks?'

'Indianapolis police,' Art said, 'walked in on a high-stakes game where this girl lost twenty thousand dollars, smart-ass. Police took the girl in and booked her. She was to spend the night in jail for a court appearance in the morning.'

'Where'd she get the twenty grand?'

Art said, 'Oh, I have your attention? She won it bettin Duke against Butler, the NC double-A championship. The girl's dad, Reno—actually he's her stepdad—runs a sports book in Indy. He raised his little girl playin poker and bettin on sporting events.'

'Losing all her money,' Raylan said, 'and getting thrown into jail, it wasn't her night, was it? Then had to pay a fine?'

'She skipped,' Art said, 'walked out and didn't show for the hearing.'

'You're tellin me this for a reason, aren't you?'

'The girl,' Art said, 'an A student at Butler, we're told is now robbin banks in Kentucky, gettin into our area of influence. Rachel and two other young ladies. Their manner of grinnin at the tellers, leads us to believe they're stoned. Three girls havin a drug-induced fling at robbin banks. Indy police look at the surveillance tapes and believe Rachel's one of them.'

'They positive,' Raylan said, 'or hoping, cause she skipped out on them?'

'Why don't you go up there and find out?' Art said. 'You'll be workin out of the Lexington office again. Pick the girl up while you're not doin anything and get the Indy cops off our backs.'

'What's her name, Rachel?'

'Rachel Nevada.'

'You're kiddin.'

'And her stepdad's Reno Nevada,' Art said, 'his actual name. Start with the Indy cops and work your way down to Lexington.'

'I got to see a picture of this Rachel Nevada,' Raylan said.

'Start thinkin of her as Jackie Nevada,' Art said. 'It's what Reno and everybody calls her.'

CHAPTER TWENTY-THREE

Jackie Nevada had walked out of the police station knowing her best bet was to get out of town. Borrow a backpack and stuff it with T-shirts and shorts; sleep a few hours, put on jeans and hitch a ride to Shelbyville: start out playing Texas hold 'em at the Indian casino with farmers and truck drivers who'd been up all night to build up her stack. She lost the twenty grand sitting in cigar smoke, the five no-limit gentlemen in their suitcoats watching her, not saying a word. She folded, threw in her ace-five against her better judgment. She would have called if these guys were wearing work clothes. She watched an ace come up on the flop and she would have won with the pair of bullets. It would've told her it was possible to take these guys; at least give her the feeling. Say, 'Oh, you waiting for me?' and raise on the ace-five. But she'd folded. Telling herself the odds said to fold. Why didn't she tell herself to fuck off? She let herself be cleaned out and was down to three hundred in her sneakers when the cops came in.

In the morning, Buddy, who drove Jackie out to 74, where she'd get out to thumb the thirty miles to Shelbyville, said, 'Isn't that my backpack?'

Jackie told him he'd loaned it to her last night and Buddy said, 'I did?'

'I'm starting out with three hundred,' Jackie said. 'I'll make enough today to buy a bus ticket

162

and only stop to play poker, all the way to Tunica, Mississippi, last stop before Las Vegas and the World Series of Poker. What I need to make is the buy-in money, win the tournament, pay off Reno and get back to Butler in time for graduation. How does that sound?'

Buddy in his hungover state said, 'Hey, why not.'

He didn't have enough gas to drive to the casino and back. Jackie told him not to worry about it, kissed Buddy on the mouth holding her breath, said, 'See you,' and walked out to the highway, Buddy watching her, the backpack hanging from one shoulder. She hadn't even raised her thumb and cars were slowing down for a look. Buddy thinking, Two minutes she'll have a ride.

He watched a car pull over and creep past Jackie for a close look and Buddy realized, holy shit, the car must be fifty years old but so what. It was a Rolls-Royce Phantom repainted its original green body color and looked brand-new.

He watched a black guy in a chauffeur's outfit get out and open the rear door, taking her backpack. Buddy watched her wave to him and get in the Rolls.

*   *   *

The chauffeur, still holding the door open, was saying to Jackie, 'The gentleman offering you a ride is Mr. Harry Burgoyne of Lexington and Burgoyne Horse Farms.'

Harry, watching her duck into the Rolls, said, 'Don't tell me you're runnin away from home. We cross a state line I could end up in jail.' He said, 'No, you're a student, huh? Don't say Butler. I had to give Butler five points the other day so I could bet on Duke and lose ten big ones.'

'I'm Jackie Nevada, and yeah, I go to Butler. I bet Duke even,' Jackie said, 'and won twenty grand.'

Harry had a grin on his face now behind his sunglasses and plaid sport coat. 'You're kiddin me. Takin bets at school?'

'Mostly,' Jackie said. She was sitting with Harry now, heads turned to each other, the Rolls cruising along the highway. 'By the time we played Duke everyone's so high on Butler, they bet the game even. I did give Butler a point to some of my dad's customers. Duke won by two, so I still beat everybody.' Jackie said, 'Actually Reno Nevada's my stepdad.'

Harry said, 'Why they call him Reno?'

'It's his name. He wanted to call me Sierra before I was born. Sierra Nevada would've been cool, but he named me after my mom instead. She walked out on us before I had a memory of her. They never married and Reno wasn't even my dad. I did see pictures of Mom posing nude in the backyard Reno left on the dresser one time and I had an intimate look at my mother. I favor her somewhat, but she's more of a babe than I'd ever be.'

Harry was frowning at her. 'You never saw your own mother?'

'Lots of people haven't seen their moms. Or their dads.'

'What're you doin now? Where you going?'

'Shelbyville, that casino called Indiana Live? I'll play poker the rest of the day.'

'I was thinkin of stoppin there,' Harry said. 'Yeah, I could watch you go through your twenty grand.' Harry grinning, to show Jackie he might be kidding.

She said, 'If I still had it I'd clean out the fish in an hour or so. Only last night at Elaine's I wasted it, lost it betting on ace-king, went all in before the flop and got beat by a pair of sevens. Reno thought I'd lose a few hundred and leave, get a little exposure to a big game. But I had all the money I won on Duke, till the cigar smokers took it away from me.'

'Honey, you're out of your league the minute you walk in Elaine's. I can't believe she let you play.'

'She looked at me,' Jackie said, 'I think she saw herself, well, at a much earlier age. The guys were okay. They smoked and talked about buying horses and running them at Keeneland.'

'Hell, that's Lexington,' Harry said. 'I won the Maker's Mark with a horse name of Black Boy and my colored chauffeur quit on me. Got in some funny business with a nurse stealing kidneys and was shot dead. I bet I know the fellas you played with. What were their names?'

'The only one I remember was Lou. He said, "I'm Lou, sweetheart." But they didn't talk much while we were playing.'

Harry said, 'The driver I had that got shot was called Cuba but said he was from Africa. I thought he was a hardworkin boy till he quit on me and I hired Avery.'

Jackie saw Avery watching them in his mirror and met his serious eyes for a moment. She said, 'I played like a girl who'd memorized what hole cards you'd look at and fold. I'm playing no-limit with five gentlemen smoking cigars, staring at me, and threw away twenty grand, every dollar I had except three hundred in my sneakers.'

'You let 'em psyche you out.'

'It pissed me off and I knew better. Don't ever play when you're mad or upset.'

'That's right, walk away.'

'I wanted to say, "Oh, is it my turn?" Something girlish to throw them off. But I never felt I had it together.'

'They scared you.'

'One hand I had an ace-five and bailed out.'

'That's what you do playing hold 'em,' Harry said. 'You get out, you don't let that lone ace vamp you.'

'Yeah, but the ace turned into a pair with the river card and a king-jack took the pot.'

'That'll happen,' Harry said.

'But if I stayed I'd of won twelve grand. I'd get the feeling I can take these no-limit guys, get down and play to win. It was one of the very few times I didn't go with my ace.'

'How many times you win with an ace in the hole?'

'How often are you dealt one?'

'You're telling me you're lucky,' Harry said. 'But you don't win at poker bankin on luck.'

'I win because I know the game,' Jackie said. 'If I don't have a feeling about my hole cards I throw them in.'

'You left Elaine's with three hundred?'

'In my sneakers. I forgot to tell you, the police came by.'

'Elaine was raided?'

'She said it happens every once in a while. Part of doing business.'

'They throw you in jail?'

'I was booked, but walked out when nobody was looking. I still have enough to start at a five-ten table. Work my way up to ten-twenty.'

Harry said, 'Honey, you're a fugitive. They're gonna be after you.'

'I'll wear dark glasses,' Jackie said.

They were both quiet now riding in the Rolls.

Maybe for ten seconds before Harry said, 'If I didn't know your plight . . .' paused, and Jackie said:

'One night I was waiting for a bus with a half dozen ad layouts, mounted, trying to hold them together, and I dropped them in the street. A man stopped by as I was gathering them up. He said, "I couldn't help but observe your plight."'

Harry said, 'Is that right?'

'That was only the second time I've heard anyone use the word.'

Now he was frowning.

'You said, "If I didn't know your plight . . . What? You don't think the dark glasses would work?'

She could tell she had him interested.

Harry said, 'I was thinking, What if I staked you?' Jackie took a moment. 'For how much?'

'Whatever you'd need to make a run. Ten grand?'

'You're kidding.'

'Honey, I raise thoroughbreds, run 'em at tracks all over the country. I don't have to kid about money. I pay a million bucks for a filly and love her like she's my own.'

'Till she runs,' Jackie said.

'Well, if she doesn't win enough times.'

'You fall for another filly.'

She could see him grinning now.

'That's right, but the amount of affection I show the girl can make her a winner.'

'How would that work with me,' Jackie said, 'your being affectionate?'

'Honey, I'm seventy-five years old. We'll have drinks and I'll make you laugh and give you a kiss on the cheek. You keep everything you win. I'll be a happy dog havin you pet me once in a while.'

'What if I'm in a game but low on chips?'

'I see you can win, I'll help you out.'

'And if I lose my stake . . . ?'

'It comes to that,' Harry said, 'I'll drop you off anywhere you want.'

Jackie leaned over to kiss his old man's cheek and tell him, 'Harry, you just made me the happiest girl in the world.'

*　　　*　　　*

It took her four hours and ten minutes to win eighteen thousand at two different no-limit tables that afternoon in Shelbyville; Jackie playing against people who hired truck drivers, people who bet on grain futures produced by farmers they didn't know or care to. Jackie was having a bottle of beer now, Harry Burgoyne a double scotch.

She said, 'All they did was try to bluff.'

'And you could tell.'

'They weren't good at it.'

'Fellas I play with at Keeneland, I think they're always tryin to bluff me. I know it, so I stay in too long, call their raise, but every time I do, one of 'em beats me.'

'I'd have to watch your game,' Jackie said, 'see

168

what you could do.'

'That's what I been thinking,' Harry said. 'Or get these boys to play hold 'em with you. They're breeders, have almost the money I do. I tell them you're my niece visitin from college. Loves poker and thinks she's pretty darn good. I say, "You fellas want to play Jackie if I stake her?" You bet they do. They win they see it as takin my money.'

Harry, sipping his drink, said, 'Keeneland, I use to do a skit for the bar crowd with a driver I had, the African colored guy. I'd chide him for the way he's dressed in my racing colors. He'd say, "But, Boss, is your wife dresses me." Watchin you play I was thinkin how I could use you in a humorous exchange, a skit we'd make up.'

Jackie said, 'You're kidding, right?'

CHAPTER TWENTY-FOUR

A former convict named Delroy Lewis ran the show: hired Floy, an eighteen-year-old street kid who stole cars he sold to chop-shops—good-looking expensive ones, Mercedes and BMW Floy's favorites—picked up mostly from big shopping mall lots using tools took him twenty seconds to jimmy the door, a half minute to start her up. Sometimes he'd settle for a Chrysler or Buick, the big Honda lately, a roomy car that gave the girls space to relax and smoke a doobie on their way to work.

Floy parked on the street and went in the apartment house had a fire escape going this way and the other down the front of the building and pushed a number.

Cassie came on saying, 'What kind a car?'

'Gray Beamer. Had it washed for y'all.'

Cassie said, 'Be down in five minutes.'

Delroy had told Floy, 'They not down in a half hour, leave. I'll give them a talkin to.'

They finally got done dressing and came out to the car looking like fashion-conscious bag ladies in their outfits they got from Goodwill, hip-huggers under their raincoats, sporty little beach hats, brims turned down, Janie wearing a Detroit Tigers baseball cap; the three carrying shiny bags from ladies' stores.

They got in the car, Kim saying to Cassie, 'You know you're wearing your fuck-me heels?'

Cassie said, 'They sound cool on marble floors.'

Kim said, 'What if we have to run for the car?'

'I could have on sneakers,' Cassie said, 'we're still fucked. You think Floy's gonna wait for us?'

'I was told,' Floy said to his rearview mirror, 'y'all take more than six minutes to come out, I take off. Delroy say to worry about my own young ass.' Floy turned in his seat to look right at the girls. 'Nobody say what you doin's easy but, come on, you walk in cool and walk out your shoppin bags full of green. Delroy told me hisself, you the best chicks robbin banks he ever had. The man loves you.'

Janie said, 'That's why he hits us?'

'You don't listen to him, what you expect? Hey, but you get home he gives you all the Oxy you want, don't he? You ladies of leisure aren't you, between jobs?'

Cassie said, 'We get picked up, you know who's going down with us.'

Floy said, 'Hey, all I am's your driver.'

'Not you,' Cassie said, 'Delroy. He never goes

170

near the bank.'

'He tells us what it looks like inside,' Kim said, 'and when there aren't a lot of people.'

Cassie said, 'Floy, what's that worth?'

'A pat on the head,' Floy said, 'the man's tall enough. The man might go fifty bucks. He holds on to his dollar, let's you do it for weed and pills.'

'And a few hundred,' Kim said, 'each time.'

'He let you out to spend it?'

'Once in a while.'

'You his bank-job slaves.'

Janie said, 'I go back to strippin I become a blow job slave. This ain't so bad, we don't ever get picked up.'

'We miss a job,' Cassie said, 'we have to do one alone.'

'You ever did it you weren't high,' Floy said, 'you wouldn't do it.'

He pulled up a half block from the bank and waited while they toked, put on shades, fixed their hats and cap down on their head good, and got out with their shopping bags.

Floy said, 'Give you a full ten minutes to do your business. You cool with it? Be cool, I see y'all a little later.'

They weren't listening.

He watched them get out and walk down the street to the bank.

* * *

They stopped at a glass-top table in the middle of the floor and used the backs of bank forms to write the notes they'd give the tellers. Cassie said, 'I like, "Give me five grand or I'll kill you."' She looked at

171

her note and added a word.

Kim said, 'How do you spell *withdrawal,* with an *a* or an *e*?'

Janie said, 'I ask for all hunnerts, the girl says she has to go get 'em. I say, "All right, a hunnert fifties." I end up taking what she gives me.'

Cassie said, 'Tell her how much you want, for Christ sake.'

Kim said, 'Why don't we write the same thing three times?'

Cassie handed her note to Kim. 'Here, write it the same way, all capitals. "GIVE ME FIVE GRAND OR I'LL FUCKING KILL YOU," with three exclamation marks, so she knows you mean it.'

Kim wrote the notes and they walked over to three different tellers.

In a few minutes Janie came away from the window first with her bag of bills. She felt awful, she had cramps. If they had to do another bank soon she'd stay in bed.

Now Cassie was coming.

'It works, doesn't it? Where's Kim?'

She was still at a window.

'Now she's coming,' Janie said.

The bank chicks walked out and got in the BMW.

*   *   *

Floy listened to the girls on the way home, back to smoking weed now and talkative, relieved to be out of there.

Cassie saying, 'We do that one before?'

Kim saying, 'Banks all look alike to me.'

172

Cassie: 'The teller goes, "This is my second robbery in the past month." Calm about it. I ask her if it was us. No, it was a guy that time. I asked how much he took. She said only a few hundred and split. Ran out the door.'

'Mine looks at the note and freaks,' Kim said. 'Kept going on about having a child at home. I told her would she please empty her drawer? It wasn't her money.'

'I told my girl,' Cassie said, 'to keep a couple hundred for yourself. How's the bank know we didn't take it? You know what she said? "Really ...?" I bet she did too.'

Floy, looking at the rearview, said, 'Y'all did all right, huh?' Watching Cassie count the take.

'Not bad,' Cassie said, touching Floy's shoulder with a couple of hundred in her hand.

Floy took it saying, 'Hey, I'll boost a car for you ladies any time you want. But how come the cops aren't on to y'all by now? Four banks already, in town or close by.'

'They think we're working girls,' Kim said, 'having fun on our lunch break.'

Floy thought they looked like weird females, walk in the bank out of sunshine in their raincoats. How come nobody seemed to notice them? He said to Janie, 'Honey, you all right? You not joinin in.'

'She doesn't feel much like doing banks,' Cassie said. 'She's got the curse.'

*   *   *

Raylan believed marshals were more like big-city cops than most kinds of federal agents. It's why he walked in on the Indianapolis Metropolitan Police

173

knowing he'd feel at home.

They met in a squad room, the detectives getting to know Raylan, asking about the transplant nurse who stole kidneys and tried to kill him. He told them about the mine-company woman who'd had a man shot in cold blood, Raylan saying he was still thinking about her. 'I was to work here, her name would be up there on your board, Carol Conlan, not yet crossed out.' He told the detectives down a long table he wished he could stay here through the month, get to see Peyton Manning and the Colts at home. He might forget about this bookmaker he was looking for. 'Reno Nevada?'

Buzz Hicks, the senior detective in the room, said, 'Now we're getting to it, aren't we? You're lookin for Reno's little girl, aren't you? Jackie Nevada.'

Raylan said, 'Isn't Reno her stepdad?'

'That's right,' Hicks said. 'The name on her birth certificate's Rachel Nevada, but Reno started callin her Jackie when she was a kid.'

One of the detectives down the table said, 'Her mom was called Jackie. She got knocked up by some loser passin through and took up with Reno. She has the child and acts like a mother till she got tired of home life and hit the road. Was Reno named her Rachel, after his own mother, but started callin her Jackie before too long. Had a soft spot for the broad walked out on him.'

Hicks said, 'Lloyd, how'd you come up with all that?'

'Talkin to her,' Lloyd said, 'while we had her in custody.'

'So now,' Hicks said, 'she's raised by Reno, this suspected colored guy passin as Latino and runnin

174

a sports book.'

'They musta got along,' Raylan said.

'Well, they lived in the same house,' Hicks said, 'till she went to Butler. Listen to this, and paid her way through college playin poker at night. The only girl livin in a house with seven guys, all students. You know what they called her? "Mother." She had a poker table, cards and racks of chips. You wanted to play you had to bring your own chair or borrow one. We went over there and talked to 'em. They said you oughta see her shuffle cards.'

'I understand,' Raylan said, 'she won twenty grand betting Duke over her school.'

'That's right, but Reno says he covered her for ten, in case Butler managed to pull off a win. We asked Jackie'—Hicks turning to look down the table—'Lloyd, what'd she tell us?'

'That game,' Lloyd said, 'Reno put up *nada*. He was too busy losin on the spread. Jackie said the students laid down twenty and that's what she picked up.'

'You look into it?' Raylan said.

Hicks said, 'What are we, the gaming commission? It was Duke minus seven, the spread *BetUs Sportsbook* was offerin online and Reno took a bath.'

'How'd Jackie take gettin busted?'

'Didn't make a fuss. I guess thinkin about the hole she was in, broke. This A student who plays poker you might say for a living. I asked the woman runs poker games we busted. Elaine? I said, "You musta known those guys'd eat her alive." Elaine said, "She lost her cool. But you could tell the girl's a player." We set Jackie aside while we're arm-wrestlin these high-priced lawyers and she

175

walks out.'

'Didn't show up in court,' Raylan said.

'Took off on us,' Hicks said. 'Reno swears he hasn't heard from her. What do you think this girl's doin now?'

Raylan said, 'Well, I hear she's sticking up banks to get back on her feet. You got tape on her?'

'Jackie and two other girls,' Hicks said. 'We have 'em in different banks in Lexington. Now take a look at what she's doing.' Hicks glanced down the table. One of the detectives—it was Lloyd—slid the stack of surveillance prints to him and Hicks passed them on to Raylan, telling him, 'We showed Reno. He said his little girl don't rob banks. These are some girls lost their way. He said, "But they're mellow, riding some kind of high." He said, "My little girl don't do drugs either. She keeps her mind on poker."'

Raylan went through the tapes, seeing the girls with shopping bags at separate tellers.

Hicks said, 'Watch 'em come away, the two looking back at the one still at a window. They're stoned. Had to get fixed to rob the bank.'

'I've heard of ones have to get ripped before they go in,' Raylan said. 'These girls look like they just cashed their paychecks.'

'What do they get paid in,' Hicks said, 'yen? Have to bring store bags to carry it?'

'I guess what I mean,' Raylan said, 'we don't see that many women stickin up banks. I think it's maybe five or six out of a hundred. Here you've got three at once. Which one you think's Jackie?'

'The one wearing the baseball cap,' Hicks said, 'down on her eyes. Some of the other tapes you'll come to, you see her lookin up.' He stood to watch

Raylan go through the prints.

Lloyd said, 'Buzz, you recall we had two girls doin banks at the same time?'

'Not around here,' Hicks said.

'Was down toward the state line,' Lloyd said, 'seven, eight years ago. They'd hit a bank in some dinky town off sixty-four and cross over to Louisville. A guy with the girls was teachin 'em how to rob banks.'

Hicks said, 'How you remember that?'

'It stuck in my mind,' Lloyd said. 'I remember a confidential informant fingered them, but they were released for lack of evidence.'

Raylan said, 'You remember what happened to the snitch?'

Lloyd was squinting, trying to recall before nodding his head. 'A guy blew off his right arm with a shotgun.'

Raylan said, 'Delroy Lewis?'

'*That's* the guy was questioned,' Lloyd said, 'about the bank jobs.'

'You mind,' Hicks said, 'if we settle on this job here?' and said to Raylan, 'That one, where she's lookin up. All of us but Lloyd said that's Jackie Nevada or her twin.'

'It could be,' Raylan said. 'I stopped by Butler and got a look at her picture. I can't see the girl in the yearbook playing to a surveillance camera.'

'We like her motive,' Hicks said. 'She needs dough.' Raylan was shaking his head. 'These two comin out, mugging right at the camera.'

'Doped up and thinks it's a hoot. It's your people in Lexington,' Hicks said, 'sent us all the bank photos. They picked out Jackie and asked for our confirmation.'

'The three almost look alike,' Raylan said. 'Young, the same size. Three girls having fun.'

Hicks said, 'Robbin banks.'

'Your fugitive,' Raylan said, 'I can see why you want her to be Jackie. I hope you're right and I'm dead wrong. But I can't see three girls wanting to rob banks. I *can* see some guy putting 'em up to it. Gives the girl's some toot and drops 'em off. I don't know for sure, but we'll find out, won't we?'

'We respect your opinion,' Buzz Hicks said, 'but hope you're wrong this time. We been followin you since you called out that Zip in Miami, Tommy Bucks? You gave him twenty-four hours to get out of town. He drew on you and you put him down.'

'And got demoted to Harlan County, Kentucky.'

'But then shot it out with that transplant nurse.'

'You're havin fun with me, aren't you?'

'Well,' Hicks said, 'you're doin a job the way we like to see it done.'

*　　　*　　　*

All the way to Reno's betting office, Raylan thought of the Jackie he saw in the yearbook photo and had copied. She could be a Miss Nevada but would rather play poker.

Raylan came to the barbershop, a few blocks from Lucas Oil Stadium. Went in and walked past three empty chairs to a door that had to be Reno's office. He knocked twice and said, 'Raylan Givens. I called you about twenty minutes ago . . . .?' The door buzzed open and he went in.

*　　　*　　　*

178

Raylan thought Reno looked Cuban, cell phones and a computer on his desk in lamplight, stacks of betting-sheet printouts and handwritten notes.

Lions and Niners 20 times reverse. Bears a nickel, New England ten.

Raylan said, 'You have to speak the language to lay down a bet?'

'My regulars, yeah, they do. Guy calls, says he wants the Saints minus seven thirty times. What's he betting?'

'Beats me,' Raylan said. 'But what if the guy loses and says he never made the bet?'

'I got him taped. I got miles of it. I ask the guy, does he want to hear himself putting it down?'

'You say you gave Jackie backup money. She says you didn't.'

'Come on—nobody coverin for her? She don't have enough to pay a win, she calls me. The ones bet with her know she's in the business; she loses, she pays. They know *me*. Listen to what I'm tellin you, all right? Jackie don't lift the twenty and takes off with it. She borrows my eighty percent to play big-time and loses it. Gets picked up in a raid and walks away. Somethin she oughtn've done. Now she's workin to recover what she lost so she can pay me back, and that's all I know.'

'She gets square with you,' Raylan said, 'then what? She gives herself up?'

'She be picked up before too long, way before she gets to Vegas. Understand, Jackie wants to play her way to the Poker World Series. See, but once you spot Jackie at a table anywhere, you look twice. You might even watch her play for a while, wonderin who she is. Jackie won't get anywhere near Vegas.'

Raylan said, 'She's not one of the girls in the bank tapes, I know that.'

'I bet they chicks can't pay the rent,' Reno said, 'and will die for some blow. I think a dude's usin them for his needs. They not chicks'd think of banks, they too loose. Any time now they gonna walk out and see policemen waitin behind cars holding guns. See, not one of those girls has Jackie's way of movin. The cops find out they don't have her and act surprised. "Man, the girl sure looked like her." All the time Jackie's at a table someplace peekin at her hole cards.'

'You don't think she'll give herself up.'

'She won't have to,' Reno said, 'she'll get picked up on the warrant and brought back here. I get one of my lawyer buddies, I doubt she does any time. Jackie don't have a record of any kind, knows how to act polite.'

'You don't walk on a fugitive warrant,' Raylan said. 'They got the stuff on you. What you have to do is find her, get her to come in before she's picked up. She tells her story and might only get a year or so probation.'

'You want you could help me out,' Reno said. 'You the one knows how to find people.'

'I'm giving you a break,' Raylan said. 'I find her before you do, she's under arrest.'

CHAPTER TWENTY-FIVE

Harry took her to the races at Keeneland and sat at his table in the Blue Grass Room: Jackie having crab legs and a Guinness, Harry, a pair of lobster tails and a double whiskey collins, while they watched the races on a rainy day, staring at the giant screen. Harry had won close to five thousand betting across the board on most races. Jackie wasn't that interested in picking horses. She made side bets with Harry and took him for half of what he'd won. Harry said, 'I'm getting an idea how you win at poker. You don't bet your hand, you bet on the serious guys at the table folding.'

Jackie said, 'What's the difference?'

She was looking past Harry, seeing a woman with teased blond hair, cool in dark shades of designer sportswear, and a guy following her through the dining room, trying to keep up in his tan suit that looked like a uniform. Closing in, the woman was looking at Jackie, not smiling until she turned to Harry and said, 'Carol Conlan, Harry,' placing a hand on his shoulder, a wide porcelain bracelet slipping on her wrist, 'how're you doing?'

Holding his drink Harry took time to come around enough to look up at Carol telling him, 'The last time I saw you was the day you won the Maker's Mark. Remember?'

'Running Black Boy,' Harry said, 'I won three hundred thousand off that stud.'

'What I meant,' Carol said, sounding pouty now, 'you do remember I was here?' Smiling now to show the pout was for fun.

181

'Yeah, Cuba and I did our routine and I sat down at your table. But hey, I want you to meet Jackie Nevada, my guest.'

Jackie watched Carol raise her eyebrows and say, 'Really,' surprised for a moment.

'I want you to know,' Harry said, 'I have a keen interest in this little girl.'

'Sounds like fun,' Carol said.

Harry said, 'Guess what she does.'

Carol took a moment. 'She's a jockey?'

'You aren't even close.'

'But she has something to do with horses,' Carol said. 'She whispers in their ears and they nod their heads?'

'She's got nothing to do with horses. Jackie's out in the world associating with people.'

'She's an exotic dancer,' Carol said.

Jackie smiled and looked at the guy in the tan suit, pretty sure it was a uniform. She said to him, 'What do you think I do?'

He said, 'Somethin I believe must draw a crowd.'

'Once in a while,' Jackie said.

'Boyd knows all kinds, good and bad,' Carol said. 'It's why I keep him handy. Harry, you know I owe my life to Boyd.'

Harry was still holding his drink. He said to Carol, 'That was a tragic situation. I guess there was nothin else your boy could've done but shoot that miner. What was his name, Otis something?'

'I couldn't move,' Carol said. 'Boyd stepped in front of me drawing his revolver—'

'I read in the paper,' Jackie said, 'it was an automatic, a Glock? If you'd like to know what I do, I play poker. Harry staked me when I was down, just about out, and takes me to poker games.'

182

'I put up ten grand,' Harry said. 'This was after she'd lost twenty thousand to some boys I happen to know. I was curious and had a feeling about Jackie, the way she talked about poker, on intimate terms with the game, and I decided why not? I gave her ten big ones, and said you lose it, I'll drop you off at the next crossroads. Well, the little girl's been on a hot streak, a few clubs in Indiana, two whole days in Louisville playin some boys don't know what hit 'em.' He said to Jackie, 'Tell Carol how much you're up.'

She said to him, 'You know you never helped me count my winnings?'

He said, 'You poor thing,' and to Carol, 'Louisville, Jackie put a wad of bills in the bank and got an ATM card. You want to know for how much? Ask her, she won't tell me.'

'Well, if she was playing against high rollers,' Carol said, 'and you say she was on a streak, I'll guess . . .' Carol paused, looking at Jackie. 'You're not saying a word, are you? If you talk about it, I might think you're bragging, so you keep it to yourself. That's admirable restraint for a young girl . . . twenty-one years old? You've been playing poker all your life, haven't you?'

'About seven years,' Jackie said.

'You started when you were—'

'Sixteen,' Jackie said, 'playing online.'

'That's close to all your life. You always play for money? What's the point if you don't, right? I suppose at school.'

'Butler,' Jackie said. 'I played every night.'

'Do you cheat?'

'No.'

'You mean you don't have to. You read people.'

'It's unavoidable,' Jackie said. 'You check out mannerisms while you're deciding on the odds.'

'All there is to it,' Carol said. 'We should get together, play a little poker.'

'She's busy,' Harry said.

'When she's not,' Carol said. 'Have a drink and chat.'

'I'm actually twenty-three,' Jackie said.

Carol gave her a nice smile. She said, 'Does it matter?'

*   *   *

Now at Carol's table in the middle of the Blue Grass Room, Boyd wasn't saying a word, hands folded in his lap. Their drinks came, white wine for Carol, Boyd, a bottle of Rolling Rock. She didn't let him drink anything hard while he's driving her around Lexington. He poured his beer, raised the glass to take a sip and placed it on the table again.

'I know what it was,' Carol said, 'Harry calling you boy. "Your boy had to shoot Otis Culpepper." Harry calls any guy under fifty boy. He calls Jackie "this little girl." Did you hear him? Jackie's twenty-three. She knew I'd caught her, so she owned up. It doesn't matter to me how old she is. She's a kid, but she's aware.'

Boyd said, 'Cause you owe your life to me you keep me *handy*? In case you want me to drive you or run an errand? You know what it's like, hear people talkin about you while you're sittin there?'

'She jumped on me,' Carol said, 'for calling the Glock a revolver. But I don't think to correct me. She said it to get my attention.'

'It's your piece,' Boyd said. 'I coulda told her

that.'

'It's like playing poker,' Carol said. 'Her turn comes, she says, "I'll raise," getting everyone's attention and reveals what it will cost the table to stay in the game. I think understating the bet would be her style. I'd love to know how much she's won, betting with Harry's money.'

'I'll ask her,' Boyd said, 'you swear you'll never mention Otis Culpepper again in my hearing.'

Carol sipped her wine.

'Why does it make you nervous?'

'You mean everybody thinkin I'm the one shot him? I don't even own a gun no more.'

'We tell them the gun's licensed,' Carol said, 'and I gave it to you just in case, that evening, once we knew Otis was armed.'

Boyd stared at her across the table.

'We tell *who* the gun's licensed?'

'The marshals,' Carol said. 'One of them called again this morning.'

'Raylan?'

'No, a Bill Nichols. He's writing a report. Wants to be sure he has the facts straight.'

'They got the sheriff's account don't they? Everything you told 'em?'

'They're not coming to get us. He'd like us to stop by the office and I forgot,' Carol said. 'He called again this morning and I told him we'd come in tomorrow.'

'It's that goddamn Raylan,' Boyd said.

CHAPTER TWENTY-SIX

Nichols was telling Raylan back in the Lexington marshals office again, Jackie Nevada was no longer a bank suspect.

Raylan said, 'She never was.'

'But could've been. Start with her droppin twenty grand in a poker game.'

'That's her motive? You lose money, you rob a bank?'

'The Indy cops said she was acting desperate.'

'Wait,' Raylan said. '*Who* was acting desperate?'

'Why're we arguing?' Nichols said. 'We're holding a twenty-five-year-old white girl walked out of a bank on West Main—it was this morning—with a little over two grand and a dye pack among the take. It goes off as she pushes open the door and colors her red for guilty.'

Raylan said, 'She's one of the girls in the surveillance tape?'

'The one Indy police swore was Jackie Nevada. She sent word from the cage she's ready to talk to us. Like she's changed her mind, gonna put the stuff on this guy has her robbin banks.'

'You know who the guy is?'

'We're gonna find out, aren't we?'

'What's her name?'

'Jane Jones on her driver's license.'

'You look her up?'

'Couple of falls for prostitution,' Nichols said. 'Jane Jones both times. Her occupation's listed as exotic dancer.'

'A stripper,' Raylan said, 'when she's not robbin

banks.'

'Good-lookin young girl,' Nichols said, 'blond. I wouldn't mind seein her act.'

*   *   *

Jane was brought in and seated facing Nichols at his desk, Raylan in the chair next to her. He said, 'Jane . . .?' She turned to him with not much of an expression, tired out. 'You look good for gettin hit with a dye pack. Your face is just a little pink. No color on your jeans or your T-shirt.'

She said, 'You should see my raincoat. You may as well throw it in the trash. I wanted to brush out my hair, but you don't have a brush you loan out.'

Raylan asked where she was from and she said Kentucky.

'But not from around here,' Raylan said. 'I think I hear Letcher or maybe Perry County in your voice. Am I right?'

'Born and lived in Hazard till I worked up my nerve to leave.'

Raylan, grinning at her, said, 'Get out. You know where I'm from? Harlan County. Worked my way out and I'm back there again with the marshals.'

Now Jane was sort of smiling. 'It's hard to escape. You have to make up your mind, you gonna go? Then get the hell goin.'

'Your daddy,' Raylan said, 'dug coal, didn't he?'

'Till a mine blew up on him.'

'The one in '96'—Raylan shaking his head—'when you were a little girl. I'm sorry I mentioned it.'

'It's all right,' Jane said. 'I came away from Hazard to better myself, I end up dancin naked and

187

robbin banks.'

Raylan smiled.

Jane said, 'It isn't funny.' But now she was grinning.

'The way you tell it it is,' Raylan said, 'like ten years from now you'll have people laughin out loud.'

She said, 'That's how long I'll be in prison?'

'This fella made you rob the bank,' Raylan said, 'didn't he get you high and you'd think it was fun? I believe you have a case against this man. What's his name?'

'The reason I didn't tell it before,' Jane said, 'I'm scared to death of him.'

'He'd beat you up?'

'He'd slap me I argue or don't answer right away. Then says in his soft tone a voice, "Baby, you know I don't like to hit you." Always this, "Please, baby, don't make me do it." He told us we had to get five thousand each or don't come home. So we go in a bank it's what we ask for. Three times with the girls and once alone, when the fucking dye pack went off.'

'How much you get to keep of the take?'

'Couple hundred.'

'Did you know the other girls before?'

'Stripped with 'em for a while. Couple of Barbie dolls on drugs. Kim and Cassie.'

'He fixed you up?'

'He'd give us a hit, tell us, "You get done, ladies, come straight home, hear?" This young guy would drive us to the bank and pick us up, but I bet anything Delroy was watchin.'

'Delroy,' Raylan said, 'got you the jobs?'

'I said his name, didn't I? It just come out.' Jane

188

was squinting at Raylan now. 'You know about Delroy Lewis?'

*   *   *

Raylan remembered having to wait for Delroy to let go of the shotgun and put up his hands. 'I arrested him one time. We didn't say much to each other.'

'In Florida,' Nichols said. 'Tall skinny guy? Convicted of assault meaning to do great bodily harm. He took a man's arm off firing a shotgun at him as the guy's pullin his gun.'

'Tryin to get it out of his pants,' Raylan said. 'The guy wanted a million bucks for the loss of his arm. The only snitch I ever heard of packin a gun. Delroy drew seven to ten for tryin to kill him.'

'What'd he make off you girls,' Nichols said to Jane, 'around forty, fifty thousand? We get him this time for bank robbery from a distance.'

'I talked to him,' Jane said, 'on the phone.'

Raylan said, 'You called him from here?' Wanting St. Christopher to stop her from telling Delroy she was being held.

'I told him I'd been picked up,' Jane said, 'covered with red dye. You know what he said? No mellow tone a voice this time. He said, "Who is this, please?" Trying to sound innocent. First time he ever said "please" in his life. He knows cops are gonna be playin my call later. I'm like, "Come on, don't fuck around, I'm in *jail*." Delroy says in a white tone a voice, "Who is this, please?" I screamed at him, "It's *Janie*. I got picked up." His white voice comes on the phone again, "I don't happen to know anybody name of Jane," and shuts off his cell. I robbed banks for the son of a bitch.

189

Now he don't even know me.'

Raylan saw he'd better move this along.

Nichols's phone rang.

He picked up and listened and said, 'Tell Miss Conlan we'll see her in just a couple minutes,' and hung up.

Jane said, 'Delroy made porno movies too, in the back of his van. Kim and Cassie were in them. I wouldn't do any.'

Nichols said, 'I'll take Miss Jones and get things started while you interview Miss Conlan.'

Raylan said, 'And Boyd?'

'And Boyd.'

'I appreciate it.'

'I told the chief why you think Boyd shot Otis.'

'I know he did.'

'The chief said he wishes you'd go back to Harlan County.'

'What was his tone a voice? You don't know when he's kidding with you? He let you set it up, didn't he?'

'You're gonna owe me for this.'

'I get Boyd to shoot off his mouth,' Raylan said, 'I'll buy you a three-dollar martini.'

'Delroy'd get us in a nod,' Jane said. 'I'll have a case, won't I? Forced to rob banks? You have to arrest him for sure now, right?' She said, 'Oh my God, I just thought of somethin. The girls don't know I'm in jail. You think I could call them? If I'm in jail they'll know I gave him up. Somebody oughta tell them.'

190

CHAPTER TWENTY-SEVEN

Delroy Lewis was a member of a biker club one time called Spades, all black guys, least fifty of 'em in black leather, the ace of spades painted on their yellow helmets. Once a month the Spades took a ride to some sleepy town in the country and fucked with people on the street. Delroy rode with the gang four times, got filthy dirty riding in the ass-end of the pack and quit the Spades.

He wore sport shirts with high collars to shorten his neck, the man long all over his six-foot-six-inch frame, 178 pounds wet, a skinny body on toothpick legs. He wore a white scarf loose around his neck and sunglasses in his hair.

This was a time before Delroy went down for shootin the snitch, the idea of Chicks Who Rob Banks came to him.

He owned a cocktail lounge on New Center Road called the Cooz Club that featured chicks writhing bare-naked on a pole that rose from the narrow strip of stage back of the bar. They'd get up there in their heels, eyes dreamy, out of focus, and the guys at the bar would bet on which chick would fall off, side bets on hitting the bartender or not. He made drinks looking over his shoulder. Once Delroy had the idea, he turned the bare-naked ladies into bank-robbin chicks and was doing fine till Janie tripped the dye pack. He'd told them how many times, check the money in bank straps before leaving and remind each other. Jane was alone and hadn't checked.

He phoned the other chicks, Kim and Cassie,

had to wake them up saying, 'Collect your clothes and valuables, any dope, get all your shit together and be ready to leave when I get there in ten minutes. You listenin?' He said, 'Jane got picked up and is gonna roll over on us. *Jane,* the chick you do banks with.' He'd have to go over there and slap 'em some, make sure they took everything they owned out of the house. Finally, they got in Delroy's car and drove out to horse country.

Going past miles of white fences and thoroughbreds raising their heads to see Delroy's Mercedes flying past.

They were approaching trees and some bushes now. Delroy slowed down and stopped on the side of the road.

'Come on out and we'll relieve ourselves together, ladies. Won't have another chance to pee-pee for a while.'

Kim said she couldn't do it with him watching.

Delroy said, 'Girl, I see you bare-ass naked every day. Get out the car.'

Once the girls were out looking for a good place to pee, Delroy took his PPK from inside his shirt and racked it. By the time he was in the trees, Cassie was pulling up her jeans. Kim was still squatting. He walked up and shot Cassie first. She fell without making a sound. But now Kim was screaming to bust a lung. Delroy shot her and she stopped. He made sure neither one had ID on her and dragged their bodies into the bushes.

*   *   *

A marshal brought Carol and Boyd to Nichols's office, rapped on the glass door, stepped aside, and Boyd saw Raylan standing by the desk, Raylan coming around it now, looking right at them.

Boyd said, 'You knew we were seein him.'

'I didn't,' Carol said, 'really. It was someone else who called, both times.'

'I'm not talkin to him,' Boyd said. 'I got nothin to say on the matter hasn't been written in reports. Far as I'm concerned the case is closed tight.'

Carol said, 'Try to control yourself, all right?'

The door opened and she was saying to Raylan, 'Well, isn't this a surprise, my old bodyguard.'

*   *   *

'I've always enjoyed watching you,' Carol said. 'Even when you were showing off and shot one of my employees . . . It wasn't in the head but in the *hair*? I asked Boyd, "He's so accurate he can do that?" Boyd said, "He wanted 'em dead they be dead."'

They took the two chairs facing the desk, Boyd gripping the arms of his, staring at Raylan sitting at the desk now holding forth. Boyd saw him waiting to try some new approach and said, 'What're you gonna pull on us this time?'

'Tell me if I have it straight,' Raylan said. 'You shot Otis while he's firing a twelve-gauge at you.'

Boyd took his time. Did he shoot Otis? *No, goddamn it,* but said, 'Yes, I did.'

'You hit him and he fired in the air.'

'I believe so, yes.'

'How many times?'

'Did he shoot? I don't know, a couple.'

'Racked the shotgun and tried twice, after you hit him in the chest from fairly close.'

193

Boyd paused, thinking of how he'd told it to the sheriff's people. 'See, Otis was firing before I shot him. After I hit him, I guess he only got off one more.'

'You thought he might hit you?'

'Jesus Christ,' Boyd said, 'you ever been shot at? I give you the benefit of knowin you don't stop and think, you're returning fire.'

'You hit him,' Raylan said, 'and he fired in the air. But you say he was shootin at you before you put him down.'

'Startin to,' Boyd said.

'But didn't hit the trailer you're standin in front of. Where you suppose his shot went?'

'I don't know,' Boyd said. 'We both shootin at each other . . . I try to see what happened now, man, it's all gunfire . . .'

'You know what I think?' Raylan said to Boyd sitting straight in his chair. 'The old man died with a loaded gun. He didn't get off a shot. Carol told you to fire the shotgun and you fired up in the air or off somewhere in the dark. But not at the trailer.'

'We didn't stop to wonder,' Carol said, 'why Otis didn't kill us. I close my eyes and I see him hurrying, he must've been afraid, but now he couldn't back down. He began firing . . .' She paused and said, 'There's no possible way you can link Boyd to the old man's death, other than obvious self-defense. The man fired a gun at us and somehow he missed, didn't he?'

Raylan said, 'That's what you told the sheriff's people and they took your word for it.'

'I think it's obvious,' Carol said, 'the old guy didn't know what he was doing.'

'Except old boys I've talked to, hunted with Otis,

194

said he don't miss with his shotgun.'

'Well, he did that night,' Carol said and told him, 'No one's perfect, Raylan. Not you or Otis or his buddies. Otis is in heaven, with his old pals from the deep mines. Coal miners get old and die from being coal miners.'

'But while they're alive,' Raylan said, 'they have a right to be alive.'

*   *   *

The only conversation in the elevator was Boyd saying, 'The man won't let go of it, will he?'

They were out of the building, crossing to the parking lot before Carol spoke. 'There's simply no way he can prove you shot Otis.'

Boyd said, '*I* didn't shoot Otis. You did.'

She said, 'What's the difference? You're standing there watching.'

Boyd paid for parking and got behind the wheel, surprised to see Carol in back. Coming here she'd sat next to him, less she was reaming somebody out as Miss Company, but never raising her voice. She still hadn't given him nothin to do in his new job, head of Disagreements.

Boyd said, 'You afraid I caught leprosy from bein in the marshals' office?'

'I'm trying to recall,' Carol said, 'when I told you to empty the shotgun, where you fired.'

'In the air. You saw me. I didn't hear you tell me to hit the trailer.'

She couldn't deny it. After a few moments she said, 'I'm not going to any more interrogations. You know we were being recorded? No, you didn't. They have all your stammering. You can act

195

surprised and stammer a little, but only when you know what you're going to say.'

'You happen to notice,' Boyd said, 'I put the spent shells by Otis, for realism?'

Boyd saw her smile in the mirror. He believed she liked his carefree attitude, long as he didn't take it too far. She was almost a nice person when things pleased her. When they didn't, he'd see her gettin pissed off at him for some picayune thing and come near firing him. He didn't think she'd try to blame Otis on him, knowing he'd turn around and drag her in. She'd be busy in court instead of doin her regular job, makin people's lives miserable.

What he needed was a threat to hang over her head. Keep her from doing something nasty to him.

Boyd was wondering, Could he get Raylan to side with him without snitchin on Carol? Remind him of walking picket lines together, seein eye to eye when it came to coal companies fuckin over miners? Say to Raylan it was getting hard to work for Carol. Hell, it was like working for Duke Power again. Remember those days we stood up together? Say this working for Carol was tearing him apart.

Something along those lines.

He started the car and said to the mirror, 'Where we goin?'

'The office,' Carol said. 'You're on your own the rest of the day, unless I need you.'

'So I should wait in the car.'

'You can't help being a smart-ass, can you?' Now she told him, 'What I've wanted to do all week is get Otis's widow off my back, Marion Culpepper. Since you're head of Disagreements you have her sign *our* agreement, where we pay her five hundred a month. Tell her we'll get her Social Security bumped up and give her the deed to her new trailer home in Benham. Even has a hot water tank.'

'I have to go all the way down to Harlan?'

'She's here in Lexington, in a nursing home we're paying for. So we don't have to drive to Sleepy Holler. Get her to sign and tell her I'll stop by tomorrow, say a few kind words and wrap it up.'

Boyd said, 'Like "I'm sorry I killed your hubby"?'

'You want me to fire you? Say that again.'

They stared at each other, Boyd coming close to saying it. Or tell her she can't fire you, you quit. What he said was, 'You know you ended a sentence with a preposition? You said, "She's here in a nursing home we're payin for."'

'Caught being ungrammatical.' Carol staring at his serious face. 'How should I have said it?'

'She's here in a nursing home,' Boyd said, 'for which we're payin the costs.'

CHAPTER TWENTY-EIGHT

Nichols got hold of Raylan and they responded to the scene in horse country: thoroughbreds grazing the pastures while the bodies of two girls shot to death lay in a thicket of trees.

'A guy driving past,' Nichols said, 'saw crows swarming into the trees. He knew something was dead, stopped to look and got in touch with police. They had it posted: look for Kim and Cassie, who'd skipped when we went to pick 'em up. That fast, while Jane's safe in custody.'

They were looking at the bodies now—cops standing around—looking at clothes torn from

197

parts of their bodies and their faces pecked to the bone by a murder of crows. 'They still have their teeth,' Nichols said, 'but no eyes. You notice? I bet they were dark. No ID on either one.'

An evidence tech watching them said, 'We're lucky we got here before the coyotes. Be nothing left but bones.'

Raylan stooped over one of the girls and the evidence tech told him not to touch their clothes. 'That blood can give you HIV positive, you get it on you.' Raylan picked up the girl's hand, a phone number in black marker witten on the palm, before it was smudged with blood.

He said to Nichols, 'She did have your phone number.'

'She hung up on us,' Nichols said. 'I'm surprised she wrote it down.'

'But no second thoughts about calling you,' Raylan said. 'She had, she might still be alive.' He stood up and thanked the cops standing around for securing the scene and told them the two girls were Kim and Cassie. 'I don't know their last names. You might have them on file for prostitution. I believe they were exotic dancers before they became bank robbers. I thank you for helping us out.'

One of the officers said, 'Detectives are coming out from downtown. You guys beat 'em to it. You want to wait and talk to the guys? They'll be working this one.'

'I think we ought to pick up the shooter, you understand, before he knows we're on to him?'

The cop said, 'You know who it is?'

Raylan said, 'Yes, we do,' and told them, 'Delroy Lewis.'

The cop said, 'You can't identify the bodies, but

you know who they are and who killed them.'

'We've got another one of his bank robber girls. She told us about him,' Raylan said. 'Thanks, fellas, I'll be in touch,' and walked away with Nichols.

'What if it isn't Delroy,' Nichols said, 'but some other mutt?'

'It's Delroy,' Raylan said. 'I can see him running a gang of girl bank robbers. Making money, maybe surprised it works. Surprises everybody.'

'What's his buddy say—he happens to have one—"The girls go down, you go with them"?'

'Delroy says, "What girls? I don't have no girls. Man, I stay far afield. Maybe get the girls a limo for the bank job."'

'He's showin off.'

'Showin how cool he is. That's the guy. A limo, everybody knows is his. He takes a few risks,' Raylan said, 'but I can't see him cutting lines in the car. That's Jane making it sound hip. I bet he doesn't go near those girls till it's dark out.'

'One of his girls gets arrested, why wouldn't she tell on him?'

'Jane did, and he blew it, pretending to be white instead of soothing her. "Don't worry, baby, I'm gettin you a lawyer gonna have your case thrown outta court." He moves someplace else and gets three more girls, gives 'em pills, tells them anything he wants and they believe him. He doesn't beat on the girls, he gives them a slap and then sweet-talks them. They get picked up, he says, "Kim and Cassie? I believe I remember those girls, my exotic dancers at the club. What is it they doin now?" We'll start looking for him,' Raylan said, 'at the Cooz Club, with backup.'

'I doubt he'll be there,' Nichols said.

'I know,' Raylan said, 'but we might find out a few things. He's a show-off. Maybe things he'd like us to know.'

'We got him for a double homicide. What else you want?'

'I won't know till we look around.'

*　　*　　*

The manager of the club, Kenneth, middle-aged in a blond hairpiece, heard car doors slam and said to Bobby, the kid at the bar sipping a glass of white wine, 'Well, finally.'

Bobby went to the store window that wore coats of pink paint on the outside, spelled out in blue neon was COOZ CLUB.

Under it, smaller in red neon, it said, THIS IS THE PLACE! The kid looked through scratches in the paint and said:

'A Crown Vic and a Chevy. Guys are coming out of the cop car and the two guys from the Chevy are holding them up talking to the guys—they have U.S. MARSHALS on their jackets—Hey, you were right. It looks like just the two guys, the suits, are gonna come in.'

'Finish your wine, Bobby,' Kenneth said, 'and get out of here the moment they ask for Delroy.'

*　　*　　*

Raylan came in, Nichols behind him, saw the manager standing by the bar, a teenage boy finishing his drink . . . Raylan said, 'Kenny?' The guy bowed his blond hairpiece saying he was, and Raylan said, 'How long you been a Kenny?'

'Well, since it's sort of my name, all my life. Have friends who'll only call me Kenneth. Oh, and Delroy, do you know what he calls me? Kennet, without the diphthong. You want to know if he's here? He isn't. I haven't seen him since, anyways, yesterday. You don't believe me, call the boys in and search the joint.'

The kid got up from the bar saying, 'This doesn't sound like any of my business.'

They let him walk out.

Raylan looked at this pink strip club going to seed, the bar with the pole up behind it. Raylan saw bare-naked girls using the pole to aim their assholes at the assholes lining the bar. Sit down at one of those tables over there and get a lap dance with moans.

Kenneth said, 'Oh,' as if he'd just remembered something.

'Delroy left you a movie he's starring in. Actually, he's the only one in it.'

Raylan said, 'He wants me to see it?'

'If you're Raylan.'

'It's all Delroy?'

'Don't worry, it isn't too long. He manages to get to the point after, well, sort of an introduction.'

Raylan said, 'Who shot it?'

'I did. I shoot all his flicks. Most of the ones where he's by himself are rather boring. His X-rated stuff I think is better than most.'

Raylan said, 'Delroy does porn?'

'Some. This one he did, you have to look at while you're here. Cross your heart and promise you won't take it with you. Promise?'

Raylan and Nichols both crossed their hearts without looking at each other.

'It'll be on that flat screen,' Kenneth said, nodding to it above the bar, 'for your viewing pleasure. Delroy said offer you whatever you want to drink, on the house.'

Raylan and Nichols still didn't look at each other.

'You want, I can make popcorn,' Kenneth said, 'in a jiffy.'

Raylan said, 'Well, Ken, I could use a beer,' and Nichols said he'd have one too.

*   *   *

The man on the screen was in sweats, a skinny six-six handling the ball with nice moves, going to the basket he stops and pops a jumper, brings the ball out and goes in and stuffs it. Now he was coming back to the camera, the ball under his arm. He raises the ball in front of him and spins it on the tip of his finger. He's looking at the camera and says, 'That's how I see the world going around, like this basketball.'

Kenneth used his remote to pause on Delroy.

'He told me he wanted to sound "not mysterious, but like it." I said, "Profound but obscure?" He said, "Yeah like that." He said we playin a game bein here. Playin it all the way to the edge and see how it comes out.'

'What he did,' Raylan said, 'was shoot two girls while they're taking a whiz.'

Kenneth clicked the remote to see Delroy on the screen spinning the ball. He lets it drop. Now he was saying, 'I can't be there right now. I happen to see outside a bank a girl I use to know mighta been Jane something? Had red dye all over her

202

outerwear.'

'I gave him that,' Kenneth said.

'Girl musta tried to rob the bank,' Delroy said. 'I did see her taken to the courthouse, the one on Barr Street? A while later I see you go in there.'

Delroy from another angle.

'Remember the time you came to arrest me and we facin each other? I'm holdin the shotgun at my leg. You told me let go of it or you'd draw and put me down. You not holdin a gun but you say that to me. Man, I had seven years to think about it. You bullshittin me or what? Bluffin? I realize while I'm in the slam you was takin it to the edge.'

Raylan said, 'Cause you don't know how far you can take it'—reciting it word for word with Delroy on the screen—'till you get there.'

Raylan said, 'Hold it, Ken, while we take you up on your offer. You think you might stir up a couple of martinis? I like the show so far, even if Delroy's fulla shit.'

*   *   *

They got back to Delroy saying, 'That man I shot you put me away for? You know I wasn't aimin at his arm. I fired and the gun jumped in my hands. See, I'd borrowed it and never fired the motherfucker till I shot the man's arm off.'

'The guy's arm was amputated at a hospital,' Raylan said. He took a sip and raised his glass to Kenneth.

On the screen Delroy was saying, 'It wasn't like I killed him. See, I hear this C.I. asshole snitch was gonna tell you people somethin he made up I done. So now I'm in a situation and borrow this shotgun to protect myself. I face him but missed. It's the first time I'm usin the piece. I mighta blown his head off but I didn't, did I? Now the snitch has a lawyer tell me he wants five million for makin him a one-arm man. I tell the lawyer I make ten cents an hour bangin out license plates, off Sundays, Christmas and when I'm sick. I spend some of my dimes on toothpaste and shave cream, buy some hooch, bet a few sports games. I come out of my incarceration with four dollars and twenty cents. How'm I suppose to pay this man?'

Delroy paused and said, 'This girl Jane Jones? She mighta talked to you by now—you believe I ever associated with a chick name of Jane Jones. She hasn't yet called you, I believe she's gonna. Claims she knows me. Wants to tell you how she thinks I make a living. She calls, I wouldn't waste my time talkin to her.'

'She already has,' Raylan said.

Kenneth looked pleased. 'It's getting good, isn't it?'

'You're in it too,' Raylan said.

Kenneth paused the video. 'I shoot his movies and tend his bar. I know nothing of his extra-curricular activities.'

'You know the girls.'

'Which ones? There always girls. But none committing felonies that I know of.'

He turned the sound on, Delroy saying:

'Raylan, I think me and you gonna have to meet sometime. I can't say when right now. You gonna be lookin over your shoulder till I make the scene. Then we gonna take it to the edge.'

Delroy faded out, his face serious; the screen turned black and the credits in reverse said:

A Kenny Flix Production
Produced And Directed By
Kenneth

They finished their drinks and Raylan said, 'Ken, will you get the tape for us?'

Nothing about crossing their hearts.

Kenneth said, 'I suppose you want the original.'

'Everything you shot,' Raylan said.

*   *   *

Kenneth dialed a cell and a voice said, 'Kennet?'

'You were right, he came with a SWAT team. I served martinis and we watched your movie.'

'Man brought a SWAT team?'

'A carload of marshals. You're a popular guy.'

'Kennet, I can't find where the man's stayin at. I don't like tryin to catch him at the courthouse.'

'Why didn't you ask? He's staying at the Two Keys. I dropped in on Crazy Night and there he was. I told you that.'

'You go there?'

'Delroy, read my lips. He's staying there,' and let that hang before saying, 'He acts as bouncer and they give him a free room and tortillas.'

'That college bar?'

'It's fun. I love it.'

Delroy took a few moments before saying, 'Man, do it in a barroom.'

'He *is* wearing a cowboy hat.'

'Like the big scene in a western.'

'That's what I just said.'

Delroy said, 'Yeah . . .' nodding, seeing it in his

mind.

'It'll be crowded.'

Kenneth said, 'I like spectators.'

CHAPTER TWENTY-NINE

'I been sittin here waitin an hour,' Boyd said. 'She calls I got to jump and go pick her up.'

Raylan said, 'Where's Nichols?'

They were in his office at the courthouse.

'He went to a meeting. Said I could wait for you long as I don't take anything. You people know how to make visitors feel right at home, don't you?'

'I should prob'ly be in that meeting,' Raylan said. He picked up the phone on the desk.

Boyd said, 'I just want to tell you somethin so you're clear in your mind about what happened to Otis. I did not shoot him.'

Raylan replaced the phone and sat down at the desk across from Boyd, staring at him. 'You're tellin me Carol shot Otis?'

'She's the only female mine-company thug I ever met,' Boyd said. 'I can't work for her no more.'

'Now she's a gun thug?'

'I'm sayin she's thuggish for a woman,' Boyd said, 'how she comports herself, talks the company line.'

'Boyd, if you're sayin Carol shot Otis, say it.'

'Raylan, I never been a snitch in my life. I would cut out my tongue first. I'm tellin you I did not shoot Otis, and I'm leavin it at that.'

'If you and Carol were the only ones there—' Raylan stopped and said, 'Did Otis fire his shotgun at you?'

Boyd hesitated.

'Or'd you pick it up once he's dead and empty the gun in the air?'

'I'm not gettin into anything has to do with Carol.'

'But you set it up,' Raylan said, 'to look like you shot him in self-defense.'

'Raylan, I swear on a holy Bible I did not shoot the man.'

'You and Carol are the only ones there, aren't you?'

'Draw what conclusions you come to, I'm tellin you I didn't shoot him.'

'But I can't arrest her for Otis,' Raylan said, 'without putting it on her, can I?'

'I'm not workin for her no more,' Boyd said, 'and that's all I can tell you. I got to go now, pick her up.'

Raylan let him walk out. He wasn't going far.

*   *   *

Carol came out of the mine company building with a couple of manila envelopes under her arm and got in front with Boyd this time.

'What did you do, go to a bar?'

Boyd came right out and told her, 'As a matter of fact, I stopped off to see my old buddy again.'

He could feel her staring at him, Boyd looking at his outside mirror, waiting for cars to pass.

She said, 'Tell me why.'

'I wanted to get something straight with him.'

She reached over, turned the key to kill the engine. 'You know I'm an attorney.'

Boyd said, 'Yeah . . .?' feeling he had the edge here.

'I've told you how many times,' Carol said, 'there is no possibility of your being convicted. You won't even be brought to trial, even if I were to admit you murdered him. I'm an accomplice, it's my gun— the company's actually. Even if I say I tried to stop you.'

Boyd held off from screaming at her, *I didn't shoot him, you did!* as loud as he could in her face.

He cleared his throat to get himself ready and said in his normal voice, 'Raylan knows I didn't shoot the man. He knows me from standin on picket lines with him, couple of coal miners on strike hopin our Higher Power's on our side and not the company's.'

Carol said, 'You told him you didn't shoot Otis.'

'That's correct, since I didn't.'

She said, 'Boyd—'

'You call me by name, you're about to yell at me for somethin.'

She said, 'When have I ever raised my voice?'

'I figure you'd fire me anyway.'

'You told him,' Carol said, 'I shot Otis?'

'What I told him was I didn't.'

'And you think he believes you.'

'Yes, I do.'

'It seems to me,' Carol said, 'nothing's changed. Whether you told him I shot Otis or not. He'd still have to prove it wasn't self-defense.'

Boyd said, 'Tell me who did it, all right? Just so I'll know.'

'What's the difference? You were there, you didn't stop me. I said empty his shotgun, and you aided and abetted. But whether you keep your big mouth shut or not,' Carol said, 'now that you've found God, you want me to give myself up so you

208

won't have to turn snitch. I'm right, aren't I?'

'You know what they say, *que sera sera,*' Boyd said.

'God,' Carol said. 'You're too dumb to be a threat.'

He turned the key and started to pull away from the curb, his jaw clamped shut, and she stopped him.

'Get out and I'll scoot over. Take a taxi to the nursing home, St. Elizabeth, the address is on the envelopes.' She handed it to him. 'Get Marion to sign wherever it's indicated and tell her I'll stop by tomorrow.'

'For what?'

'Thank her for being so cooperative. God, talking to her on the phone was an extreme test of will. Tell the old lady she's getting five bills a month and that's it.' She said, 'Boyd,' her tone becoming almost soft, 'let me do the thinking, okay?'

*   *   *

The taxi driver said, 'You going to see your fatha or your mama in this place?'

'My old mom,' Boyd said, holding the envelopes on his lap, the one with the deed not as fat as the one with the agreement the old lady had to sign, three different places.

'Is nice you go see her,' the driver said. 'You bring her some candy?'

'She eats sweet stuff she gets pimples.'

'Yes? How old is she?'

'I believe goin on eighty.'

'She still has teeth?'

'I haven't examined her mouth, but I believe they

209

long gone.'

'Get her some candy she can suck on.'

Boyd could not tell where this guy was from, but not anywhere close to America. 'She's old-lookin from the life she's had, married to a coal miner.'

'He die?'

'Yes, he did. Was shot.'

'Oh, you know who shot him?'

'Yeah, but I'm not tellin.'

'You say okay? You not gonna shoot him?'

Boyd said, 'Where you from?'

'I come here from Albania,' the driver said, 'but I'm not Muslim. I have to shoot some guy, I do it.'

He pulled into the drive of St. Elizabeth's, the nursing home. Boyd got out and paid the driver, telling him, 'You oughta try to control your emotions, partner,' and went in the building: two stories of red brick with white trim, a nice-lookin place to end your days. But wasn't at all nice inside. It smelled of old people wettin theirselves all day long. A woman took him down an aisle, around the corner and down another aisle to Marion Culpepper's room.

*　　　*　　　*

There she was sitting in a rocking chair, a quilt over her legs to the floor, limp hair stuck to her head, eyes sunken, not showing much life in there. She had oxygen tubes stuck in her nose, the line going underneath the quilt to the floor. As a representative of the coal company, Boyd said, 'Ms. Culpepper, don't you have a cozy setup here.' The room had the rocker and a straight chair, a chest of drawers, a bed you pressed a button and it changed its shape and, on the wall, a picture of Jesus showing his Sacred Heart.

It was a room at the end of the trail.

Boyd said, 'Hey, you got your own bathroom.'

Ms. Culpepper said, 'Wasn't you suppose to bring a jar?' Boyd frowned. 'I only was given these papers.'

'I told Sista to find when somebody was comin.'

'I never heard from her,' Boyd said.

'Miz Conlan'd never bring any.'

'As I say, I only brought these papers for you to sign, the deed to the house and how much you're settlin for. It says five hundred, cross it out and write in what you want or you won't sign it. You can discuss it with Ms. Conlan, she's the one wrote it up. Or,' Boyd said, 'you can sign it, and I'll get 'em to write any changes you want.' He thought a moment and said, 'I tell you what, you sign the papers, I'll run out and get you a jar of shine.'

'I miss Otis,' Marion said.

'I 'magine so, but you're gonna be with him pretty soon, aren't you?'

'Doctor says they's years left in my bones. I'm only sixty nine. He told me I only had a touch of black lung, my cooked lungs was from smoking reefer all my life.'

Boyd said, 'Try to get some Oxy off the nurse.'

'She said I need to be in pain. I'm not takin any sass off that company woman no more. She's always short with me. I hear her yellin I get what she gives me or nothin. I said, "Where you think we're livin, back in 1940?" It all started with that god-damn fishpond of Otis's. I threaten to cook the fish, he'd go up on Old Black and shoot us squirrels. One time he got us a buck.'

211

Boyd said, 'Ms. Conlan's stoppin by tomorrow. Whyn't you come out'n demand what you want?'

'Six hunnert, I ever speak to her again. Up from five hunnert, what I been tellin her. Hey, you work for her, don't you?'

Boyd said, 'I'm in charge of'—came close to saying Disagreements, but changed it to—'drivin her around.'

She said, 'You was with her, wasn't you? The night Otis come up to you?'

Boyd straightened, saying to the widow, 'Ma'am, I did not shoot your husband.'

'I know that,' Ms. Culpepper said. 'I've heard her talk and now I've heard you talk, offerin to go out and get me a jar. Get two, please. I suppose you don't have much patience, but she don't have *none*. She like to get things done right now. She come to get these papers signed, you now what I'm gonna do?'

Boyd shook his head.

She threw off the quilt covering her legs and was aiming a shotgun at him.

Boyd said, 'Jesus Christ.'

Ms. Culpepper said, 'My Lord and Savior.'

'You surprised me's all.'

'I'm gonna scare her good. Thinks I'm about to shoot her, but they's no shells come with the gun. Was Otis's, a state trooper give me. I asked him, "Say I want to go out and shoot a turkey for supper?" He says no, he can't bring me no shells since I'm stayin in this home. He believes it's against the law.'

'What you need shells for?'

'Shoot the company woman, she comes in tomorrow.'

'Whoa,' Boyd said. 'You can shoot that gun?'

'Near good as Otis.'

Boyd took his time before asking, 'How many loads you think you'd need?'

'Jes one,' Ms. Culpepper said. 'It'll put her down. Maybe one more if I need it.'

CHAPTER THIRTY

Liz Burgoyne came in the sun parlor from the patio to see Jackie Nevada waiting, getting up from the sofa, and it made Liz think of Raylan, the time she walked in and he asked her about Cuba stealing kidneys. Liz crossed the room in jeans and cowboy boots offering her hand, saying:

'Jackie Nevada. Harry's told me about his poker-playing buddy. He makes you sound like a little girl, but you're quite something else, aren't you?' Liz smiling now. 'Harry mentioned you're wanted by the police?'

'It's a misdemeanor thing,' Jackie said. 'I didn't show up for a hearing.'

'Picked up in a raid,' Liz said. 'Harry told me about it. He said you like Manhattans, is that right?'

Jackie said, 'If that's what we're having.'

*   *   *

They were both on the sofa now, the nearly empty pitcher on the cocktail table, both smoking cigarettes.

'You ever cheat?' Liz said.

'Why do only women ask that? You mean at

213

poker.'

'Or on a guy.'

'Poker, I've never had to.'

'You're that good?'

'You have to work with another player. Didn't you see *Rounders*? They cheat playing with a bunch of cops. I've never cheated on a boyfriend either. Right now I don't have one, but I live with seven guys. You know what they think is funny? Farting.'

'Why do guys love to fart?'

'They're expressing themselves.'

'You hop in the sack with any of them?'

'Nope. There's some fooling around, girls come for a party and we get high, but I don't recall anything really inappropriate. You might hear a girl tell some guy to quit grabbin her ass. We have great parties.'

Liz said, 'You like to go down on guys?'

'Not *guys*, no. But I have polished the occasional knob.'

'Wow,' Liz said. 'You're not bashful, are you?'

'You know what I'm talking about or wouldn't of asked.'

'You have to meet some of my friends from olden times, they'd love you.'

'I'm not a lay,' Jackie said. 'I've only gone to bed with three guys in four years, ones I thought I was serious about.'

'What happened to them?'

'They graduated.'

Liz poured the rest of the Manhattans.

'You like to do it standing up?'

'I never have,' Jackie said. 'In movies they look like they're ringing the bell, but I think it would be uncomfortable.'

Liz said, 'I bet I know the movie you're thinking of. The girl walks in the bar—'

'That's the one.'

'She can't get any attention and yells out, "Who's a girl gotta suck around here to get a drink?"'

'She gets into the cute guy's pants, in the booth.'

'Then you see them in back doing it standing up.'

'You ever do it with a black guy?'

'No, and I'm not racist,' Jackie said. 'Or maybe I am and don't know it. I've never had any chills and thrills yet when I meet black guys at parties. I know you have.'

'Our driver at the time,' Liz said. 'Harry thought was from West Africa, so Cuba always had to put on an accent, one he picked up from cabdrivers.' She said, 'I can't imagine Harry trying anything with you.'

'Why?' Jackie said.

'He's too old. He might ask you to strip, promise he'll just look.'

'Would that upset you?'

'Not in the least, if he can pull it off.'

'He sure goes to the bathroom a lot.'

'His tired kidneys,' Liz said. 'And here's your boyfriend now.'

Harry came in from the hallway telling Jackie, 'I got three guys so far want to play you: my friends the breeders, Ike and Mike, and a World Series of Poker pro they dug up called Dude Moody.'

Jackie was nodding.

'He's been at the final table. I think he won a couple of bracelets. They call him Moody Blues or just Blues.'

'I said to Ike and Mike, "For Christ sake, what do you guys need help for?" And there's a guy in

215

town I asked to stop by. You met him, Liz, Raylan Givens? The marshal lookin for that driver we had. He called, I asked him to come by for a drink and say hello.'

Jackie said, 'Harry, don't tell him I play poker, okay?'

*　　　*　　　*

Jackie watched Raylan take off his hat shaking hands with Harry and they stood talking for a few minutes. Now they were coming over to the sofa, Raylan saying, 'Don't get up, ladies, you look comfortable.'

'We *have* had a couple,' Liz said. 'Raylan, it's so good to see you. It seems to me that you and I sat here having martinis one time. Harry, where were you?'

'Tendin business. I believe I was helpin a foal come into the world. She's still lookin like a possible.'

Jackie saw Raylan stare at her for a moment and turn to Liz again, Liz saying, 'This time my guest said she might try a Manhattan. They seemed to've worked just fine.' Jackie wondering how she'd be introduced. These people got in conversations and forgot she was there.

Not Raylan.

Harry said, 'Liz makes it sound like she's never had a Manhattan.'

Jackie watched Raylan smile, being polite, watched his eyes come back to her. She said through her buzz, 'Hi, I'm Jackie.'

Raylan came over to shake hands telling her not to get up, but she did and stood with her feet

216

planted.

'Harry's latest partner,' Liz said.

Raylan gave her hand a nice squeeze and said, 'Is that right?'

Jackie told herself she'd get out of this or she wouldn't, and said, 'Harry's my banker, he stakes me to poker games, but doesn't pay too much attention.' Smiling then to show she was being funny. 'He has no idea how we're doing.'

No one laughed. Liz said, 'If you've been playing no-limit for the past week, you're winning, or Harry would've left you off somewhere.'

Harry said, 'You make me sound heartless.'

'I'll bet,' Liz said, 'she's up at least a hundred grand.'

Raylan said, 'You play poker as an occupation?'

She said, 'I'm not sure. I'm looking at it.'

'You were in a game,' Raylan said, 'in Indianapolis recently that was raided, weren't you?'

Jackie said, 'You know how much I lost?'

Harry said, 'You never want to be in a game when the cops bust in. They take all the cash and chips as evidence. What happens to the dough after that?' Harry said to Raylan. 'Maybe you can tell me.'

'Isn't part of my job,' Raylan said.

'I'm always careful,' Harry said, 'pickin games for Jackie. What I do is call the chief of police, tell him who I am, and say I want to play some poker without gettin in the way of a raid. I ask him if there's a police fund-raiser I could help out.'

Liz asked Raylan if he had time for a drink. He said, glancing at his watch, he'd better get back. 'We're tryin to locate a guy wants to shoot me on sight.'

Liz said, 'I'd think you'd have them lining up.'

'Well, some are dead,' Raylan said, and looked at Jackie. 'I'd like to hear more about what you're doin. I haven't played a lot of poker but've always had a good time. Are you stayin here by any chance?'

'Till we hit the poker trail again,' Harry said. 'Jackie's takin on some guys tomorrow in a big cash game.'

Raylan touched his coat pocket and said, 'Excuse me,' taking out his cell phone and turning away.

Jackie watched him, telling herself it was a case they were putting him on and he had to leave right now, forget about her walking out of jail, and heard him say, 'Come on, you're kiddin.' He turned his back to them now and stepped away to listen. *Come on, you're kiddin,* his voice raised but not much, was all she heard. She watched him fold his cell and come back to stand with her as he told Liz and Harry, 'I'm sorry, but that was my job callin.'

'About the guy who wants to shoot you?' Liz said.

'Something else,' Raylan said. Then paused, like he was getting around to what he wanted to say. 'You don't mind, I'd like to have a word with Ms. Nevada.'

Liz said, 'I hope you're not going to cuff our guest. Are you?'

'I'm not arrestin her,' Raylan said. 'There's something I'd like to talk to her about.'

Jackie gave Liz a shrug and walked out to the hallway with Raylan.

'Where we going if you're not turning me in?'

'I want to talk to you,' Raylan said. 'The first time I came here I said, "This's a sun parlor? I'd like to see what they call the living room." Liz told me it's been a sun parlor for eighty-five years.'

Jackie stopped. 'If you're not arresting me, where we going?'

'Forget about Indy,' Raylan said. 'I'll appear at your hearing and tell the court you owed a shylock and was hopin to pay him out of the twenty grand you blew.' Raylan, turned enough to see the Burgoynes watching, said, 'Come on,' and they continued walking down the hall, Raylan telling Jackie, 'I stopped at Butler and saw your picture in the yearbook. I said to myself, Whatever it was, you didn't do it.'

'I have no idea,' Jackie said, 'what's going on.'

'I want to take you out,' Raylan said, 'if you're not playin tonight. You are, I'll come and watch.'

She said, 'Like a date?' Thought for a moment and said, 'You know those two girls who were murdered? I'd love to see where it happened.'

'There's nothin there now but police tape.' He paused a moment and said, 'Hey, you want to come with me? I'll show you a scene hard to believe.'

*   *   *

In the car now Jackie said, 'My first murder scene. I'm excited.'

'It isn't called a homicide yet,' Raylan said. 'I'll warn you, don't get too close to this one.'

'Liz said to remind you, I'm a poor college student just trying to get by.'

'Playin poker,' Raylan said. He believed it put her out in the world so their age difference didn't mean a thing.

'High stakes every evening,' Jackie said. 'Hands

become a story you'll be telling weeks later, about a guy who's trying to scare you out, raises and reraises, going for it. Thirty-odd thousand in the pot when we come to the flop. You know he'll bet. But I think he's bluffing. I've got two pair, jacks and tens. Either one shows up I've got a full house. He bets fifteen thousand. I see him and raise him ten. The poor guy, he's playing a girl when the truth hits him: he's about to get cleaned out. There's an advantage in being the only girl at the table. It makes the guys act cool and want to show off. Harry's problem, he can't tell when they're bluffing. I think they always become quieter, like they're holding a serious hand.'

Raylan said, 'What's the flop?'

Jackie said, 'You haven't played much hold 'em, have you?'

*   *   *

Police cars lined the drive, uniformed officers stood around in St. Elizabeth's lobby, residents watching, asking each other what in the world was going on. A city detective waiting for Raylan took him through the halls to Ms. Culpepper's room, telling him, 'Our response on this was less'n twelve minutes. Anybody in the room when it went down is still in the room.'

Raylan asked him, 'What was the weapon? I believe I was told a shotgun.'

'A Remington 870 with a slug barrel, one load fired, one still in the chamber. It belonged to her deceased husband, Otis.'

Raylan said, 'They let her keep a loaded shotgun in her room?'

'It's the first thing we asked. If she didn't have

the slugs hidden, somebody went out and got 'em for her. We haven't asked about it yet.'

'I was told Boyd Crowder came with Ms. Conlan.'

'That's right. He brought documents he wanted the old woman to sign.'

'How about Carol, Ms. Conlan?'

'She's still lying where she fell, I think blown off her feet. The slug hit her in the chest and messed it up some. Nothing's hardly been touched. Mr. Crowder says the old woman fired the shotgun under her quilt and it set the quilt afire.'

'Where's the gun?'

'Being checked for latents.'

'You know Boyd's prints are on file.'

'We're already inquiring.'

Raylan turned to Jackie and took her into the room with him.

*   *   *

Boyd was at a window on the other side of Ms. Culpepper in her rocker, a new quilt over her legs, her eyes looking dazed or stoned.

Boyd turned to Raylan saying, 'Finally . . . Man, I'm the one told 'em to get the marshals and ask for Raylan. He'll tell you I'd never use a shotgun on a woman. Would I?'

'Not ordinarily,' Raylan said. 'Boyd, you didn't shoot her, did you?'

'You ask me that,' Boyd said, 'knowin, or soon to find out, I never touched the gun? I gave Marion, bless her heart, some of her medication right afterwards.'

Raylan saw Jackie start to look down at Carol's

221

body, next to the bed, and turn away quick. He watched her go to Ms. Culpepper and take her hand, crouching down to speak to her, Jackie knowing more about life than any twenty-three-year-old college girl, exposed to the world having Reno for a dad. It seemed to have been a pretty good thing.

Boyd said, 'I was at the table gettin out papers for Marion to sign and bam, the quilt catches fire and I see Ms. Conlan fall against the nightstand knockin things over, I believe her soul leavin her body before she hit the floor.'

Raylan said to Boyd, 'I bet if I retraced your steps last evening, I'd find myself in a gun shop buyin shells.'

'And I bet a hundred dollars you wouldn't,' Boyd said.

'You have a wino buy 'em for you?'

Boyd said, 'Raylan, leave things lie, all right?'

Raylan motioned for Jackie to come over.

'What'd she tell you?'

'She said if anybody cares,' Jackie said, 'God let her blow out that woman's lights the same as the woman did Otis's. She said she spoke to God about it and God told her forget it, she'd done all right.'

Jackie gave a shrug looking at Raylan. She watched him step over to Carol's body lying by the bed, bloody from throat to chest; watched Raylan stoop down and use two fingers to close the woman's eyelids and crouch there looking at her.

Once he got up he motioned to her and they left the nursing home. He did speak to the city detective again, but was quiet in the car driving away. Jackie waited.

Finally she said, 'What's wrong?'

'I knew her pretty well,' Raylan said. 'Enough that I didn't much care for her. She was the company and did whatever she wanted.'

'But seeing her dead,' Jackie said, 'was different.'

'Killed with a shotgun.'

'By an old lady. You think she'll go to prison?'

'I doubt it. But you don't know which one to feel sorry for.'

'Indiana they speak Hoosier,' Jackie said. 'Come down here you're in a different country.'

'Coal country,' Raylan said. 'Carol's from West Virginia, she shouldn't of been surprised.'

Jackie said, 'Ms. Culpepper said the company woman came in and told her how nice it was to see her again, and Ms. Culpepper shot her.'

'Being cordial,' Raylan said, 'instead of wondering what the hell that was under the blanket. You live down there you get to know people's ways. You hear Boyd? He said, "I never used a shotgun on a woman." Carol knew everything but who we are. She was good at sounding West Virginia when she wanted but, I'll say it again, she didn't know our ways.' He looked at Jackie and said, 'You want to get a beer? It might do you good.'

CHAPTER THIRTY-ONE

The way Harry set up the poker show—once he decided Raylan and Boyd didn't have the money and Carol Conlan was no longer available—he'd stage it as a guys-against-girls thing and have it shot professionally on HD video, in his poker suite at home, a Burgoyne Farms Production, with refreshments.

Jackie said, 'You want us drinking?'

'Don't poker players drink when they're not on TV? I want the atmosphere real. The guys are Kwami and Qasim Mu'tazz, breeders from Saudi Arabia. I know they drink. I got to be careful doing the play-by-play I don't call them Ike and Mike.' Harry said, 'And joining the two Arabians will be Dude Moody, winner of two World Series of Poker championships. If Dude wants to smoke he may. You see him on *Poker After Dark* he's rollin a dead cigar in his mouth.'

'And the girls?' Jackie said.

Harry was showing her the poker suite: a well-stocked bar, bookshelves and shots of horses on the paneled walls.

'I'll introduce you as the Butler champ.'

'Butler doesn't have a competition.'

'You beat everybody there, don't you? And we have two of the top names from the women's poker club here in town, Vanessa Russo and Leanne Lynn, always competitors.'

Jackie said, 'That's it?'

'Start playin for a hundred grand, top prize, and we'll keep the local girls in for a while. Then you go no-limit with the boys.'

'You're doing this,' Jackie said, 'so you'll have a video to show at Keeneland.'

'If it's any good,' Harry said. 'Everything anyone says will be in it. I think that part'll be betten'n the poker. But there's always suspense when you raise a bet. All you have to do is sit down with the pros and see if you're any good.'

He sounded serious. Jackie said, 'Don't you love me anymore?'

224

'Course I do. I'm checkin, see if you're ready. You win, I suspect you'll be on your own from now on.'

'And if I lose my bankroll?'

'We'll still be buddies,' Harry said, 'won't we?'

*   *   *

Raylan and Boyd sat at the back end of the suite by a screen that would follow the action: a camera mounted above the poker table, and a young guy with a Sony Handycam, putting it on the players as they came in the suite. Harry, by the bar, introduced the players.

Harry: 'Twice poker world champ Dude Moody, here all the way from Cypress, Texas, to be with us.'

They watched Dude come away from the bar in his white Stetson, holding a lowball glass of Maker's Mark. He touched his brim to the camcorder and took a seat. Dude rolling a cigar in his mouth.

Boyd: 'Smokin it too. They don't allow it he's on TV. Raylan, did you get a good look at Ms. Conlan?'

Raylan: 'I did. I noticed she was dead. Boyd, how come you're here?'

Boyd: 'Ms. Conlan invited me. I identified the body and the company had a funeral home come by and pick her up. She was lookin forward to this game.'

Harry was introducing the Mu'tazz brothers. 'My good friends Kwame and Qasim from Saudi Arabia, successful at poker as they are breeding horses.'

Harry: 'And now the ladies. Jackie Nevada, who's been playin the big boys lately and winning. And Vanessa Russo and Leanne Lynn, local women's club champs.'

Vanessa raised her arm in the sleeveless dress and waved to the camera.

She reached the table and the Mu'tazz brothers were each kissing her hand.

Boyd: 'I believe Vanessa forgot to shave her armpit this morning. You notice some fuzz?'

Raylan: 'Just the one?'

Boyd: 'Far as I can tell. I saw Ms. Conlan's armpit she's layin there dead? It was clean as could be. You could see one of her knockers all bloody.'

Liz, as she joined them: 'What was all bloody?'

Boyd: 'Ms. Conlan's chest.'

Liz: 'I'm so sorry she couldn't make it.'

Boyd: '*Poker After Dark,* you see their hands on the screen, you know what's goin on. I think this is gonna be boring.'

*   *   *

Harry: 'You want some background music?'

Vanessa: 'You got anything inspires poker?'

Leanne: 'I like it quiet so I can think.'

Vanessa: 'The one turns me on is Taylor Swift.'

Dude: 'That little girl?'

Vanessa: 'She'll pack a stadium.'

Dude: I don't mind Brad Paisley, he change his name he wouldn't sound queer. Him and Kenny Chesney'd swap names they'd have it right.'

Vanessa: 'What're you talkin about?'

Dude: 'That Zellweger girl was married to him a week and walked out.'

Harry: 'Why don't we get the cards in the air?'

Boyd: 'Dude don't find Kenny to his taste. That Vanessa, she looks like she'd make a meal of Taylor

226

Swift. How old you think she is, her twenties?'

Liz: 'They're all young, the girls. Would anyone like a drink?'

Raylan: 'Not yet, thanks.'

Boyd: 'You know how to make a Sazerac?'

Liz: 'With my eyes closed.'

Boyd, to Raylan: 'Your girlfriend hasn't said a word.'

Raylan: 'She's waitin on everybody to shut up.'

Vanessa, to Dude, who's coming from the bar with another bourbon: 'You gonna drink all night?'

Dude: 'When I'm playin women I do.'

Leanne: 'All the talkin, I can't concentrate.'

Dude: 'Honey, we haven't started yet.' To Harry: 'What's the blind?'

Harry: 'How about four and six hundred?'

Dude: 'We playin in the schoolyard? Bump it up some.'

Vanessa: 'You're dumber'n you look, sittin there with your cowboy hat on. I read you like a book, you and your bracelet. What're you gonna do after, go round up the herd? You guys and your hats.'

*   *   *

Boyd, to Raylan: 'She see yours yet?'

Raylan: 'I'm keepin it hid.'

Liz: 'They gonna play or not?'

Raylan: 'Bet you a buck they don't turn a card.'

*   *   *

Dude: 'A man wears a hat it becomes part of him.'

Vanessa: 'Cover up your bald head, less you're wearing a hairpiece.'

227

Dude removes his Stetson to show Vanessa a full head of dark hair. He leans toward her at the table. 'There a few strands of gray—but go on, pull on it, stick your nose in my hair and satisfy yourself it's all mine.' Dude straightens. 'I see you got kinda pink hair now. Any your other hair pink?'

Vanessa: 'I can't sit here and look at you no more. You are so fucking out of it. You win cause you bet enough nobody can call. That got you the bracelet?'

Dude: 'A pair. Honey, the boys I play all got enough to call my bets. Give me a seven-deuce down and I'll beat you playin for anything you want.'

Vanessa: 'You're a big-mouth stuck on yourself—'

Dude: 'Sometimes.'

Vanessa: 'You prob'ly think Lady Gaga's a chick from outer space.'

Dude: 'You mean wearin raw meat on your body makes you an alien? I thought it just made you un-hygenic.'

Vanessa, staring at Dude with cold eyes: 'Why don't you throw that stinky cigar away and get your yellow teeth cleaned? I don't think I can look at you no more.'

Dude: 'If we're gonna continue exchangin pleasantries why don't we forget the whole thing? Less you want to put all you brought on one game.' He waited.

He watches Vanessa and Leanne put their heads together for a moment. Now they both get up from the table and walk out of the poker suite.

*   *   *

Boyd, to Raylan, both sipping Sazeracs: 'You called it, partner. No poker this evenin for the young ladies.'

Liz: 'Jackie's still sitting there.'

Raylan: 'She wants to play, foolin with her chips, but doesn't say a word.'

Dude: 'I'll tell you what. Let's see if we can be polite to one another and wrap this up.' To Jackie: 'What's the most you ever lost?'

Jackie: 'At one time? Twenty grand.'

Dude: 'You piss it away?'

Jackie: 'I got mad.'

Dude: 'Finally met some players, huh?'

Jackie: 'Cigar smokers. I lost my cool but got it back, in case you're wondering.'

Dude, reaching over to pat her shoulder: 'Let's see how far bein spunky gets you.'

The hired dealer in his vest and bow tie finally sat down at the table and dealt each player two cards down.

Jackie peeks at her hole cards: an ace and a seven.

Dude: 'Hundred thousand to open,' and throws in his chips. 'If that's okay with you people.'

Jackie and the Saudis see the bet, the Saudis quiet, not looking happy this evening.

The dealer burns the top card and deals the flop: an ace, five, four.

Jackie now has her pair.

Dude throws in chips, betting another hundred thousand.

The Saudis fold and leave the table. Done with this nonsense.

Jackie sees the Dude's bet.

Dealer: 'Pot's six hundred forty thousand.' He deals the next card, the turn, an eight of hearts on the board.

Dude: 'I'm gonna leave it up to Miss Spunky. See where she's at.'

Jackie: 'A hundred thousand.'

Dude stares at her before adding chips to the pile on the table.

Dealer: 'Pot's eight hundred forty thousand.' He then deals the river card face up on the table. 'An ace of clubs.'

Dude: 'Well, hey, we both got aces paired. You got a good kicker under there?'

Jackie: 'Bet and find out.'

Dude: 'I do, I don't see you got enough to call. Hon, I don't want to take any more your lunch money.'

Jackie, bringing a checkbook and pen from her jeans: 'You want to bet, go ahead.'

Dude: 'Check, I'm gonna rest here.'

Jackie writes a check to CASH and drops it in the pot. Jackie: 'Eighty thousand to you, Mr. Moody.'

Dude, pausing: 'You're a tough little girl, aren't you?'

Dealer: 'Eighty thousand to Mr. Moody.'

Dude: 'What's the pot?'

Dealer: 'One million when you call.'

Dude, staring at Jackie: 'A big moment in your life, huh? Waited for the river to fill your hand? It didn't, you have to act like it did. I'm callin your bluff, hon.' Drops chips in the pot and shows his hand. 'Beat two pair, aces over cowboys.'

Jackie, turning up her ace in the hole: 'A set, Mr. Moody, three bullets.'

CHAPTER THIRTY-TWO

If Raylan wanted to say anything to Boyd and Liz he'd have to wait for them to quit talking. He watched Jackie at the poker table looking up at Dude Moody, listening and close to smiling at him. He'd turn his head and say something to Harry and her expression would lose interest.

Boyd was telling Liz about Ms. Conlan's end, Liz saying 'Really . . .?' following every word. Raylan thought Carol dying of gunshot was excessive. Ten years would've been more like it. Boyd, he'd have to forget about Boyd's part in it, even if Boyd had given shotgun shells to the old lady. Raylan would be kicking a dead horse.

Now he felt involved, or wouldn't mind it, with Jackie Nevada, sitting there, her head bent back, looking up at the Dude. Now he was kissing her on the top of the head, the Dude bending over her, Jackie looking like she was hunching her shoulders. Now Harry was busy talking to the Dude and Jackie got up from the table and came straight over to Raylan.

He said, 'I hear you beat the pro.'

'All three. You know how much I won?'

Raylan shook his head.

'A million bucks,' Jackie said.

'Come on—'

'Two-twenty from the Saudis and the rest from Dude. A million fucking dollars.'

'Took you only one game?'

'Dude was tired, thank God, or we might've

played some more. He told me nice going, I did all right for a girl and kissed me on the head.'

'I saw that part.'

'Harry'll put their checks in my account.'

'Were you nervous?'

'A little. But I knew I'd win.'

'How'd you know?'

'I told myself I'd hit on the river and I did.'

He'd ask about 'the river' another time.

Raylan said, 'So you won't need a bodyguard. I was lookin forward to it.'

'I thought you'd want to guard me,' Jackie said, 'so I won't run off again.'

Raylan said, 'I could handcuff us together.'

She was looking right at him. 'And throw away the key?'

'We're gonna have to be separated once in a while,' Raylan said, 'to go to the bathroom. But being cuffed together's a good test of compatability.'

She said, 'We need to test how we get along?'

'You're right,' Raylan said. 'Tell me what you'd like to do.'

She kept staring at him.

'Go someplace and have fun.'

Raylan took a moment to see them in the Two Keys Tavern, going up to his monk's room on the second floor. He said, 'You know what tonight is where I'm stayin? Crazy Night.' He said, 'You like to act crazy?'

Jackie said, 'I love to act crazy.'

*   *   *

Delroy said to his phone, 'Kennet, nobody seen him

at that bar. He's livin there, ain't they gonna see him?'

'You think your guys are alert?' Kenneth said.

'I get 'em what they need, stand around there all night. They like to feel relaxed.'

'While they're in a nod, the Lone Ranger comes in and goes to his room. Delroy, you continue to be your own problem. Forget the guy. God, he arrested you, that was seven or eight years ago.'

'I made up my mind,' Delroy said. 'I got me a cowboy hat I stuck in a bucket of water, get it to bend and shaped the motherfucker how I like it to look. I'm on face Raylan Givens in a shoot-out at the Two Keys saloon.'

Kenneth said, 'Get someone to count to three and you go for your guns? Delroy, you're wasting your life doing street drama.'

'My hat's black. I pull it down on my eyes . . . See, I don't want him to know it's me right away.'

'Del, you're quite tall.'

'But I want him to know it's me that second he recognizes my stature and I shoot him in the head. Last thing he's thinkin about. Kennet, what's the last thing goes through a bug's head he hits the windshield? The bug's ass. I'm goin down to South America or someplace after. Once I stick up a bank for travel money. Or get some chicks to do it. You know why it worked with chicks? Nobody ever seen it before.'

'Delroy, listen to me. It didn't work. You're wanted on sight for murder. You'll be caught and go to prison. Your next jolt will be life, at best, without parole. You know what Raylan Givens is famous for?'

'Drinkin shine?'

'Shooting people.'

'Sneaks up on 'em, like he done me, and gets the drop. See, this time I'm puttin on the show. I know my moves leading to shootin the motherfucker in the head. I tip my hat to the crowd and walk out the saloon.'

'And then you go to South America or someplace.'

'I been thinkin of Haiwaiya.'

'Delroy, Crazy Night at the Two Keys, some of the students go a little nuts and wear nutty outfits. Or sorority girls come as hula dancers. One time I heard, *Playboy* bunnies.'

'I'm gonna wear my hat.'

'Throw the fucking hat away. You have to wear something so he won't know you.'

'You see me dressin like a bunny?'

'That's not bad,' Kenneth said, a fingertip touching his lips. 'Not a bunny, but some kind of . . . awfully tall broad in a dazzling frock. Or . . . I don't know, something else.'

'Man, tall chicks rub up to me all the time. Know I'm lookin for one don't get lost in my embrace.'

'I see you as statuesque, a fucking knockout from *La Cage aux Folles,* a tall, bawdy bimbo.'

'You see me wearin a dress?'

'A frock of some kind.'

'What do I do for tits?'

'Come on over while I'm thinking about it.'

He realized he may have to shave Delroy's entire body, but decided not to mention it.

'I'm trying to think of what we have here at the Cooz besides G-strings. I'll look around. Delroy? I'll get Bobby over to do the makeup. All the black drag queens love him. Bobby'll give you smoky eyes with long lashes you can flutter at Raylan.'

'What do I do for tits?'

'If Bobby want you to show cleavage you'll have it.'

'I was thinkin,' Delroy said, 'I could be a Arab. Cover myself with a sheet.'

'No, you want the exotic RuPaul look.'

Delroy said, 'Kennet, where do I keep my piece?' It was always something with the big boy.

'That's right,' Kenneth said, 'you'll need your gun, won't you?'

* * *

Two and a half hours later, from the time Bobby arrived with his suitcase of makeup and armloads of dresses he'd borrowed from friends—'Costumes, really, from two of the most popular drag queens in town,' Bobby said—to Delroy looking at himself in the full-length mirror in Kenneth's bedroom, both Bobby and Kenneth waiting for Delroy's reaction.

'He's still awfully tall for a girl,' Kenneth said, 'but he looks delicious. I love the rich pouty lips with the lighter skin tone, the eyelashes . . . Delroy, bat your eyes for us. Give us a flutter.'

Bobby said in a murmur, 'He doesn't know what you mean.'

Delroy was staring at his long, slim figure in the mirror, turning his head from side to side appraising himself.

Bobby, his hand over his mouth this time, said to Kenneth, 'He hasn't said a word. You know he does have quite a sexy figure. I was afraid he might be all angles.'

'I'm wondering,' Kenneth said, 'if a simpler dress

without the distracting sequins might work better. It's awfully busy. But, I have to say, I love it. Delroy in the sky with diamonds.'

'It's short,' Bobby said, 'but his knees aren't bad, are they? You like the earrings? I love the way they swing when he turns his head. The pumps, I'm sorry to say, are the largest size of sling-backs I could find.'

'His feet do look like they might burst out,' Kenneth said, 'but I don't know what else we can do. He can't wear his own shoes, and his sandals are much too gauche with the frock. But who's looking at his feet? Delroy, what do you think?'

'I look like a homasexual.'

'You're a cross-dresser,' Kenneth said. 'You don't have to be gay to like wearing women's clothes. It shows a certain flair. You don't march with the common man.'

'You think I look all right, huh? Not too way-out?'

'You're dazzling.'

'But where do I put my piece?'

*   *   *

At half past nine they were in the Chevy on their way to Two Keys on South Limestone and talking about Delroy Lewis, Raylan thinking he shouldn't of brought him up. Now Jackie was into it, asking about him, now as far along as:

'You think he'll pick a spot and be lying in wait?'

'He could walk up behind me in a street fulla people, press his gun in my back. Or he finds out I live upstairs over a saloon.'

'How would he?'

236

'I'm big as life at the Two Keys, administering the law for my board. A snitch can live off stuff he finds out about and sells it.'

'I think you'd like what's his name, Delroy, to find you.'

'It might be the only way to have it done. Tryin to look at all the faces in a crowd wears you out.'

'We don't have to go to the Two Keys,' Jackie said. 'Harry got me a suite at the Hilton I still haven't used. We could stay there for a while, order room service on Harry, a bottle of champagne to celebrate.'

'Champagne,' Raylan said, 'can give you a headache.'

'You don't have to drink the whole bottle.'

'You don't?'

'Everything in moderation.'

'And you won't ever get in trouble?'

'I think if I were a guy,' Jackie said, 'I'd be a lot like you.'

'I bet you're like Reno.'

'Cause I gamble? I'm only somewhat like Reno. I'm smarter than he is, but he knows more about people. You know who I try to be like? Me, on a good day. I'm nice because I'm winning pots.'

'One with a million in it. You should be the happiest girl in town.'

'I don't stop to think, Am I happy? I am most of the time, I guess. But it comes and goes.'

'But you like being up. I can tell you how to maintain that high.'

'Yeah . . .?'

'Become a U.S. marshal.'

'You're serious?'

'I don't know, I may be.'

237

'To me,' Jackie said, 'to win a mil tells me I can do it. I knew I could beat what's his name, Moody, almost right away.'

Raylan said, 'I noticed you had your checkbook out. What if you had to write one to stay in? You didn't, cause the Dude, with five maybe six Maker's Marks in him, tells himself you're a girl . . . '

'*Only* a girl. But a nice one.'

'You didn't have to write a check for seventy grand.'

'I would've if he made me. I knew I had him beat from the moment I saw my ace in the hole.'

'You had good cards.'

'I had great cards. When do three aces lose?'

Raylan said, 'But not till an ace came bobbin up in the river.' Both smiling because they felt like it with each other.

Jackie said, 'I might as well tell you now, because I know I will later. I've got a serious crush on you. I'm excited by how cool you are. You carry a gun and've used it.'

'Yes, I have.'

'But you don't jog every morning or do anything you don't like, and you're not married.'

He said, 'What if I was?'

'I don't know. I'd still want to go to bed with you.'

'So when we start thrashin around under the covers, I'm not makin you do it.'

'Well, you are,' Jackie said. 'We could even take a shower together, first.'

Raylan said, 'Before my heart starts racing and we bang into somebody's rear end—'

She said, 'You want to stop at the Two Keys.'

'For a minute. Stick my head in.'

'You think he's there.'

'I'm right half the time when I get the feeling. Wait in the car, all right? I don't want to take a chance losin you before we get to the hotel.'

Was she laughing or what saying, 'Tell me you can't wait either.'

'I'll swear to it,' Raylan said, pulling up in front of the Two Keys. He'd already thought of kissing her here in the car, but it might be something he'd think about later as a bad sign, so he didn't kiss Jackie. He left the motor running, said, 'I won't be five minutes' as he got out.

Jackie watched him duck under the rail, go up on the porch and through the door. She took the keys from the ignition and got out to follow her new boyfriend.

* * *

Delroy sat at a table, his back to a wall, his two dopehead homeboys watching the place for him while he sat there drinking soda, raising the glass left-handed, his right one on the shoulder bag with the Smith .357 in it.

He'd told them already, 'All you two mopes have to do is get his attention when I touch my platinum head. You boys like it? I'm growin to. I get him he don't know where to look as I take the stage. What time is it? Kennet squeeze my titties so tight I said no, I be flat-chested. I'm still like nothin nobody ever seen.' His homeboys, mopes on weed, were the same age as most of the people in here, but street in their ways, what they were wearing, easy to pick out of the crowd.

Delroy walked in, people took one look at him

239

and began to cheer—man, look at this dude? A with-it crowd of his people. They made Delroy feel fine, like he belonged.

He watched them shooting goldfish with their water pistols. He read the signs on the walls, how much it would cost 'em to get drunk. He might be early, but would sit here an hour before giving it up.

The mope sittin with him slid out and was gone through tables toward the bar. He couldn't see the mope now, he was too short. What he saw was the hat, over there in a crowd, the cowboy kind of hat he was waiting for.

Now the mope was on his way back, eyes open for a change, wide open. Stood long enough at the table to nod his head, face telling nothin. Now was moving toward the other mope, out of the way.

There was Raylan among the tables looking around. Delroy watched the man's gaze move over the room, coming around to right here, Delroy wearing his platinum wig, drag queen makeup shining on him, and stopped.

*   *   *

Coming in, Raylan went up to the bar for a shot of bourbon since he was here. He saw the homeboy, out of place, staring at him. The homeboy turned, moving through the tables, and Raylan followed him up the aisle now till he saw the drag queen sitting at a table against the wall. Raylan kept walking toward the queen, the homeboy moving off to one side now but still in Raylan's vision.

He said, 'Excuse me, but if you're not Delroy Lewis you gotta be his ugly twin sister.'

Delroy, surprised, started to scowl at Raylan.

240

'How you know it was me?'

'You're waitin for me, aren't you?' Raylan said. 'I saw your movie, I know what your intentions are. I could pull right now and shoot you. Before you get your purse open.'

He watched Delroy touch his wig.

And the homeboys started yelling at each other.

Raylan held his gaze on Delroy. He said, 'Even if I looked to see what they're doing, you wouldn't get your purse open in time.' Raylan said, 'You want to do it right here, all these people watchin?'

'They don't bother me none,' Delroy said.

'They bother me,' Raylan said, pulled his Glock pointing it straight up and fired a round into the ceiling.

There was no sound in the bar. Now that's all there was: people screaming, chairs scraping, glass breaking as the crowd in the Two Keys dropped to the floor, some of them running out the entrance.

Raylan held his Glock at his leg.

'Same as last time,' Delroy said, his fingers inside the shoulder bag on the table now in front of him.

'You're dressed different,' Raylan said.

'You held your piece at your side like that,' Delroy said.

'The same one,' Raylan said.

'I had a shotgun,' Delroy said, 'thinking could I raise it before you got one off.'

'I run into this kind of situation on the job,' Raylan said. 'You made up your mind to give up and you're still alive. But for how long?'

He saw Delroy raise the purse in his left hand, aiming it at Raylan, and Raylan shot from the hip and saw Delroy sag back in his chair still aiming the purse and Raylan shot him again.

Raylan took time to approach the table, Delroy facedown on the surface, still holding the purse out in front of him. Raylan looked at the two homeboys staring at him and told them to go on out of here before police arrived, and they ran. Now he was aware of a hum of voices in the bar, Raylan touching Delroy's throat for a pulse but didn't feel one. He turned now, pressing the marshals number on his cell and saw Jackie Nevada standing there watching him. She appeared different now, looking right at him without knowing who he was. He walked over to her to stand close, saying, 'Remember me?' Her eyes raised and she was smiling, trying to, but she did wrap her arms around him, holding on tight, and everything seemed okay.

*   *   *

Raylan told Jackie, 'You know when I fired the shot at the ceiling? I mighta hit my room upstairs. It wouldn't of hurt it any, unless it put a hole in my extra pants hangin from a pipe.'

They were in the Hilton suite now that Harry had got for Jackie. Perfect. Nobody knew they were here.

The phone rang.

Art Mullen said, 'Were you gonna tell me what happened or keep it to yourself?'

Raylan heard the shower turn on.

'I didn't want to wake you up.' Raylan had his shoes off and his pants. 'How'd you find me?'

'Bill Nichols. He told me you shot Delroy and are now staying at the Hilton with the girl you went after. Is that correct?'

'I'm keeping an eye on her till I get her back to

242

Indy.'

'She sittin there with you?'

'Wait,' Raylan said. 'No, I hear the shower runnin. Art, I'm not payin for the room. Mr. Burgoyne got it for Jackie. I'm gonna sleep on the couch.'

'Be the first time in your life, won't it?'

'Art, I'm not gonna take her to that room I was using. This girl just won a million dollars. I'm not gonna sit in a chair out in the hall.'

'You saw her win a million bucks?'

'One hand of hold 'em. She's twenty-three, about to graduate and poker is her life. She isn't the least interested in an old fart like me.'

'"He said humbly,"' Art said. 'I'm not telling you how to bring her back. Long as you don't run off to some island. She in love with you yet?'

He could hear the shower, the bathroom door left open.

He said, 'Ms. Nevada is all the way into poker. She has the . . . stuff to make it work.'

'You were gonna say "balls," weren't you.'

'Art, I'm gonna take a week off after I get her back to school. She carries a three seven five and she's a nice girl. Art, tell me you're done.'

*   *   *

He put down the phone, tore the rest of his clothes off and ran to the bathroom and paused, got ready. He opened the shower door saying, 'Hi, are you decent?' Saying, 'You're way more than decent.'

She said, holding up her hands, 'I've been in here so long I'm starting to shrivel.'

'I'm sure not,' Raylan said, giving her a poke.

243

'Talking to your boss turned you on?'

'Something around here does. I wonder if it's this bare-naked girl in here with me?'

'Watching me so I won't run away. You do backs?'

'Fronts and sides . . . Let me lather you up.'

She said, 'No, let me work on you.'

He was at the place where he was thinking of ways to keep this going while Jackie was soaping every part of him.

Run out and bring in some champagne.

Say, That's my cell, and run out.

Take a couple of deep breaths and think of cleaning your weapon. Your gun. Then step back in. This was for fun.

She said, 'If I joined the marshals, could I be your partner?'

'I'd make it happen,' Raylan said, giving his new partner another poke.

* * *

She said, 'Remember *Young Frankenstein*? The monster gets it on with what's her name and she starts singing about finding the sweet mystery of life?'

'What made you think of that?'

'I don't know,' Jackie said.

CHIVERS LARGE PRINT
–direct–

If you have enjoyed this Large Print book and would like to build up your own collection of Large Print books, please contact

Chivers Large Print Direct

Chivers Large Print Direct offers you a full service:

• Prompt mail order service

• Easy-to-read type

• The very best authors

• Special low prices

For further details either call Customer Services on (01225) 336552 or write to us at Chivers Large Print Direct, **FREEPOST**, Bath BA1 3ZZ

Telephone Orders:
FREEPHONE 08081 72 74 75